LOST
BELIEVERS

A NOVEL

IRINA ZHOROV

SCRIBNER

NEW YORK   LONDON   TORONTO   SYDNEY   NEW DELHI

Scribner

An Imprint of Simon & Schuster, Inc.

1230 Avenue of the Americas

New York, NY 10020

First Scribner hardcover edition August 2023

SCRIBNER and design are registered trademarks of The Gale Group, Inc., used under license by Simon & Schuster, Inc., the publisher of this work.

For information about special discounts for bulk purchases, please contact Simon & Schuster Special Sales at 1-866-506-1949 or business@simonandschuster.com.

The Simon & Schuster Speakers Bureau can bring authors to your live event. For more information, or to book an event, contact the Simon & Schuster Speakers Bureau at 1-866-248-3049 or visit our website at www.simonspeakers.com.

Interior design by Kathryn A. Kenney-Peterson

Manufactured in the United States of America

1   3   5   7   9   10   8   6   4   2

Library of Congress Control Number: 2023011352

ISBN 978-1-6680-1153-9

ISBN 978-1-6680-1155-3 (ebook)

For Felix

Nowhere does time fly so fast as in Russia.

—Ivan Turgenev
Fathers and Sons

You should lie down now and remember the forest,
for it is disappearing—
no, the truth is it is gone now
and so what details you can bring back
might have a kind of life.

Not the one you had hoped for, but a life
—you should lie down now and remember the forest—

—Susan Stewart
"The Forest"

LOST
BELIEVERS

PART I
ЧАСТЬ I

CHAPTER 1
Глава 1

Agafia was walking along the rows of susurrating wheat and potato stalks when the valley exhaled a peal of thunder. Booming in the near distance, it brought to mind the rumbling rains that had put out the most recent grass fire. She pushed a finger into the soil to feel for moisture and squinted at the incongruously clear skies.

It had been a hard winter and the spring had brought wildfires and unpredictable weather. Summer had rolled in slowly. A sheet of thin wispy cloud had blocked out the long gray season before itself dissolving into blue skies. Work came easy when the sun shone the family's way, without the heavy blanket of snow to burden their movements. They had spent those early warm days rushing around the homestead, every atom in their bodies sped up by the thawing air. What they accomplished early—the planting, the cleaning, the preparations—would determine the whole year ahead, and the weeks had filled with organized chaos.

Dima had chopped wood, Hugo and Natalia had hacked at the still-cold ground to prepare it for planting, and Agafia had walked the dug rows inserting seeds into the dirt one by one. She was the one they trusted to make things grow, to eke out something from the unwilling ground. Sometimes Agafia had become distracted, her concentration blurred by the emerging greenness just beyond the field. It's that when the seasons changed, her feet and fingers extended beyond her gloves and shoes, unfurling like ostrich fern fiddleheads. Her siblings also changed, turned their broad faces to the sun to warm like smooth river stones and tucked wisps of hair behind their ears to open them to the sound of rushing water. Natalia wasn't prone to let Agafia dream long—she had shoved her in the side, urging her progress. Agafia had resumed her rounds, murmuring to each seedling under her breath as she covered it with soil. She hadn't been sure the seeds were still good.

But sprouts had pushed up in green lines and Agafia had crossed herself, her pointer and middle fingers extending out to touch her forehead, just above her belly, then one shoulder and the other. Amen. Here they were with a garden in full bloom, their fortunes tenuously reversed.

The thunder worried her.

■   ■   ■

The helicopter was a hulking metal box painted olive green and stripped inside except for two seats and instrumentation. Its lumpy chairs gave off a mild animal smell, unwashed camel hair or squirrel fur. The mission was classified as highly important, and Galina, its leader, had no trouble convincing the military to hand over the helicopter for the entire summer. She told the general that the work would ultimately benefit him anyway. The general hadn't argued, just signed over the machine, like he didn't think it capable of flying far anyway.

"Find your own pilot," he told her.

Blue eyes pinched into slits of concentration, her pilot maneuvered out of the valley. Snow still sat in the shadowy crevices of the north-facing slopes. White strips of it on the dark rock transformed the mountain face into a zebra haunch. She almost expected the noise from the helicopter to scare the animal, for the giant mountain equid to take off running below her. Instead, a freakish stillness. The helicopter's sharp blades cut through the valley's silence, each rotation slicing the air into ribbons.

The pilot steered to an opening where the land stepped up from the water more gently, and scanned for breaks in the birch and cypress. On the horizon, the river meandered toward flatter land, the stream splitting around pebbled banks and reuniting in wide stretches etched with rapids. Galina clicked a small Zenit camera pressed against the helicopter's window glass. She squinted at the ground, looking for outcrops visible from the air and signs of faults. She creased her brows, progressed the film, and refocused the lens on the ground below.

"Should we look for a landing pad?" the pilot asked. He looked like he belonged in the navy. He wore Breton stripes and a silk scarf tied jauntily around his neck. He jabbed a thick finger at the radio buttons and Galina adjusted her headphones.

She pointed to flatter land, to note it, but said, "Not yet."

The pilot drew on the stick, sending them forward. Galina lofted the camera to the glass and scanned the horizon with the lens out of focus. In the viewfinder, the river and forest dissolved into painterly splotches. She picked up the intercom but didn't say anything.

The pilot started to draw a grid with the helicopter, running long lines north-south, each lap ticking its way east. The magnetometer trailed behind the helicopter, pinging. The machine penetrated till and forest to measure the magnetic field below them, uncovering the blob of metal ore hiding in plain sight.

Moscow probably vibrated with unbearable heat by now, but here the valley's tendershoot vermilion signaled the early start of summer. That morning she'd loaded black-and-white film into the Zenit, to capture the contrasts in terrain, simplify the aerial maps to their basic hues. But in her mind, she recorded the oversaturated colors. *Remember it*, she told herself. *Remember it*.

In her hands, the lens bumped the window, glass clinking glass.

■ ■ ■

Used to be, when Agafia worked or strolled or slipped into bed at nighttime her mind raced, tripping over itself. Now, unless she made herself sit and think about something, her mind settled into a cool still lake, unmoving. As she toiled in the garden, this lake stretched in front of her for miles, a well of serenity and boredom. She was thinking about how she didn't think about much anymore when the thunder interrupted her thoughts. It came from the mountains.

The men were gone somewhere, but her sister worked by her side. Natalia tugged at weeds in the potato bed, pulling them out one by one. In the summer the family worked so much that there wasn't as much time for prayer, and Natalia used each uprooted weed as a notch on her *lestovka*, counting off recitations as she cleared the beds.

"Don't you hear that?"

Natalia had a way of shutting out the world.

Agafia sat down on the ground and gazed toward the noise.

"It's like the rain is running toward us."

Natalia rarely said much, but she stopped weeding and looked in the same direction as Agafia. They watched a dark speck emerge in the valley. A small object approached from a distance, carrying a large noise.

"It's for our sins," Agafia told her sister. They trained their eyes on the horizon, following the object as it receded then returned, like a fly, back and forth, its hum expanding and contracting in the air.

"We were so lazy this winter!" Agafia said, panicked. "I barely moved from my cot."

Natalia hushed her. "Let's go inside," she said.

The sisters crept through the greenery, keeping to shadows until they reached their house. The one-room hut stood in a small clearing, watching like a sentry over the river, the garden, the mountains and forest. Inside, an audience of four beds stood around a masonry stove. A nest of blankets lay on the stove, the prized sleeping place in winter. In every corner clutter climbed toward the eaves except the east-facing side, where icons and a large metal cross, all eight points dulled by age and groping fingers, occupied a clean three-legged table. A shelf wedged into the log walls protruded at waist level. Agafia retrieved a prayer book from the shelf and the sisters squeezed in front of their makeshift sanctorium. Natalia started. *O Angel of God, my holy guardian, preserve my life in the fear of Christ our God.* Her voice spilled from her mouth, a vomit of noise, a barely controlled scream. Agafia joined in. *Glory: now and ever.*

Inside the hut, the women's prayers shape-shifted like swallows' murmurations. Prayer a physical presence, growing and shrinking and changing form as its keepers ululated and hummed. There was the blocky Russian stove, the small mantel of books, the birch boxes, and there was their prayer. It took up more room than the furnishings.

■ ■ ■

Galina was the boss of the whole operation. She signed off on the budget, on the summer camp preparations, on the employee roster, on the canisters of helicopter fuel and boxes of canned meat stacked in neat rows at camp. On the 5 a.m. wakeup call. She stalked the rows of tents in the morning fog with a flyswatter, hitting each tent wall twice to rouse the team. From inside, the men—and all five were men—would plead with her.

"Galockha, two more minutes, sweetheart."

It was her first time truly in charge, leading a team surveying the land for a new iron mine. She'd run two field seasons, the first to examine a large area and make rough maps of the deposit, the second to gather rock samples and figure out where, exactly, a mine should be located. She had not asked for these responsibilities and assumed them reluctantly. She wanted to be woken, to be told what to do, for someone else to give the journalists quotes and count the canned meat portions. To be a piece of a solution, not its architect.

The helicopter turned around to run another line on the grid, still no flat, stable land in sight for the machine to land. She considered clicking on the headset and issuing an order for the pilot to return to camp, but instead she sat back. If she didn't say anything, maybe he'd run the grid back and forth and back and forth until they ran out of fuel.

Galina imagined the helicopter a Trojan horse soaring over the mountains, and she Odysseus, preparing to unleash destruction on the kingdom below. Tasked with evaluating the iron deposits, she'd be the one to order the charging of the rock. Drill rigs and front loaders groaning, the mountains would submit like the Trojans. She pressed the button on the transmitter.

"You ever feel bad telling them where to dig?" she asked the pilot.

"It's not God's work, is it?" his voice crackled back.

They veered off the grid, toward a mirage of flatness.

Galina had decided to study geology after her mother took her to the Orlov Paleontological Museum. She was young, and for nearly a decade her father held to the hope she'd change her mind and enter the university's economics department, like he had, so she could eventually work on some government planning committee, like him. He revered geologists for making progress possible, but he despised their bohemian bent. They had a reputation for beards, liberal politics, and drinking, and he didn't want his daughter in their milieu. But when Moscow State University sent her an acceptance letter in the mail, she rode the metro to campus the same day and filled out the paperwork in the run-down geology building. Her first act of rebellion.

Classes started soon after. She left the house at sunrise and didn't return until dinnertime.

She made friends whose parents didn't work for the state and got a whole new education. Everybody she met understood more about the world than she did. When she ate with her parents in the evening she stayed quiet, as she'd been taught, while they discussed politics. But inside she was a desert bloom, a vastness suddenly quenched and turned radiant.

An old lecturer with hair growing out of his nose and a jewel thief's air led the introductory class. He dimmed the lights and clicked through colorful slides of kaleidoscopic minerals. Garnet, calcite, pyrite, hematite. Oolitic limestone. Tennantite. He laid out small white boxes, nests full of rocks, for the class to identify. She'd scratch their surfaces with her teeth to test for grittiness, and drip acid to see if they'd reveal their properties. At night, lying in bed, she replayed the day's slideshows in her head. Geology all wizardry and divination.

Her favorite class was stratigraphy, taught by a short woman with a squeaky voice. On field trips, the professor brought along the pointer she used in class and poked it at the striped road cuts. She teased out the rock's history from the tan lines she found on its surface, painting old landscapes for the students on the sides of roadways. She found time tucked into thin black stone layers and led them through years of drought to desiccated river bottoms millennia old. A magic trick. The rock faces spoke along with the professor, and when she moved on they closed back up, a book slammed shut.

Galina took applied geology classes too, with patriotic guest speakers and field trips to big open-pit mines and terrifying underground ones. Galina liked to suit up, clipping the headlamp battery on a wide leather belt and wrapping a kerchief around her nose and mouth to keep out the dust. She'd heard that dissidents were forced to labor in the nation's mines, and though her father denied the rumors—"Not since Stalin's death!" he'd say, as if offended by the notion—she looked for them during mine visits. At a distance she spied men scratching ore into piles. She searched for their faces with her headlamp, catching skittish eyes and framing sweat-slicked brows in yellow light. Always a foreman made them turn away.

Galina obsessed over the mines. Civilizations, she knew, rose from rock. The newspapers printed mineral production figures that ran for pages, incomprehensible rows of numbers that in their sheer overwhelming quantity implied a steel-hardened future. The dust-covered men underground translated into rows of data, and that translated into tractors and bridges and munitions, and that was progress. Galina ran her finger along the rows of numbers, smearing ink, until the pages became greasy and unreadable.

The economic geology professor noticed her enthusiasm for the mines and began to groom her. On trips, she directed questions directly at Galina, pulling her to the front through the scrum of students as they examined gleaming veins of ore. On exams, she received an abundance of notes for her efforts. And when she finished the class, the teacher, a reserved woman so tall that she entered the mines folded low like a leggy heron, gave her an orange hard hat.

"Make use of it," she had said, and slapped her on the back.

Before she'd even graduated she received a letter in the mail inviting her to work as a mine geologist for the state's Moscow office. *You'll train under senior geologists on some of the biggest, most exciting projects in the Union,* the letter read. *We hope you'll use your knowledge to divine the rocks, decipher what the raw landscape can offer to our people.* The bureaucrat tasked with typing it grew, at times, poetic in his acknowledgment of the exciting opportunities that awaited the recipient of the form letter.

At dinner that evening, Galina had gushed to her parents about her news, taking the letter out of her purse and reading passages aloud. Her mother had placed a hand on her father's arm.

"Your father called an old friend in the geological division," she'd said. "The man owed him a favor."

Her father had barely put down his fork, a speared cutlet midway to his mouth. He'd looked up at Galina and nodded, to accept her thanks, though she had stayed quiet.

It had been a good education. Years of work helped open mines across the vast Union, and aerial photographs of blasted horizons decorated her new office, each a medal for her labor. But since her promotion, since she'd come to Siberia, all she desired to do was walk, play hide-and-seek with outcrops of gunmetal-gray mountains, and sketch along riverbanks. Camera tightening noose-like around her neck, she snapped several photos in a row, to stitch into a fresh panorama.

■ ■ ■

Agafia's ma, Nadia, had given birth four times. The first three came into the world in their old home, in a village where the smell of hay drifted on neighbors' voices. When she first bent over with pain in the church, women carried her to the town's wooden bath and brought stacks of towels and metal bowls to the banya. They boiled water on the banya's heater and wiped her with warm cloths, heaping heavy mantles of prayer on her small, laboring body. The first birth broke her body in half, followed by her heart; the child died in her arms before she could memorize his face.

Before baptism. They buried him in the cemetery's pagan section, alongside the old souls struck down by unholy deaths, those who had lived unholy lives, and Nadia's brother, killed by a lightning strike. Whenever Nadia pondered the child, all she had to conjure him was the small, nameless wooden cross her husband erected over the creature's body as she lay recovering.

The second came quick and painless. The boy emerged with lungfuls of air, wet and perfect and curious. She named him Dima and swaddled him in yards of white cloth, singing to him every waking hour of every day. Curls cupped a heart-shaped face and his alabaster skin glowed like the icons' in the town church.

When Dima was five, she made Natalia. She slid out of Nadia without anyone's assistance, independent from her mother the moment a neighbor pinched off the black-eyed girl's umbilical cord. Nadia admired and feared her first daughter. The girl's quiet stilled her surroundings and slowed time. If Nadia weren't so sure of her offspring's holiness, she might have thought her a devil instead. Natalia straddled that fine line.

Things were getting bad by then. Beardless men with rifles slung against their backs showed up regularly in the village demanding that the children go to schools outside the community and the adults to factories to work. Nadia and Hugo thumbed through their handwritten books, two-hundred-year-old tomes Nadia's mother had given the couple on their wedding day, for guidance. These changes all around them, they concluded, were signs of the

Antichrist's nearing. To preserve their old ways, they'd have to go to the mountains, far from temptation and worldly sins.

Only then could they be saved.

The family didn't wait long—their books described in great detail what happened to people who didn't heed the call to flee. Hugo and Nadia packed what they could.

For generations, the Kols' people had traded tales about a utopia, somewhere east, where people like them lived safe from the Antichrist. It was a place called Belovod'e, where the trees grew as tall and straight as their faith, the winter frosts were thick, and real priests, serving barefoot, still swept the ground with their robes. One hundred forty churches rose from Belovod'e's fertile soil. Upon arrival, refugees underwent three baptisms in the river to wash away the impurities they had carried. Travelers from all over had searched for this refuge, but it had been hard to find. As the Kols prepared to flee, Nadia's mother gave them a pamphlet she'd long kept in one of her books. It had directions, landmarks, distances, promising deliverance to Belovod'e. Maps with detailed topographical markers, town names, and friendly shelters along the way folded out of the leaflet.

Nadia's family had always spoken about Belovod'e—White Waters—as if of heaven, a place as fantastical and as true. But the directions were a revelation. Why hadn't they gone? Nadia's mother couldn't say. Nadia and Hugo traced the map's faded lines east, calculating the journey's toll. The names and landmarks rang vaguely familiar, though neither had ever gone far from their village. They set off on a gray morning in the summer of 1934, on foot, dragging along a cart packed with their belongings and their two living children.

Hugo lost count of their steps when he counted to eternity.

They stopped when they reached a clearing by the river, a thick carpet of grass ringed with dense forest. In some ways it was as the brochure promised: they'd traveled a long, long time and found tall trees, clear water, the land free and rolling, no sign of the Antichrist. They prayed without hindrance. But no priests greeted them, no one welcomed them from their long journey. There was not a single person within screaming range. Hugo jabbed his pointer finger at the map, which had run out months ago.

"A little farther," he said.

But Nadia shook her head, so they unpacked, without reaching Belovod'e. She slipped the leaflet back into a book. With no priest present, they didn't dare call it baptism, but they entered the water reverently and dipped each other in the current, tired hands cupping their heads, floating, letting go of past lives and future ones. *The frost here*, Nadia thought, *will indeed be thick.*

Agafia was born there. Only five-year-old Natalia and Nadia's own husband, Hugo, attended her in this last birthing. They hadn't built a bathhouse, so she crouched on the tundra-grass mattress by the hut's stove. Nadia thought she would die pushing life out in such empty vastness, staining the white winter with her labor pain. But Natalia placed a cool small hand on her mother's forehead. The pain in Nadia's belly melted away and Agafia's tiny squawks joined the taiga chorus.

The newborn's wail announced her to the wolves. Wildness must have seeped into Nadia, who pumped it through her umbilical cord and her thin blood to this second daughter. The girl internalized the feral world outside, half human, half mossy wood. Chest full of woodpecker thumps, pine knots in her calves. The others tolerated the taiga's harshness and learned to ask it for forgiveness. To survive. But Agafia, having known nothing else, thrived in the secluded brutality of her home. In this way, Agafia stood apart from the rest of the family, building a home in a nook of Siberia far from any settlements.

Years had sped by since Nadia had passed away, but whenever Agafia prayed she still appeared by her side. Nadia had passed down her books to her daughter, the travel guide to Belovod'e still tucked like a bookmark between pages covered in Church Slavonic script. When Agafia was alone she studied it, imagining herself moving along the map's twisted routes. If anyone else was around, she kept it hidden in the thick leather tomes, which contained their community's history and their prayers, one bolstering the other.

"You'll memorize the prayers soon enough," Nadia had told her young daughter. And she had.

Agafia held on to these devotions as if to buoys, bobbing with them in the open waters of her isolation. They were company, compass, structure. They were a home, however cramped. In times of uncertainty, she felt the bigness of the books' promises crash against the smallness of the world they contained, like great blocks of melting ice on a river eager to flow free.

■　■　■

The pilot turned on his headset and let it sputter before addressing Galina.

"Look," he said, pointing below them. A jute rug, woven neat and tight and straight, lay below them.

"What is it?" she asked.

He hovered over the carved hole in the forest, waiting for it to reveal itself.

"Are there any settlements in the area?" he asked.

Galina had pored over the government maps at camp before they set out that morning. They detailed where oil and gas deposits might be, but the thorough geologists who drew them had marked just about everything else on the maps too. Mineral deposits, roads, railroads, rivers, villages. Down to the individual warming shacks hunters built atop the tundra to shelter them as they gathered ermine and fox furs. On the map for the section they were flying, nothingness reigned. It was as if they'd drawn the map in winter, and the drafter had transferred the unblemished whiteness of the plain onto his page.

"Nothing," she said.

The pilot hovered, then looped around and approached from the other side.

"Looks like a garden," he said.

"That's impossible."

Galina unscrewed the lens from the camera and switched to a longer one. The new lens swooped out of the helicopter into the immensity below. She clicked off several frames, wound, zoomed, clicked again.

"Let's go," she said.

Thundering, the machine bored through the landscape back to camp.

"A bear couldn't claw his way out of this valley," the pilot mused as they reentered the mountains.

At camp, Galina grabbed a piece of bread from the communal table and shut herself in the photo tent she'd brought along. She wound the film onto metal cages and let them fall into the chemical-filled canisters to develop. In the still dark, she could almost hear the silver salt falling from the film, settling like snow at the bottoms of the cylinders. The timer showed two more minutes. She thought about her old roommate, who'd taught her to develop film and photographs. He'd used the same lens on his camera and his homemade enlarger, switching it out as needed. He'd set up the darkroom in their tiny bathroom and spent his waking hours in there in a chemical daze, happily printing. Galina had to use the neighbor's bathroom. Now she understood why he locked himself in there for so many hours; the small, confining tent and its warm smell of chemicals in the midst of the open, unsettled taiga restored a sense of reality, something controllable and self-made. The tent fit around her and cradled her with its smallness, protection from the bigness of what lay just beyond it. The timer clicked off in her hand.

She rinsed the film, yanked it from the holder, strung it garland-like across the tent to dry, and crawled out. The pilot brought sandwiches and they sat down on a hammock to eat. Around them, the men lounged about like a colony of cats. They didn't exactly know the extent of the deposit, so their exploration area was vast; surveying such a large tract took long days of tedious work. Galina had drawn a grid on her map that she and the pilot traced in the air with the aerial magnetometer while the rest of the team walked the same north-south tracks on the ground, measuring the strength of the magnetic field at close range. To stay the course on the ground the men had to break trail. With saws and hatchets, they downed trees and cleared debris, leaving behind shorn lanes. Pointed poles hung with red flags protruded every hundred meters, marking plot points.

"Maybe it's an undiscovered tribe, like in the Amazon, that no one's ever made contact with that's been living in that valley for millennia," the pilot said. Crumbs flew out of his mouth as he laughed. His thigh pressed against hers.

She took a bite of the sandwich. The cheese had melted and solidified so many times that the chemical structure of the block had altered. It crumbled out and landed in her lap.

"It means they haven't tasted the delicacy our dear leaders call cheese," he said, and brushed the brittle crumbs from her knees.

"We must immediately bring them Russian bread!" Galina said. "These poor people have not lived until they've tasted it!"

"You know, first contact is never good for the contacted," he said, suddenly serious. Too serious, like he was actually being funny again.

"Human contact in general rarely works out too well."

Galina leaned back in the hammock. Clouds gathered in great massifs above the trees.

When she awoke the pilot was gone, tinkering with the helicopter.

She fired up the generator, plugged in the enlarger, and stuck one of the dried negatives in a tray. For a moment light illuminated the tent, then extinguished. She slid the paper into a tub and rocked it back and forth. Grays solidified into blacks. An image floated up, conjured from emptiness. Galina transferred the print into the fixer solution, turning it picture-side down. When the timer sounded, she pinched the photo with a pair of rubber tongs, and carried it out of the tent to the pilot. She pointed.

He put down his tools.

"It's got to be a garden," he said.

"Let's fly over it again."

■ ■ ■

The taiga made living such a project, its endeavor invited introspection. How had she got here? Agafia contemplated it constantly. The way some people ponder their existential purpose in the world, she wondered about her physical presence in the taiga. She knew her family had walked there. She knew it was Peter's fault.

The long past came in snippets, in stories. Of long-haired cousins dancing with full-bearded men, fields with night-black soil, the yeasty yolk of community warm and rising.

Impressions rather than details shaped the past. Her people had worked the land and venerated it. Their priests wore finely embroidered robes and led them to the Lord and the river. Even in the midst of chaos and war, her people relied on the monastery's guidance and lived simply, in ways godly and independent.

Change came in the 1600s, when the czar Aleksey Mikhaylovich and Patriarch Nikon started to reform the church. That time defined Agafia's fate so much that its retelling was a birthright, her own terrifying heritage. Nikon issued new books, new orders for prayer, new routines. Frantic councils met to discuss the altered church rules—three fingers instead of two to make the sign of the cross, standardized prayer books, a four-pointed cross instead of the usual eight points, processions to flow against the sun rather than toward it, three alleluias instead of two after the Psalms and the Cherubic Hymn. All of it all wrong. The bureaucratic pivots tentative steps closer to Christian statehood, on the one hand. A smidge toward eternal damnation, on the other.

Her people, steady as the seasons, refused to change. They'd gained their Lord through routine; the particulars of their liturgy were the essence of their being. To change the symbols in their worship was to alter the nature of their God, to write His name in a new way was to rewrite their understanding of Him. There was a break between her people and the reformers—the schism. The czar made her people into pariahs, and they gained a new name: Old Believers.

The next czar, Peter, brought new trouble, new pressures to change their long-rooted ways. His ultimatums drove them farther north, east. Peter and the Old Believers were the Russian continuum personified. He looked toward the future. Agafia's people's job was to preserve the past. They were bound to clash.

Some Old Believers met the conflict with fire. It was after the schism. Armed sentries terrorized the countryside with orders from Peter, to shave beards, farm differently. Signs of the end times seeped into daily life. In village after village the elders decided Peter was too close. They chose to cleanse themselves with fire before the Last Judgment rather than continue to live in Peter's sin. The elders lit kindling in oil-soaked churches full of congregants. Flames climbed the wooden pillars, lapped at the ceiling, spilled outward toward the walls where the flocks huddled.

Agafia's ancestral village suffered this fate. But her people had resisted the sin of immolation. They watched their church burn with their neighbors inside, and then they pushed, each body a lowered plow on the ground, through the tundra, stubbornly pointed north. They carried small icons they'd rescued from the church and brought them to new villages, to bald settled bowls of land cultivated by distant kin. But the epidemic of mass suicides followed them; always in a church, always the whip-loud crack of the flames out-thundering the screams of the people burning inside. The family stayed only briefly in each village. It was the start of their long wandering.

For generations—even after Czar Peter died—the Kols' line led peripatetic lives. Each new ascendant Russian leader found something to punish in the Old Believers. By the mid-1800s, though, Hugo's grandfather landed in a village called H. The settlement was full of refugees who'd once fled burning churches and unchristian mandates from local overlords. He stayed, helped build a new house of prayer, settled.

Hugo was born in that village. He met his Nadia, started a family. But bad luck found them again, in new form, when Stalin came to power. The Kols, like so many others, decided to flee. They sought escape in Belovod'e but had only made it to this empty valley.

The hut, this piece of land. The second origin tale.

Agafia knew she came into the world on the right side, the righteous side. Her people came from the earth itself, molded by God's hands from black soil, limbs carved from whole birch stands, hair poured from melted amber, hearts hardened in the icy water of the Baikal. But until the schism, until Nikon and Czars Aleksey and

Peter came along, her people were ether. The conflict gave them blood, body, history. Loneliness.

It's strange where one finds company in the solitariness of one's convictions. She was a girl the first time she saw Peter. Natalia was tying a fine shawl she'd managed to keep from the bugs around Agafia's head, tucking witchy wisps of hair under the fabric and smoothing it down with clammy hands.

"Hold still," Natalia said.

"Is this Mother's shawl?" Agafia asked. Nadia already dead a child's lifetime long.

The fabric constricted Agafia. It dulled sound and squeezed her head. The man came up behind Natalia, to inspect the knot she was tightening under Agafia's chin. He didn't say anything, just stared, and Agafia startled.

"What are you looking at?" Natalia asked.

Agafia jutted her chin at the man standing behind her sister. He was thin, tall. Brown hair lay in waves on his head and he focused on her with intense, bugged eyes. He sat down across from Agafia, picking his teeth. From his pocket he took out little wooden men and began to line them up in battle formation, a boy at play. Natalia gazed across the room, then turned back to her sister to finish the knot.

"I don't see anything," she said.

Agafia never mentioned him again, but soon he started appearing more frequently, talking. He told her stories about old Russia and foreign women and horses he'd loved.

Sometimes he seemed to speak in a different language and Agafia did not understand him. At the riverbank, washing clothes, she heard the raspy breath of someone planing wood and woodpecker-sure hammering. He was building something. When she went to investigate, she found nothing.

She figured out, of course, his name: Peter Alekseevich. Some called him Peter the Great, though not her people. He was the reason for the family's first fleeing, and every one after that. The desolation. He'd found her. She came to understand his appearances as warnings, the physical manifestation of her own dark history strolling in the forest beside her, his body full of blood and ghosts. Peter both present and invisible, like history itself. After each visit, she doubled down on her piety, trying to shape it into something tangible from the muddiness of her heart, fire it into something durable with the heat of her wanting.

She believed. She really believed. She didn't even know that not believing was an option. The faith taught to her from the womb on, the ritual that sustained her tether to the Lord, it was air and she knew she had to have it. But when she shaped her bowl of devotion lovingly with her prayers, its walls came out uneven as a braided shoal, porous as the sand on her tongue. Sometimes, when Peter appeared, Agafia worried her prayers were devoid of inspiration, lacking the vividness that true faith required.

The morning of the great noise she was preoccupied about this very thing. The thundering from earlier had trailed off in the distance, overpowered by the mosquitos' buzzing. So early in the summer and they already gathered in great masses. Still Natalia stood praying, head down. Peter hunched in the corner, the length of him bent under the hut's low ceiling. Agafia tried to quiet her mind, to focus on the recitations. But Peter distracted her, took her mind off the supplications so they rolled off her tongue without substance.

"What was that?" she whispered to him, cutting her eyes at Natalia.

"I guess the world has come to you, all this way," he said.

He fingered the books on the shelf. His name peppered the tomes' pages, cursed in the Old Believer chronicles. Agafia feared he'd harm the books, but they stood undisturbed under his hands. Next time she glanced up from her prayer, he was gone.

Hugo and Dima returned soon after from their chores. As the thundering passed overhead, father and son had crouched on the ground and uncovered their heads. When it retreated, they hurried back, to see if the world still beat on.

The sisters put on potatoes to boil. Most of last season's crop had already disintegrated and bloomed with mold in the pantry. They filled a pot of threadbare metal, blackened from years on flint-coaxed fires. Agafia lifted the pot and emptied the water outside, then dumped the small, disfigured crop in the middle of the table. Hugo pulled sheets of freckled skin off the tubers and wiped his fingers against the table. *All that history,* Agafia thought, *to get here.*

■   ■   ■

After the war, steel production in the Soviet Union grew, surpassing European nations in its output. Railways connected ore to distant coal mines and processing facilities sprouted tumorous add-ons with the signing of each five-year plan. By the time Galina entered the university in the early 1960s, most industry had slowed, but iron mines kept opening.

She had a professor who took her senior class to Vyksa to show his students how steel was made. The professor had advertised the visit as a history lesson, and said they'd get to see ancient processes they had learned about in class. Instead, he brought them to a working steel mill.

In a locker room, the air so full of metal she tasted it on her teeth, Galina and her classmates put on heavy coats, dark glasses, and protective leather gloves. A worker led them out on the floor, where patriotic posters hung from rafters. The furnaces looked like the cold chambers in a morgue, except tongues of fire leapt out and licked at the huddled students when the compartment doors opened. The professor tried to explain what they were looking at over the machinery's banshee screams. It wasn't necessary. The students who had paid any attention in class could see that the workers manned ancient open-hearth furnaces from the previous century. So many things were like that in this country, history and present all at once. History and future.

The workers allowed them to bang on freshly pulled steel with hammers, to show their visitors the product was strong, not brittle. When the class left, each student received a metal pin, a tiny cauldron filled with red acrylic, shiny and bright as the molten metal.

They rode a chartered bus back to Moscow. Students kissed in the darkness, the bus filling with private hushed noises. The driver refused to stop for bathroom breaks on the seven-hour drive. Galina had sat up front and watched the man piss in a bottle as he drove, swerving just slightly as he readjusted his pants and tossed the urine out the window. It had made her jealous, that adaptability that only men and cats seemed to possess. The old professor sat next to her on the drive back. He smelled of hooch and beets, earthy, as if ready to be buried.

"I've been taking students there for three decades!" he said. "Nothing ever changes."

"Must make your job easier," she said.

He dug around in his bag, then shoved his hand toward Galina, opening it. Identical cauldron pins spilled out of his fist, and they both laughed.

After that trip, she'd concentrated on iron, in rapture to its strength, its possibilities. She apprenticed with geologists who worked in iron and read unassigned books on the mineral's development. By the time she graduated, she was a fledgling expert.

Still, it was her father who'd gotten her that first work assignment. Her expertise a bonus to her connections. She wore the cauldron pin on her first job to remind her of her passion, her worth. But her father kept meddling, pulling strings that outpaced even her ambition. She knew, of course, but didn't say anything. Instead, with each new job, each mine, she transferred the pin to a new uniform to keep herself focused.

Then came the latest promotion. Another unsolicited favor from her father, secured without her knowledge, had put her in charge of this mission. Her assignment in the taiga was to find the iron in the mountains, to trace on maps the deposit's reach, give it shape and life and narrative. She'd have to calculate its size, translate its worth to tons. She had to do her part to send this rock to the Union's ancient furnaces, so it could be turned into steel. Something about her rise, though, soured her dedication. When she started in the position, she transferred the pin to a new jacket out of habit, the power from the talisman fading.

Out of professionalism, she continued to fill her field journal with her efforts: notes on surface deposits and crooked traces of the mountains' uplift. Sketches from the helicopter showing geological unconformities and lines of bent strata. The journal a daily diary that linked her fate with the mountains'.

The day they first spotted the garden in the taiga, she turned to a clean page and dated the top, July 11, 1973, signaling a new entry. She labeled it *HOMESTEAD* and boxed in the word with a heavy hand. *Maybe they're miners just like me*, she thought. She wrote: *Performing an aerial magnetometer survey, we spotted what looks like a settlement.* Then she stuffed the notebook into her bag and motioned to the pilot that she was ready to go.

The blades of the helicopter waltzed into a frenzy, their rotation quickening until they turned into a solid mass that lifted them off the ground, and they headed back into the valley. The pilot clicked on the headset but didn't say anything, just held his finger on the relay button, the mouthpiece hovering in front of his lips. She made him nervous. Galina saw his pupils, tiny rosebuds, loosening with anticipation. She turned away.

The homestead lay some twenty kilometers from the camp, Galina estimated. A quick trip in the helicopter. They needed to continue the survey, but she instructed the pilot to fly back to the section they'd completed that morning. The silence between them stretched the minutes. She clicked on the headset but couldn't think of anything to say.

"Have you ever been to Siberia before?" she mustered.

The pilot choked into the headpiece, a barky exhale, as if she'd caught him off guard. "Yes," he said, "I've spent a little time here."

"Oh." She hadn't expected that.

The pilot pushed the helicopter forward, until he came to hang above the spot Galina had captured on film. Low green stalks pushed from the crenellated soil, dancing in the helicopter's wash. A stack of chopped wood lay piled on the roof of a dwelling. By the hut, another garden, enclosed by a crude wooden fence. No people in sight.

■ ■ ■

The thunder returned, booming. The family huddled together, hands clasped into knots, eyes upturned to the web-filled corner of the hut. They'd grown accustomed to living with the specter of the Antichrist, yet they hadn't heard him bellow so close. So viscerally. Hugo squeezed so hard Agafia imagined her fingers breaking, bones splintering like twigs in wolves' teeth.

Peter, seated beside her, chuckled. *If Peter is by my side, what is out there?* Agafia marveled.

"Why don't you go see?" Peter said.

She stole a glance at the others.

"You don't even know what you're scared of," he taunted.

He stood up in the hunched way he had in their low hut and opened the door. A gust of debris blew in, swirling. Agafia watched him fold to fit through the door and unfold on the other side. He stood within view, back to her.

Natalia jumped to close the door and crossed herself.

"Maybe it's not Peter!" Agafia shouted over the thunder and the prayers.

Natalia silenced her with a hand.

The thunder pulsed in Agafia's ears. The appeal of their life here, specks in the nothingness of unwanted lands, depended on the homestead's unapproachability. She had never strayed far, but believed Hugo when he told them that for unimaginable distances in every direction they were alone. He made it seem like even the Antichrist would not attempt to scramble into this corner of the world. But this wasn't the first time something from the outside had encroached on them. In her youth, she'd seen the spring melt carry tree trunks, stripped of their canopies and lashed together into great big wood rafts. Hugo told her then that it was worldly industry, men cutting wood to bring to the cities. Some of the wood sank, muddying their stretch of river and killing off fish for years.

Maybe this, too, was something worldly. From out there, beyond her valley, beyond the ascetic gifts of her faith. Agafia was the only one in the family who'd never experienced worldly things. Not up close, not firsthand. In the pure cradle Hugo had carved out of Siberia, the worldly remained mostly theoretical. Distant. Having never touched it, Agafia feared it only in the abstract, and the abstract can be hard to fear.

She unlinked her fingers from her father's grasp and ran out of the hut before Natalia could stop her. She ran into the sun and stood under a great big bird. An enormous body hovered above her, bobbing slightly up and down, kicking up a gray cloud of dust around her. Peter had his hands on his hips and his head thrown back, studying it.

"There are people inside it!" he yelled to Agafia. "Flying people!"

She gazed up, past the thing, into the sun, the light blinding her. She couldn't make herself look for the people. Instead, she searched the foreign object's perimeters, taking in its angles and curves, its green coloration as if attempting to blend in with the trees. It looked hard and heavy, and she pondered how it managed to stay in the air and feared it would fall and flatten her. Peter grinned at her; spit flew from his moving mouth, but she couldn't make out his words. In the machine's roar, the world had gone terrifyingly silent. The wind from the machine whipped at her shawl and tore at its knots until her hair loosened and floated around her. Long, honey-brown locks tangled about her, wild, dancing. Warm urine ran down her leg, soaked into the long gown she wore. She was heavy and flushed. She didn't know how long she stood there, neck craned and eyes upturned. Eventually the thing receded above her, as if she'd won a face-off. It rose above the surrounding tree tips and pitched toward the mountains, taking with it the noise it had brought.

When quiet returned, Agafia washed herself in the river, rubbing her legs with smooth pebbles. Pills of skin rolled up on her thigh and she splashed at them. Fish appeared, O-shaped mouths searching for the debris of her body in the water. She grabbed the net she kept on the bank and scooped a lenok, sunset-orange spots flashing as she lifted it out of the water and walked back to the hut cradling it in her arms. Had she conjured the visitor with her sins? Her body powerful and out of control. Nausea tightened her throat. She spit.

She chopped off the fish head with an axe and set it in water to boil. Its eyes turned milky in the warming pot. Natalia dumped the guts outside, packed the flesh in birch bark, and set it in the oven to bake. The pantry was practically empty, and while they waited for the fish to cook Agafia swept out the small shed, carpeting the mud outside with scraps of rotten potato and wheat chaff. How routine the end days now appeared. Peter sat inside the pantry, watching her. "It was just a worldly visitor," he said.

The hinges of the door had deteriorated years ago, the metal rusting and flaking until it broke, and the door leaned against the wall. When she finished, she lifted it into position, and returned to the hut. Dima had made mint tea, and they sat in silence sipping it.

"What could it be?" she asked her brother. "Maybe it's something worldly?"

He shrugged. The siblings looked at their father, who had spent the most time around worldly things. Hugo shook his head.

"I've been gone so long," he said.

■ ■ ■

As a child, instead of a dollhouse Galina had a ceramic hut on chicken legs. Sculpted from clay, it was one of the few things her mother brought to the new apartment when she married. Before bed, Lida recited stories about Baba Yaga, the old witch who chased children who strayed into her woods. A cape of white hair trailed behind the witch when she flew, bony legs tucked into a mortar, gnarly hands steering with a pestle. The screechy calls of a trapped fox echoed in her wake. In Lida's telling, desperate to get her daughter to sleep, Baba Yaga was more eccentric than dangerous, an unconventional aunt. Galina, sheltered and perpetually attended, asked, "But how did the children get there?" She wanted to go too. The doors on the ceramic house did not move and the openings were too small for Galina's dolls. But she lay for hours in front of the empty sculpture, peering into the small windows and wishing the chicken legs would stretch and turn the hut just the slightest bit. In Lida's stories, Baba Yaga's house rotated round and round like a spinning dervish, shedding wooden roof tiles and hay. Galina would look away, pretending not to see, only to whip her head around, as if to catch the hut in action. Sometimes in the mornings, Galina found the hut turned, the door to the wall, her mother grinning from the kitchen.

That afternoon, leaning into the helicopter window until her force about tipped it, she finally glimpsed the old witch. Her untamed hair blowing around her in the helicopter's wash, skirt rags spread out on the air so that she seemed to float, eyes trained on other dimensions. Galina had made the pilot hover and hover because the image of the woman undone by the helicopter's gusts was hocus-pocus, a fable in flesh and bone. What was she? Had it been real?

"Do you see her?" she kept radioing, hand clasped on the pilot's arm. "Do you see her?"

There she stood, Baba Yaga protecting her hut from Galina, who had finally managed to find her in the wood.

That evening the pilot came to her after dinner, by the river. Galina had lit a small fire from driftwood, and it made a warm porthole for their faces in the cold blue of the latitude's summer night light.

"I was just thinking about Baba Yaga," Galina told him.

He smiled, teeth showing. "I thought she was supposed to embody nature, the forest, its creatures. But in stories she was so ugly."

"I thought she was just a lonely old witch."

"Not all witches are bad," he said, and shrugged. He passed her a military water canteen. "From my personal stash. A friend makes it."

Alcohol wasn't allowed in camp, but she sipped the moonshine.

"Floral notes on turpentine," she said. "Excellent."

They passed it back and forth without talking. When the fire died, she faced him.

"Should we go visit the hut?" she asked. "We have to go survey that area anyway."

"You're the boss," the pilot said, and nodded.

The next morning, Galina packed camping gear, food, cameras. She folded triangular hats out of newspapers to shield their heads from the sun. Afraid of who the homesteaders might be, she packed gifts: a small transistor radio, a bagful of honey cookies, a sack of their best tea.

The pilot loaded the helicopter. He followed his internal map and the greasy red arrows on Galina's aerial photographs, retracing the way to the settlement. He found the flat spot Galina had pointed out and landed on loose rock, still several kilometers away from their destination. They loaded each other down with backpacks full of supplies, then headed toward the red flags the line cutters had hung. Pretending still, to themselves, they'd come to perform the ground survey.

They sang songs as they walked, gathering bilberries. Galina led, breaking trail through forest padded with still-soggy grassland, the suction of the ground adding percussion to their voices. They looked like state-sponsored Pioneers on an outing for fresh air and adventure, cheeks pinched pink by the outdoors. Animals scattered in the wood as they approached, their fleeing a swish of shrub leaves and creaking fir trunks. Fox paths led them to the edge of the forest and into open fields. Stands of Siberian iris the color of deep northern dusk hushed and intoxicated them under the beating sun. The pilot pulled up irises as he walked. With a knife, he cut off the roots, filling a pillowcase with soil-covered bulbs.

At lunchtime, they stopped at the water's edge and ate bread with cheese sweating from the afternoon heat. Spring snowmelt still fattened the river, pushing it into the forest edge. Tree trunks emerged from the black mirror of standing water. Pale-green grass peeked out of the shallows. Over their sandwiches, the geologists speculated about who they'd encounter. Rogue fur trappers, Tolstoy disciples, diamond miners, lost souls, Baba Yaga.

They found the first flags after lunch. Galina unpacked the hand magnetometer, aimed it at the ground, recorded diligently the gammas it measured. She pictured the octahedral crystals of magnetite suddenly aware of her presence, perking up. In her notebook, Galina noted the regolith that hid the rock below, concealing what her instruments discerned. They packed and proceeded toward the next flag, in the direction of the settlement. From there, they'd have to veer off the grid.

A warm aimlessness dissolved inside Galina. She hadn't spent much time in this part of the taiga. Other field expeditions had taken her to more industrialized land tracts. Even when she'd had opportunities to walk fields and switchbacks and valley floors, her gaze had been peculiarly strategic. The mountain there for her taking. She'd spent so much energy trying to prove herself, that she belonged there; the work had consumed her like a strange vortex, swallowing her. Now she focused on the vistas. The ground beneath her sank slightly as the permafrost softened under the sun's warmth. Each footfall released a spore cloud. The mountains razored up to the edge of the sky. It all looked untouchable, too breathtaking to take, to tarnish.

They walked slowly, detouring and exploring, until the light turned the dusky color of Arctic nighttime, and pitched camp in a field. Wolves howled very far off, their song muffled by a foggy veil wrapped around the meadow's rim. The pilot threw iris roots into the fire to perfume the air. Galina watched him through the campfire smoke. Eyes beholden to distances, fingers roughed by metal, one gold chain slung around his tanned neck.

■ ■ ■

That night, Agafia looked for guidance from a ghost. She slept on a pyre of stones in the meadow where her mother stopped trying. That was in the winter of 1950, when Agafia was ten years old, before her sister tied the dead woman's scarf around her head.

It had been an especially hard season; when Nadia retrieved food from the pantry little puffs of mold exploded at her fingertips. She told the children to stay in the hut and tend the fire, but they stuck their faces to the window and put their ears to the walls. She dragged the burlap bags of spoiled potatoes out into the snow and spread them onto the clean white surface, staining it with the rot.

They heard her wailing in the snowy meadow where Agafia now lay amid wildflowers. Nadia crouched there for a long time. New snow began to fall, covering the moldy potatoes with a layer of cleanliness, hiding the hunger spelled out on the snow. Then she walked back to the hut and gathered everyone around her.

Agafia had tuned in and out as her mother spoke. Nadia didn't have too many lessons to impart. She sucked air through her teeth and gazed at her children, marveling at the strong bodies she'd succored with her own small one. Hugo stood in the corner, disapproving.

"If not fire, then hunger," he'd told his wife when she shared her decision to forfeit her food portions to the children. "It's the same thing."

But Agafia's mother ignored him; she lay down and she did not get up again. The blankets around her shrank, vacuum-sealing her body as she wasted away. Hugo rose earlier than normal and returned to the hut later, though the winter presented few opportunities for activity outside the house. Each night he dragged a sled filled with river-smoothed boulders. He piled them around the perimeter of the hut, encasing it.

Nadia's breath grew quieter, but she lay in bed an entire forty days, holding on despite everything. Her last exhale was a gale-force wind that blew through the house, leaving her children chilled and disheveled. Even as an adult, Agafia feared the wind more than she did the cold, the snow. But she also spoke to it affectionately, as if to her mother.

Nadia died in the last days of that February. She ceased to whistle, and both inside and outside the wind calmed. Hugo combed her hair, braided it. He wrapped her in a single blanket and placed a prayer scroll in her hand. She lay like that among them in the one-room hut for two days. On the third, each of her children delivered a last kiss and Hugo carried her out feet first from the hut.

There was no procession to accompany him and nowhere far to go to reach the burial place, so he made one lap around the house before carrying her to the meadow. Without a casket, he let her body sink into the field's winter cover. The ground was too frozen to dig; with the others' help he hauled the stones that lined the outside walls of the hut and piled them higher and higher over Nadia's body. They moved slowly, to conserve calories. They unsheathed the house and covered her, building a short mound atop her body until they could no longer roll the stones.

He questioned whether the cairn was sinful even as he worked.

Summers the stones drank up the sun hungrily and the family sat around the heap, leaning on the heat of Nadia's tomb. The warmth held into the night; it pulsed against Agafia as she draped her body around the rocks.

She tried speaking with her mother. She wanted to know if it had been worth it, to leave them. She needed to know what loomed beyond their nest, the beauty that awaited her. To know if magic existed beyond their valley. Instead, Peter strolled up, stretched out on the grass below her, and fell asleep. Agafia tossed and turned that night, waiting.

She woke to trilling birds. No thunder, nothing out of the ordinary. The stone bed where she'd slept made all her joints hurt, and she stretched in the lush grass at the tomb's base. She didn't return to the hut for prayers but recited them from memory, sitting on the ground. She directed them at the treetops, the sappy trunks that held them up, the sun.

The family hadn't built a church, perhaps fearing they'd have to burn it down, or hoping they wouldn't have to stay long enough to need it. Its conspicuous absence an ode to the unsettled nature of their quarantine. Instead, Agafia imagined twisted spires rising over the meadow, flowers' balm in place of incense's fog, the priest's drone drowned out by the seesaw crane call. Here was a church of sorts. Didn't her people say the forest grew all the way to heaven?

She went to the garden and ran her fingers through the bolting potato plants. In the winters, the family ate potatoes nonstop. Tubers in the summer, when fish and berries and edible leaves of all sorts abounded, churned her stomach. She was a bear, fattening for the sparse cold winter, which came, an onslaught, each year. Try as she did, though, she couldn't sleep through the long winter, so she got down on her knees and began to weed.

■ ■ ■

The hut faced Galina and the pilot as they approached, its small, dingy window openings unblinking, heavyset hips bulging. The roof was thatched with debris, hanging over the structure like a mushroom cap. The worn wood of the walls softened the rough construction, and the garden that buffered it from the forest lent it the air of just another house on the outskirts of town, a stretch of dirt road away from the neighbors.

The pilot knocked. He hadn't realized how strongly his knuckles would land on the dry wood and stepped back, startled. The door, aslant against its frame, creaked open. Galina held her breath for Baba Yaga. Instead, an old man stepped out. His clothes matched the wood of the hut, a flat gray-blue that made his teal eyes pop in a face full of beard and brow. He stood silent under the roof's lip, looking out at the sky and trees as if seeing them for the first time. Inside the hut, other voices rose and fell, but he didn't pay them or the pair of newcomers any mind. Hugo absorbed the surroundings, inhaled deeply, grasped the doorframe as if seeking balance on a precipice. A fugitive taking a moment before he's caught.

"We're geologists," Galina said. "We're doing some field work in the area."

Hugo raked his beard with a thick-fingered hand.

"We've brought some gifts," Galina went on, and held up a satchel filled with offerings.

The man made a noise of acknowledgment in his throat, then ducked behind the door. At the geologists' feet, drying fish scales shone pearly in the sun. Potato peels and small animal guts twisted together in the grass in front of the homestead's door. All around the house, refuse in different states of decomposition littered the ground. A woman's voice rose inside, a cry or exclamation. Other voices gathered around it, a flock of birds. Galina slid a backpack from her shoulders and let it fall on the ground amid the food scraps. She rolled down her sleeves against the mosquitos and flies and waved her hands at the bugs making for her face. She looked for the long-haired woman in the dark of the hut's opening.

The old man emerged again a few minutes later. A younger man and two women followed him out and lined up, as if for inspection. Each had broad shoulders and slack, weathered skin.

Galina recognized the woman with the hair, now hidden. She smiled slightly.

"What do you want?" the old man asked.

"We didn't know anyone was out here," Galina said. "We're camped nearby. Spotted your homestead when we flew over."

"Sorry if it scared you," the pilot added.

The younger people muttered behind the man.

"How far did you come from?" he asked.

"About eighteen kilometers," Galina said. "Just a straight path, that way." She pointed toward the canyon. The witchy woman turned to follow her finger.

"There's a settlement?" the man asked.

"It's just us. We're geologists, here for the summer. Working."

"Working." The man nodded and looked at them. "Leave now," he said. "Don't return, please."

Galina protested, offering the gifts they'd carried, but the man was already ushering the others back into the hut. Before he shut the door, he crossed himself. From inside the house came cries and something like song.

CHAPTER 2
Глава 2

After the geologists left, Agafia moped for days. She spent all her time at the river filling metal pitchers of water, walking out to the rapids and curling her toes around stones to keep her balance. On the riverbank, she picked her teeth with stiff blades of grass and launched pebbles toward the opposite shore. She loosened the knot under her chin and slid the scarf down around her neck. With her fingers, she recentered the part of her hair and then refolded the layers of her rags, so the seams of her being lined up. She felt dirty, but also excited and warmed from both inside and out. When Peter came to see her, she snapped at him.

"A devil you are for sending them here!" she said.

Peter bounced on his feet. "I'm afraid they'll teach you about worse devils than me."

Together they walked along the water toward the garden. Usually she tried to avoid Peter, hiding from him or ignoring his entreaties into conversation. But the geologists' visit confused her, scrambling everything. Only sinful Peter could understand her desire for the sinful company of the geologists.

"Imagine," she said, "flew over us just like a bird!"

Peter, so reverential whenever a question of technology arose, marveled along with her. "A ship for the sky," he said. "If that had been around in my time, I could have seen my land from the air."

He stopped to consider the notion. "Do you think it would have looked vaster or diminished?" he asked.

Agafia stepped onto the soft, plowed soil of the vegetable plot and looked for the most overgrown rows. The visitors were the first people she'd ever seen in her thirty-some years who weren't her family. They spoke differently and dressed differently; the woman wore pants and her hair fell by her ears, like a man's. Agafia's books had taught her to fear many things and described dangers in meticulous detail. Yet she didn't quite know where the geologists fit. She didn't even know what a "geologist" was. As she weeded in the garden, she hummed to herself. *Maybe they are worldly but innocent,* she thought. *Maybe I can have a friend.*

The next day Agafia woke early and sneaked out of the hut. She intended to trek to the geologists' camp. She left in the penumbral morning sliver between daylight and northern not-quite-night-light, with Peter by her side. A splotchy effervescence settled across her cheeks and grew brighter as she walked. She rushed along after Peter, then slowed to pace herself. When she stopped to rest, Agafia peeled boiled young potatoes, hanging the skins on flower stalks and stiff weeds. When the light hit them, they glowed like paper lanterns. After lunch, she marched into the fully risen sun, holding up a flattened hand over her eyes. She spread her fingers wide, then narrowed them, letting cones of light enter in the slots between her digits, then slowly shut them out.

She left the valley's lush grass and stepped onto mountain scree. She hesitated for a moment in the massif's shadow, but Peter waved her on and she proceeded, as if following the geologists' scent. Maybe the afternoon breeze whipped up instructive spoors, or perhaps it was Peter's wake in the distance ahead. The deep contrasts in the afternoon light made it hard to see. The geologists had said it was a straight shot to camp. She walked for hours.

The pilot noticed her first. He'd been lounging in a hammock with a pair of binoculars when he saw someone approaching from the mountains. He pulled on his army boots and ran to her shirtless, yelping and waving with excitement to the unexpected guest. When he reached her, Agafia turned her back to him and closed her eyes.

"Come! Come!" he said, barely noticing her modesty.

He led her the last kilometer to camp. Galina laid food on the table, metal plates laden with state delicacies—sardines, canned meat, crackers crumbling in the corners, a feast for tamed senses. Agafia refused everything. Instead, she rose from her seat and silently began to run her fingers along the objects on the table.

Things. She'd counted her things in her mind as she lay in bed the previous night. A gown; a long coat for the winter, patched with fur; several hole-riddled shawls which, when she layered them on her body, transformed her into a grand paperbark maple. Three books dating to the late 1800s, inherited from her mother and filled with the daily prayers and divine services. A nesting bowl collection of birch boxes, for storing seeds, grains, nuts, berries, emptiness. A tundra-grass mattress. A skillet with a worn bottom that she had to lean left in the fire, stirring its contents askance. She recounted what lay in the cemetery of things that could no longer be cajoled into usefulness: sheaves of moth-devoured cloth, chips

45

of blackened metal still curved into the bottoms of pots and pans, small wooden and cardboard boxes that had come from the world a long, long time ago.

At the geologists' camp many more things spilled from containers and covered surfaces. Even as Galina apologized for the lack of cultivated hominess, Agafia inspected the piles of objects.

"This." She pointed. "What is it?"

"It's a radio," Galina said. "A machine that allows us to listen to songs and news from Moscow. The sounds travel through the atmosphere by way of electromagnetic signals."

"This."

"It's a magnetometer. We use it to figure out how much iron there is in the rocks."

Agafia caught Peter out of the corner of her eye but refused to turn her head in his direction.

"This," she said defiantly.

On the table lay a folded-up multitool. The pilot picked it up and drew out a blade, a tiny scissor, a screwdriver, a bottle opener, a diminutive saw. As he pulled more blades out of hidden pockets, the metal bloomed, each instrument a gleaming petal. Agafia leaned in and touched the tips of the miniature knives with her fingertips.

"Sharp!" she exclaimed. Nothing like the dull lengths of metal she used to make tattered cuts in meat and vegetables as she cooked. She grabbed the pocketknife out of the pilot's hands and turned it over in her own, sliding the implements in and out of their places. The blade release refused to yield and she sliced at her palm, then dropped the thing, shocked. When Galina rushed to help her,

Agafia stomped her foot. She pressed the bleeding palm to her dress and picked up the tool again, rolling it in the cloth, as if to conceal it without anyone's noticing.

"You can have it," Galina said. "It's yours."

Agafia, without acknowledging Galina, had already tucked the gift into her skirts, and proceeded down the table, inspecting.

"This."

She thrust her chin at the table, where the pilot had left a razor from the morning's wash.

"This," Galina said, "is used to shave."

Agafia heard a burst of laughter from Peter, who had forced men to shave though it was a sin.

She inspected the geologists' camp with her fingers, a blind woman inching her way through the modern world by touch, smell, taste. The objects—blankets, tents, drying clothes, food items, tools like hammers and the thin, hollow screws they used to bore cores from trees—made up whole classes of textures, colors, and smells that she'd never encountered. She walked over to the photo tent, where Galina had been developing photos that morning, and then to a string tied taut between two trees, where she'd hung up photos with wooden clothespins to dry. A print of Agafia's homestead swung among pictures of familiar mountains and aerials of the twisted rope of river.

"That's a photo of your house," the pilot said to Agafia, pointing. "From the air." A gray patina covered the photos like daguerreotypes because Galina had been impatient with the fixer.

It lent them an otherworldly cast, as if she'd captured memories instead of land.

"As if the snow cranes could paint," Agafia said, and looked up at the pilot. "You're a giant snow crane."

From then on, the pilot was known only as Snow Crane.

"Can I take a photo of you?" he asked.

"That is worldly," she said, waving him away.

He unclipped a photo from the line; when he handed it to her she accepted it with her bloody hand, hiding the paper in the folds of her dress, which absorbed everything like a voluminous suitcase.

That night Snow Crane came to Galina's tent and she allowed him to enter.

"Why did our things surprise her?" Galina whispered.

She had set up a tent and cot for Agafia right next to her own. She lit a small lantern so she could see Snow Crane's face. He shrugged.

"Maybe the family has been living out there all alone for so long they haven't seen these things."

"But why?" She leaned closer to his face. "Why would anyone do that?"

"A million reasons."

When Galina was in school, everything surprised her. Fellow students grew exasperated whenever she would ask why someone acted this way or that. She'd been so sheltered, an innocent, confused by reasonable people's irrational behavior. One night a girlfriend of hers got sick of her questions about something, she couldn't remember what now. "This Soviet system," the friend said, "don't you understand it makes normal people act crazy?" Galina hadn't understood.

"What kinds of reasons?" she asked Snow Crane. But he'd

fallen asleep facing Galina, their knees bent and kissing in the cramped tent.

In the morning, as Agafia repacked her things into her shawl to head home, Galina came to her.

"Do they know you're here?" she asked.

Agafia shook her head.

"How long have you lived there?" Galina asked.

"My whole life. My family came out there in the nineteen thirties. You're the first visitors we've had."

"We're the first people you've ever met aside from your family?"

"Yes!" Agafia clapped her hands, delighted. "Won't you come visit us again?" she asked.

"I'm afraid your father won't like that."

"He'll come around," Agafia said, and lunged to hug Galina.

■ ■ ■

The next week Galina and Snow Crane detoured again from their ground survey route. They brought bags of grain and military blankets for the family. Agafia bounded to them; she wore the pocketknife around her waist on a leather belt and had cleaned the tool so that it shone resplendent in the sun. Behind Agafia, the old man emerged. He approached slowly and tentatively. Guilt ate at Galina for making him resign like that to her presence, but she did not leave. Hugo motioned for the group to follow him. He led them to a clearing behind the house. Everyone spread out into a big circle, the geologists with sun-scraped faces, Agafia grinning, her people carefully avoiding the newcomers' eyes.

"We are the Kols," Hugo finally said.

They went around and introduced themselves. When they finished, a quiet settled among them.

"We brought some gifts," Galina said. She took out a flashlight and clicked it on to demonstrate how it worked.

"That is worldly," Hugo said. "We cannot accept it."

They did the same for each new item Galina pulled from her carefully prepared package—a sleeve of crackers, cans of meat, a sleeping bag, old newspapers. The year-old papers would bear fresh news to them, she had mused as she packed. Snow Crane dug around in his bag until he found a cloth bundle.

"Salt," he said, extending his hand.

Hugo bared his brown teeth and accepted the parcel.

"Lick your fingers," he said to his grown children, "and dip them in here. Then lick again."

"Three, two, one," Agafia counted down.

They thrust their fingers into their mouths. The salt dissolved on their tongues, the flavor sharp. Agafia, Dima, and Natalia coughed and examined the remaining crystals on their fingers.

"We ran out of salt a long time ago," Hugo said, cackling.

He caught his breath, his face slackened, and he began to pray. The others joined him, bending to the ground in a steady beat, song coming from deep in their bodies. So rarely had she encountered prayer that Galina didn't recognize it at first. She pursed her lips and cast down her eyes, not knowing how to act. Her school classrooms had been covered with posters proselytizing godlessness. In one, a beaming, cherubic cosmonaut, red space suit tethered to a rocket in a starry sky, floated high above onion domes. *There is no god!* the poster read. Staring at his beatific smile in class day after day, Galina believed him. That was the extent of her religious education.

The Kols prayed, undistracted by the onlookers, until Hugo looked up and, as if remembering an old joke, began again to chortle about the salt.

"What religion do you follow?" Snow Crane asked.

"We're Old Believers," Hugo said. "We're just believers." He hadn't had to explain himself to anyone in decades. "We follow the pre-Nikonian Russian faith."

"True Christians," Natalia added.

"You were persecuted so you came here," Snow Crane said, as if translating for Galina.

The Kols nodded.

"We came here."

"We are the keepers of memory, of the past, which will save us," Agafia said.

"And the future?" Snow Crane asked.

She'd never lived for the future, for it was not guaranteed, threatened by starvation and the Antichrist in equal measure. The past was concrete, written, her inheritance.

Hugo looked stunned to find himself in the taiga, its mercurial grandeur forever sneaking up on him. The geologists had intruded on the Kols' homestead and life, but they too were mere squatters on this brutish land. Together they were nothing more than visitors, each passing through for their own purposes. How easy it was to relinquish one's claim on this place. It never quite welcomed anyone like a real home. The idea of their mutual foreignness—the geologists', the Kols'—in this meeting place relaxed them all.

They talked into the night, a friendly interrogation of their respective foreign worlds. The Kols told stories of their harvests, of the traps they built to ensnare deer, of how the snow piled around them in the winter and encased them in wind-carved white walls. The geologists regaled them with tales of new railroads crisscrossing the entire continent, of electricity and the density of cities, where, they said, little huts like the Kols' were stacked one on top of another to make apartment buildings, where they lived.

But the changes the geologists longed to share with the Kols were so vast and otherworldly that the prospect seemed to stunt them. Impossible to explain the late twentieth century to someone living in the seventeenth without it sounding like science fiction. The geologists grew pensive. The quieter they became, the rowdier the Kols grew. The struggles of their daily survival rolled out in expansive prose. The smallest details received lengthy treatment in their repeated tellings, each family member's version overlaying the previous person's. An a cappella of the mundane details of endurance.

At a lull in the conversation, Snow Crane said, barely audible, "Stalin is dead, you know."

The old man crossed himself.

"But Peter still lives," Hugo said.

■ ■ ■

Galina and Snow Crane left early the next morning, promising to come again. The geologists waved at the family as they grew smaller with distance, turning back every once in a while and lifting again their arms as if in exaltation. The Kols stood together, watching them retreat. At a bend in the trail, Galina and Snow Crane's bodies slipped out of view, but their presence lingered among the Kols, like a smell. Agafia wondered what her family would make of the visitors she'd invited into their solitary world. Their appearance was a threshold in her mind. Each person would have to decide what had changed for them in the presence of strangers and what would remain the same and how the family's life would shift. And then they'd each step over the threshold into an altered way of being.

"Well?" Agafia asked no one in particular.

"Well," Hugo sighed.

More and more Hugo appeared weary of the taiga and suddenly old. He'd known strangers once, had fled them all those years ago, and Agafia worried he'd forbid further interaction with her new friends. But Hugo leaned on his knees, groaned once with pain, and picked up his walking stick.

"I'm going to go harvest in the garden for dinner," he said.

It was a tacit approval, a signal that he would not stand in her way. Agafia bit her lip and turned to gaze at her sister. Natalia was already padding off after Hugo, her arms full of birch boxes, skirt swaying against encroaching weeds. Natalia lived in her head, her fingers constantly counting the steps on her worn *lestovka*, her eyes either upturned in prayer or downturned in task. In those early hard years in this meadow, when the parents were preoccupied with constant challenges to the family's survival, Agafia was often left in her sister's care. It was quiet Natalia who'd taught Agafia to talk. The girl would bring her young sister to the garden and urge her to name the world around her. *Potato, turnip, soil, pine, pebble.* For all

Siberia's vastness, Natalia had made the world small with her sparse basket of words. Named, the world shrank. The smallness she cultivated was her way of controlling the difficulties at hand, but Agafia longed to lap everything up. The sisters weren't close, and Agafia watched her go after Hugo with sadness.

Only Dima remained with Agafia, still looking after the vanished figures, dreamily scratching his beard. If Natalia made the world small, then Dima exploded it into a kaleidoscopic riot of possibilities, his bliss a radiant heat, like the sun. Agafia and Dima had leaned on each other growing up, and as adults they maintained a childlike attachment full of inside jokes, the physical roughness of juvenile play, the intense connection of bonded escapees. Agafia poked Dima on the shoulder and jerked her head sideways, so that he rose and followed her.

They picked their way along the riverbank on a path they often took to reach a favorite swimming hole. The river pooled there into a wedge of deeper water, but not so deep they couldn't reach bottom. Brother and sister shed their clothes into neat piles on the gravel shore and entered the stream. They came here in the summer after a hard day's work, and babbled as the river rushed around them, a third voice in their conversation. Hugo had found them in this secret spot before, admonished them for bathing naked, forbade it with anxious insistence. His vehemence had scared Agafia, as if her brother's skin was a source of sin, so always she kept a distance. But the water felt too good. She floated supine, her hair rippling in the slight current, breast breaking the surface, legs sinking slowly to the sand. The vague threat of strangers had always hovered over their hut like a weather system. Now their appearance had finally parted the skies, and more than anything, Agafia thought, the day felt normal and clear. She let her feet touch bottom and stood up.

"Are you scared?" Agafia asked.

Dima's face was half-submerged, mouth open so that the water ran through it as if he were a filtrating fish. He spit a stream toward Agafia.

"I'm not scared of anything," Dima said.

Agafia knew this to be true. Sometimes she thought he wasn't even very scared of the Antichrist, eschewing prayers when he could, but then he'd stun her with an act of resolute piety and she'd reconsider, thinking his fearlessness a result of his sureness in the Lord.

"Do you think they're bad?" she asked.

Dima watched the goose bumps on his arm rise. The water was cold even in summer, even in the sun.

"I don't know," he said. "They're probably unbelievers."

"Promise me you won't leave me for them," Agafia said. Her brother had sometimes confided his desire for something more. For children, a wife. Dima sank again in the water so only his eyes floated above its dark surface. He blew bubbles with his mouth and disappeared into them.

"Dima!" Agafia shouted.

The water roiled with his exhale. After half a minute he came up and splashed her.

"Don't be stupid," he said.

"Should we pray?"

She began to recite the morning prayer for the second time that day.

Lord Jesus Christ, Son of God, have mercy on me, a sinner.

She bowed until her lips touched the water, then continued.

I have sinned immeasurably; Lord, have mercy and forgive me, a sinner.

To pray was to work toward believing and to labor in the taiga was to slog toward survival and that was good and important and to try new things was to tempt trouble but she resolved anyway to allow the lure of strangers to break open her world so that she could know a bigger life. And she would have Dima by her side, and because God loved him they would be protected, Amen. She dipped to wet her hair and let the current carry her until her bottom touched the scree in shallower water. She stood and dove back into the pool.

■ ■ ■

At camp, Galina's team was busy with the daily tasks of field life and their mission. Over breakfast, in pocketed military pants, loose button-down shirts, kerchiefs tied slack around their necks, the men checked the previous day's notes with each other and made lists of the outstanding tasks before setting off. Galina liked the incremental progress of a large assignment, how something as astounding as tapping the earth's innards started with some hammers and the tear-shaped hand lenses that hung from each geologist's neck. Simple tools that a mountain should be able to withstand. Rather than making the work more prosaic, each step became more inspired. They were mere mortals against the alp, like David and Goliath, improbably—inevitably—coming out on top.

The men trekked into the mountains, hands clasped easily

around pickaxes balanced behind their backs. They stopped to measure outcrops or jot comments into notebooks, observing the rock. The team hacked off stone shards into labeled sacks and boxes, weighing their bags down as the work progressed. They returned to camp each evening to fill in the blank spaces of the underground maps they all held in their heads.

Nights, a tenderness bloomed; the sun barely set, the five geologists marked time with campfires. The smoke kept the bugs away and the ritual drew a line from one day to the next. They had built a pit and each evening took turns lighting the fire. Once the flames peeked over the rocky rim and crackled steadily, the camp gathered on the logs they'd laid in a circle to talk and watch the blaze dance. Sometimes they spoke about work or told jokes, but more often they talked about books, kitchen concerts where they'd crossed paths, the summer gardens at their dachas, and who made the best plov. On especially pleasant nights the orange glow loosened lips and they dared to imagine their futures. Mostly the future was abstract, incomprehensible, a fugue. For each of them, it seemed, the future was elsewhere, but no one knew where. They told of their surreal bureaucratic efforts to flee the Union, the serpentine paths and Escher-esque angles they worked to secure a visa and a plane ticket out of the country that clung to them unrepentantly.

Galina mostly listened. Geologists were an independent breed, she'd learned that from the beginning, in school. In that way, she hadn't fit in with her classmates, then colleagues. She was a rule follower, a daughter of the ruling class, despite the small distances she'd put between herself and her father. She had believed in her assignments. In her country. Most of the other scientists she'd met believed only in the goodness of field season, when they fled the cities for the anarchy of the forest, the mountains, the plain. In emptiness they found freedom. In camp they shed their guard. Its remoteness unclenched their jaws and relaxed their psyches so they felt more like men and less like prey. They grew new skin, new ways of being; this molting a treasured part of their profession.

This season, Galina felt it too. She relaxed into the evenings. Her mind wandered. To the tanned arms of her colleagues, the translucent moon, something funny Agafia had said, the fragrant bank of the river just below. A guitar circulated; each person would strum a chord as he talked, then pass it on.

"Well, boys," she'd say, "play something already."

She was done striving, she was ready to live. This time, the taiga was changing her too. Thawing her as if she were summer permafrost—around the edges, to start. From the melt tumbled her ambition to open the mine, that old urge to please her father, the need to do anything at all other than walk.

The walks dissolved her, reshaped her. Sometimes she walked toward other valleys, other possibilities, looking for a different entry to the past or a pleat in the present. She was mining for understanding of the affections that unfolded within her, for Agafia, for Snow Crane, for the land.

■　■　■

Every few days Snow Crane and Galina left instructions for the line cutters and other geologists and set out to see the Kols. They packed sacks of buckwheat, clothing in assorted sizes, what tools the team could spare. The Kols began to accept the gifts the geologists brought, tucking them into the hut's eaves, squirreling away provisions. Warmth crept in between the two groups. They were two Russian civilizations discovering each other, two distant time periods brought together by chance. When two rock faces—one older, one much younger, with time lost in between—touch, geologists call it an unconformity. The maw of time that separated Agafia's and Galina's worlds also scrambled easy understanding. They talked about this often, probing how to reconnect each other's realities into something linear.

One afternoon they sat in the sun watching chipmunks chase each other in the tall grass. The garden was in bloom and the sun glazed them with viscous warmth. Languorousness begot gab and Agafia began to ponder aloud.

"If the Lord is our father and the land is our mother, then somehow we are all siblings here," she said. "And just like Natalia and I are so different you'd barely know we share blood, we're all so different you'd barely know we came from the same Russia."

She said it in the singsong patois that rendered all her declarations—about potatoes and growing seasons and the winter and the summer and her very existence—into homogeneously toned hymnal verses. As if song could be the only path to such hard understanding. For children to learn the alphabet, teachers made up songs, and to learn fundamental truths, Agafia did too.

Agafia seemed a child to Galina, though they were roughly the same age, in their thirties. She groped at the world like a fledgling, curiosity not undone by the stacked years of adulthood. Other times Agafia appeared ancient. She looked decades older than Galina, as if carrying the centuries of her people's struggles on her skin, and she spoke in proclamations that acquired a timeless sort of wisdom in their incomprehensibleness. Suspended in the liminal space between her innocence and her weighty history, Agafia was clear-eyed about the change the geologists brought.

"Now I have met so many people," Agafia mused to Galina. "There's my mother and my father, Dima and Natalia. And now you and Snow Crane and the geologists. Each new person opens up the world in new ways."

This pondering eased Galina's anxiety about being an unwanted guest, and she returned regularly. Once she and Snow Crane arrived just as the family was setting off somewhere, laden with bags.

"Come, come," Hugo called.

"We're off to work!" Dima said.

They padded down a well-worn path toward a smaller clearing where Dima and Hugo had been building a second hut. Hugo hung back with Snow Crane, confiding as he walked.

"I regret my children can't marry," he said. "To live here is to wait for extinction."

Snow Crane had noticed the careful way Agafia tended to her brother, coquettish and admiring as she picked a flower from the meadow to tuck into a buttonhole or turned her eyes up to listen when he spoke.

"Is that why you're building the hut?" Snow Crane asked. "To not tempt sin?"

They had tempted it too long, Hugo lamented, but each year one disaster or another distracted them from the work of making a second dwelling. They were finally getting around to it now.

"Dima will live here when it's finished," Hugo said. "A little personal space is good even in the taiga."

At the new site, a cabin smaller even than the main house rose from the muddy clearing.

Young, straight pine trunks lay in piles. Dima had arranged the timber rim of his quarters, sunken in a square hole he'd dug out to the depth of his knee. When he stepped inside the wreath of logs, the tiny, one-room rectangle practically hugged him.

"It'll be easy to heat!" he said, grinning.

He unwrapped an axe that Snow Crane and Galina had brought him on a previous visit and started to hack the logs down to size. The thwacks reverberated in the valley like dull bird calls. Hugo had gone to gather peat moss to chink the room against the cold; a heap of it already sat in wait. And Snow Crane set to carving notches in the logs, to finish the walls.

Sweat dampened Snow Crane's shirt and clamped his hair to his forehead as he worked. He found a rhythm, sank into it. The work came back to him so easily, as if his hands had a harder time forgetting than his mind. He'd done this sort of thing before, his hands told him, he'd chopped wood in Siberia. This time, at least, it was summer.

Silence settled between the men, only their tools calling out to each other, like song. Then Dima started up an actual song, which rose and fell with his axe. It was a call and response ballad, and after some rounds Snow Crane joined in, so that their voices braided into a fine refrain that pulled the work along. Hugo returned with more moss; he took up the tune too, his voice lower, thinner than the younger men's, filling in the melody as the moss would soon fill the cracks between logs.

When they stopped to rest, Hugo stepped back to admire the day's effort. The family hadn't built anything substantial since just after their arrival in the valley decades ago, and the sight of new human trappings on the familiar, harsh terrain filled him with melancholy joy. He recalled, aloud, the village where he'd once lived, how carved animals decorated huts' exteriors so that everything, even the structures that lined miserable, muddy roads, felt alive. Pigs whittled in relief grazed by the front doors; wild cranes and red roosters, to ward off fires, congregated between windows edged by filigreed wood trim.

"I'll carve some animals for my hut!" Dima said. "Snow Crane will bring me tools."

That's how it was, the Old Believers quickly accustomed to their friends' generosity, replenishing some of what they'd lost in their isolation. The geologists fulfilling their requests when they could, emptying their own matériel bins to bring the Kols food stores, supplies, the world. The unconformity between them thinning.

■ ■ ■

At the geologists' camp, work proceeded too. The aerial surveys Snow Crane flew collected rough measurements of magnetism in the rock below. Higher gamma readings hinted at rich iron spreads. Preliminary maps drew a perimeter around the ore, a lasso catching the iron in concentric outlines. Galina and her crew traversed the mountains with waterproof notebooks, sketching and sampling at outcrops, refining the map with ground measurements. Disoriented compasses, thrown off by the magnetite below their feet, hinted at the deposits' vastness.

It wasn't a secret, really. More than one hundred years ago a man with the last name Ambler discovered the continent's vast iron deposits while surveying the land. Galina's mission was to map them more precisely and decide whether there was enough mineral to call in the drill rigs; to poke holes in the rock, like neat rows of swallows' nests, and stuff them with explosives; to make way for a procession of barn-sized trucks. The compass, its needle drunkenly pointing south instead of east, north instead of west, said yes. She ambled on, in homage to that explorer of the past, taking stock of the black rock chips she found shimmering on the surface and in riverbeds. She carried a matchbox-sized red magnet, shaped like a horseshoe, and when she lowered it to the ground, debris stood on end, reaching. In some eroded openings, the ground showed its hand, revealing striped stone. The undulating bands of rock varied in thickness and stretched like gentle waves frozen solid. Looking at rock, Galina's eyes lost focus, and she rubbed at them, trying to clear away the vibrations. The stripes sparkled black and magenta. Ground-up Milky Way dust and wine.

In school she had learned that these striped iron formations developed at the same time the world over. Most geological processes are repeatable; the earth slowly recycles itself, breathing and roiling, its processes slow but witnessable. But anywhere you went, these iron-rich rocks were the result of a one-off oxygenation unfolding some two billion years ago. Bacteria in the soupy ancient oceans learned to make oxygen, and this oxygen hugged the iron floating in the water and fell to the shallow ocean floor along ancient coastlines, layer by minuscule layer, until ferrous molecules stacked many meters high. The atmosphere was so full of oxygen and the ocean lay so very far from this place now that she found all of this impossible to imagine.

People had theories about the stripes. Her favorite held that the iron-rich layers had formed when the oxygen made by bacteria bonded with the dissolved iron in the water, making a new insoluble molecule that fell to the ocean floor. But the bacteria didn't yet know how to live in the oxygen they produced. If there was too much of it, the bacteria died off. With no oxygen to bond with, the iron stayed dissolved, and instead red, cherty layers spread over the mineral-rich ones. Until the bacteria made a comeback. Over and over, proliferating and poisoning themselves, not learning the lesson for nearly a billion years.

How odd that the Kols, trapped in a century relegated to antiquity, would choose to live on ground that was a snapshot of the world at the dawn of life. As if this stretch of Siberia, so magnetized, attracted fragments from a long-stretching history. Like a box of mementos, faded letters, favorite bobby pins, an empty bottle of perfume, notebooks full of cursive, spent pens, a threadbare handkerchief, the things that made a person, who could not bear to throw them all away. They, and the Kols, were dragged into this tear in the universe's fabric, here where Galina stood.

This stretch of Siberia was odd for another reason: it shouldn't have existed. Some four hundred million years ago, mountains grew there. Rock budded, climbed skyward, folding and deforming. During mountain building, stone—which is time—is scrambled and torn. Chronology is mixed and relaid. By the time tall mountains stand, the neat strata of stone that once lay in their place have been melted and shuffled so that the past is unrecognizable and confused. Chaos reigns in the rocks. But here, an arc of ridges framed an older deposit of banded iron; the iron flats formed two billion years ago were left undisturbed even as mountains rose. How could that be? Unimaginable.

Galina checked and rechecked her findings, doubting them. Her understanding of the geology around her was fragile. She followed her figures like strands of thin hair, untangling with care what she saw from what she knew to be possible. Often the data left her disoriented, hemmed in by mountains she could not understand.

Unable to conjure reasonable answers from the maps and little boxes of samples she collected, she asked Snow Crane to fly her around. The flights were expensive, arguably unnecessary and unscientific after the air surveys were completed, but Galina coveted this bird's-eye view of the area. She needed to see it as a multidimensional map, with the eye of the omniscient rather than the scale of the human. The flights were limited to the two of them, Snow Crane controlling the machine, Galina straining her eyes out the window, notebook in hand, drawing what she saw with as steady a hand as she could manage. That was easier on some flights than others. The machine hurtled through the air with barely controlled urgency, tossing around anything unsecured in the stripped interior. Against air currents and speed its metal skin provided the delicate protection of an eggshell.

As the summer wore on the rapport between Galina and the pilot took on a certain comfort. She'd chosen Snow Crane for the expedition because he was trained as both a scientist and a pilot and she found him competent, scholarly, and attuned to the pulsations of the earth, a kind of shaman geologist who also happened to be able to fly. Her supervisor had told her that most of the people who'd apply for positions with the mission, so remote, would be dissidents. Galina had flagged his résumé in part because he had no record. At the interview they spoke easily of mountains and ambitions. He avoided personal questions. He appeared apolitical, asexual, atheist. She hired him.

He was a good employee in the field. He cleaned and maintained the helicopter, running oiled rags through the crevices of the interior and polishing the exterior. He attended to his machine like a feline in the act of vigorous self-maintenance, contorting his body into knots to reach forgotten nooks. He moved his lips as he worked, but emitted only the slightest noise, murmurs emanating from him as frequency rather than sound. He kept immaculate records, reported on time for missions, kept a clean tent in camp, and followed Galina's orders. Even when he drank in camp, which they all did despite the ban on alcohol, he eventually slunk off to his tent with a journal and a flashlight while the others cackled around a fire; not antisocial, but private, Galina told the others, who joked about him when he retreated.

During their flights, she'd turn on the headsets that connected her and Snow Crane in the impenetrable noise of the helicopter cabin.

"Testing, testing," she'd say into the headpiece.

And he'd reply, "Yes, yes, yes, loud and clear."

At camp, in the silence of the forest, an apprehension stifled their conversation, but the roar of the helicopter blades and the hiss of their friction in the air allowed for honest talk. They spoke openly, their words traveling through the headsets, competing with the noise of the machine. It was for this she grew to like the flights as much as for the bird's-eye vantage. And, at times, Snow Crane broke his own rules. He flirted with Galina through the headset, eyes focused on the horizon and his control panel, not once turning to look at her as he spoke. He described accurately the curve of her nose and lips, and how her chin sloped down into the smooth skin of her neck. Like the curve of a freshly sharpened ice skate blade, he said, with not even a dimple to break the line. He stopped at the suprasternal notch. This didn't go beyond the flights.

They spoke of other things too. Snow Crane told her about his first memory: his mother, in a thin floral dress buttoned down the front, holding a metal watering can. Standing it in the kitchen sink, she turned on the spigot. She moved the stack of chairs from in front of the balcony door and unlatched it. When water ran over the can's lip, she carried it to the balcony, spilling dollops as she walked. The drops, like overripe fruit, burst on the linoleum floor. Snow Crane followed her, his bare feet stomping on the little puddles, slipping. Plants grew in jars, bottles, and metal boxes on the balcony. None of them ever flowered—his mother complained that not enough light reached the shadowy perch. Pretending to be Mowgli, he crouched amid the leafy greenery as if in the jungle, the worms and spiders he found stand-ins for Bagheera and Baloo. When his mother wasn't looking he plucked a leaf from one of the bigger plants and shredded it with his clumsy child fingers, then stuck his hand through the balcony rails and let leaf strips sail down to the ground, riding the air so that they danced side to side before vanishing from sight.

His mother kept a chair on the balcony and that day they sat out there for what, to his impatient inner clock, seemed like hours. He climbed onto her lap and she read to him about trains that criss-crossed the entire Soviet continent, and planes that could travel faster than anything else, and cargo ships and taxis and even bi-cycles. It was a book of propaganda about Soviet transportation. Blue block prints of each machine floated at odd angles on the canvas-colored book cover. She balanced the hard edge of the book on his belly until a slight red indent grew on his skin. Snow Crane fell asleep on her, pressed to her chest, warmed by the Moscow summer heat. Maybe she sang, or hummed to him. When he re-called that idyllic afternoon, it seemed like the kind of thing good mothers like his did. Sing.

He told Galina about his last memory of his mother: A knock on the door, waking him. Shadows crept along the darkened walls, velvety shades of black gliding by each other like manatees.

"Manatees?" Galina asked.

He'd read about them in an illustrated book about North Amer-ican animals, he explained.

He heard his mother's voice, and then a man's voice he didn't recognize. Wearing nothing but his underwear, he crept out of his room. Yellow light filtered through the gauzy fabric his mother had rigged around the bulbs instead of lampshades. The man was trying to usher her out of the apartment, but she kept saying Snow Crane's name, over and over. When she spotted him peeking out from behind a wall, she grabbed him and the man took a step back, surprised that the woman's incantations had conjured a real, human boy. Sweat started to drip down the man's face and he blot-ted it with a striped, dusk-colored handkerchief.

"We'll see to it that the boy is taken care of while you are away," the man said. Then added, "I'm sure you won't be gone long."

Snow Crane described his mother's curled lip. How she opened the drawers of the bookcase and rummaged behind a stack of books, a set of cut crystal glasses, loose papers, faded folders. She produced a box and from it she took out a small stack of bills. She offered it to the man. The man blotted his head again, shook it side to side.

"Oh, you're an honest killer?" his mother asked.

She told Snow Crane to go back to sleep, but he backed up against a wall and refused. His mother sat down next to him. Then the man sat, his back to the wall across from them. For a long time, the three of them just sat there. Eventually Snow Crane's eyelids began to droop, weights pulling them down like heavy garage doors, closing off the watchman behind them. He slumped onto his mother. When he awoke the next morning in his bed, a tartan wool blanket weighed him down. His mother was gone.

Galina learned that he grew up in a government orphanage that isolated promising children and trained them for future military posts. He lived at the orphanage until he turned sixteen.

At sixteen he moved from the orphanage's communal quarters to the military dormitory and eventually learned to fly.

"I suppose I'm from a bad family," he said, "but I don't know anything about that."

Pilot school: in the book his mother read to him, flying meant freedom, but the training bewildered him with its rules and endless classes and studying. The other boys all came from prominent political families, seemed to know each other, and carried themselves with an ease Snow Crane found foreign. Weeks passed before he entered a cockpit. It was a Lavochkin La-250, a long fishlike plane that tended to crash on test flights, so the officers kept it grounded.

Several more weeks passed before one by one the students joined pilots on short flights.

Snow Crane flew in an Su-15, the plane on which he eventually earned his hours. He was good at flying, had a natural touch for maneuvering any aircraft with grace. He remembered, again, the book his mother read him as a child, with the various modes of transport soaring in different directions in blue ink on the cover, and how the plane spoke to him the least. Trains and bicycles and even cars captured his imagination; in trains, one could drink tea with mysterious passengers in each compartment and get off at unfamiliar stations with names like Chita and Birobidzhan. Bicycles allowed him to revel in the force of his own legs, and cars opened horizons. Planes seemed to him like utilitarian machines, inelegant birds full of speed but no sense of adventure. Even so, the views and stillness at thirty thousand feet calmed him. Eventually he went to university, to study geology, and now here he was.

Galina listened, pen tracing mountains and the catenary dips between peaks. In her sketches the mountain ridges took on the look of handsome jawlines and brows.

She spoke, too. Her parents, she told him, were party officials in Moscow. She'd grown up in the strange center of their country's political machine. As a child, she recited patriotic poetry at meetings, rode in parades, marched with the Young Pioneers. She recognized dinner guests on political posters and from a young age carried within her the comfort of a person unquestioned. Her parents' standing lavished her with opportunities: special schools, trips, books, travel.

"I've gotten the best of what the state has to give," she said. "I am the poster child."

She'd come to think of herself that way, as a real-life representative of a fabulous dream.

Like a beautifully furnished show house. A sample.

Snow Crane's laugh was warm even through the headphones' static.

"I'm sold."

Agafia often came up in conversation. Snow Crane spoke tenderly of her naïveté, the hallucinatory way her eyes shone when she encountered new things or people.

"Do you remember the time she watched us unload the food?" he asked Galina on one flight.

Another helicopter had dropped off fresh supplies, bags full of buckwheat, black bread lined up in neat symmetric rows, jars full of farina, cans of condensed milk. As the group unloaded the shipment, Agafia sniffed and touched each piece.

"She's never acquired food in any way other than to grow it or to trap it," Galina said.

"And yet other things don't shock her at all!"

The helicopter gave Agafia little pause after the initial meeting. The photos Galina printed made her curious, but the enlarger barely registered with her. It was the matches, lighters, the stacks of secular books, the walkie-talkies that held her in their grasp. The utilitarian made miraculous by her unknowing.

After speaking of Agafia they'd be quiet for stretches of time.

Once, sitting absorbed in their thoughts, they spotted a pack of wolf cubs frolicking in the meadow below. When Snow Crane lowered the helicopter closer to them, they ran off a distance; but as long as he hovered at a certain height the pack stayed in the clearing and they could observe the pups as they rolled around, wrestled, and learned to hunt. Galina drew them in her notebook.

"Just you wait!" Snow Crane exclaimed into the headset, and turned his head in time to catch her smile.

A popular cartoon at the time followed a disheveled wolf as he tried to outsmart a wily rabbit. The wolf wore garish suit jackets and smoked cigarettes. The rabbit sported fetching overalls with a slit for his pom-pom tail. Always the rabbit managed to outsmart the wolf and the segments closed with the dejected, injured wolf shouting, "Rabbit, just you wait!" That became a joke between them. When the ore behaved unexpectedly in the rocks they examined, when it slipped out of their grasp just as they had their fingers on it, they'd sit in the sprawl of papers and rock samples and tell the rocks around them, "Just you wait!"

■ ■ ■

A couple of weeks passed without Galina and Snow Crane visiting Agafia. Like a watchman, she kept an eye on the valley opening through which they'd come, but eventually she grew restless. She decided to go to them. As she walked, Peter trailing behind her, the sky turned the same color as the mountains, collapsing everything into a flat, gray ocean. A lightning crack announced her arrival and rain soon flooded every low spot in camp. People crowded into the communal tent, where Galina hooked a tiny television to the generator. Fumes from the generator seeped in through the tent walls and everyone's eyes glassed over into shiny marbles. On the TV, tiny ballerinas in grainy white tutus fluttered in and out of formations like iron flecks shifting to a magnet's pull. Due to the poor connection, static kept rolling across the screen. Each time it cleared, everybody cheered. Agafia didn't dare look at the screen of this incomprehensible piece of technology; she retreated to the back of the tent and Galina.

"I'm going to go lie down," Galina told Agafia. "There's a tent set up for you next to mine."

As the big tent emptied out, a clear sight path opened to the television. It glowed lunar blue. Agafia stood to go, but then turned to look at the radiant screen. She swept the tent with her eyes to check for Peter and did not find him. The more time she spent at the camp, the more she allowed herself. Plates of food from cans, gifts, clothing. Some things she accepted more than once; others she rejected if offered anew, just in case. She had to relearn what qualified as worldly out in the actual world. Agafia moved toward the flickering box, groping along the chairs in a diesel fume haze. She settled on a low wood stool.

One man remained by the TV. She sat off to the side, chin planted in her hands, her shawl across her knees, eyes wide, pupils dilated and focused on the dancers. How could something so beautiful be bad? She stared down at her new rubber galoshes, a gift from Galina, then the dancers' pointed feet. The ballerinas emerged one by one from behind the curtain, stepping carefully down a ramp, tutus bouncing as they floated into formation. They looked like leggy blue herons. Layered tulle extended into wings and carried them across the stage when they jumped.

The man let out a low moan.

Agafia turned to check on him. His pants were unbuttoned and a hand disappeared into their folds. He watched the dancers.

Agafia gathered her shawl and ran. She stood in the middle of camp loudly whispering Galina's name until she opened her tent, calling to Agafia. Agafia crawled in, crossing herself, body on fire. That glint of aggression in the way the man glowered at the avian dancers. The odd angle of his arm, muscles strained. She'd once watched a wolf hunt a deer and saw the deer's muscles tense before the predator revealed himself. As if the doe had received some cosmic warning. *Danger!* That's how she felt: she sensed the sin without knowing it. The small tent pushed the women together. Galina wrapped one arm around Agafia and with the other she stroked her head until her breathing evened out and she calmed. Agafia appeared a big woman—sturdy and tall—but holding her, Galina realized her smallness. She was like a mummy, swaddled in a tightly wound knot of cloth.

"No one really touches me," Agafia said.

Her mother used to hold her like this, by the stove. Or Agafia would crawl from the bed she and her siblings shared when they were little to her mother's bed, tuck herself into Nadia's wisp of a body to warm herself. Nadia's papery skin flammable against Agafia's, which remained somehow supple even in hunger.

"It feels so good."

Agafia fell asleep in Galina's arms, and Galina sat up for hours holding her and listening to the rain on the tent. The canvas wasn't very waterproof and by the time they woke in the morning a puddle had seeped in, soaking the sleeping bags.

. . .

In the morning, Agafia walked home more slowly than usual. She made a pouch out of a shawl, tied it around her waist, and meandered from the muddy path collecting open pinecones. She picked nuts out of the cones to eat as she strolled, running her tongue along the inside of her mouth to feel the nuts' greasiness. The shawl, too, filled with cones, a gift for her family from her travels.

Agafia returned to a quiet house. Hugo was out, but Natalia and Dima lay in bed. They'd mentioned they weren't feeling well when she set out to the geologists' camp, but she'd made them tea and hadn't thought much of it. Now it smelled like sickness in the hut. She put water on to boil, removed her shawls, and wrapped them around her sister. Agafia never got sick. *I am an elk and a fox and a bear*, she told herself. When the water boiled, Agafia steeped herbs. After they drank the tea, the siblings went back to sleep.

The next day, they were worse. Brother and sister rallied for the morning prayers, then stood swaying in the hut's entrance to wash themselves with the fresh air that lapped at the doorway. They did not take any of the food Agafia prepared. Dima dampened the shawls Agafia had arranged as pillows with his sweat, paddling under the blankets like a swimmer lost in a too-heavy sea, sinking. Agafia touched her lips to his forehead and felt him burning. She applied cold, flat stones to his hot head, but the fever persisted and he grew more agitated.

Hugo left early in the morning and returned late, busying

himself in the garden. He spent hours putting the finishing touches on Dima's hut and gathered plants for eating and medicine.

Agafia took the herbs Hugo brought and put them away into birch boxes. She didn't know much about using them, groped her way to healing by sniffing at the leaves: this one smells good for the stomach; this one has a cooling quality, so it must be good for Dima; this one a peppery taste, hot, perhaps to wake Natalia. She was one with the elements, but sometimes she feared the elements didn't know that. Her mother had died before she taught Agafia practical lessons in apothecary and survival.

Over the next week, Dima's and Natalia's legs swelled and they left their beds less and less. Hugo attempted to pray with them. Natalia interpreted Hugo's recitations as messages from wolves, and when her father's beard brushed her face she puffed up her shrunken body and stared defiantly into his eyes, as if to fight him off. Dima demanded more urgency from Hugo, hitting the hut's wall when Hugo failed to elevate his voice in prayer. Dima accused him of betraying God for Peter, and flung dried grass from the mattress at Hugo, screaming.

Agafia began to grieve. Entering each new day without Dima would be a diminished way to live. Even the loss of her sister, who had always seemed at least half gone, stunned Agafia.

She cried and roamed alone, spreading her angst in the wilderness like seeds on the wind. But without people to return to—people to be with—grieving tangled too tightly with regular life. Days passed in solitary fugue.

"I hate to see you so down," Peter told Agafia. He picked at his nails with a sharp knife, but he sounded sincere.

"I didn't really think anyone else would die," she told him.

They walked into the forest. She carried a large birch box to collect partridgeberries, but it stayed empty.

"Yes, there is that touch of everlastingness about this place."

He tapped a large tree trunk and looked up, assessing its straightness.

"I used to think eternity was possible," he said. "In some ways, anyway." Agafia kicked at a mushroom, releasing a mist of spores.

"What ways?"

Peter drummed again on a tree—*tap tap*—and squinted into the dark canopy.

"I saw eternity all around me, in the cycles I observed. The moon, the tides, the regenerating forest. I saw existence as more circular than straight, where life perpetuated life. But nature is nature and man is man. I was sad I could not be a part of it all forever."

Agafia crossed herself. How odd that the Antichrist, who signaled the end of things, would speak so much about eternity. She kicked at another mushroom. Eternity wasn't trees, it was heaven. Her brother and sister would be there soon. And yet. In the forest, trees swayed to silent music, their branches like upraised arms in ecstasy. The ground's springy top layer buoyed footfalls and sent up the smell of pine. She sometimes preferred the graspable forest to something as immaterial as heaven. At least she could visit Dima in the wood.

Back at the house, she placed fresh cold compresses on her brother's forehead and leaned in to feel his hot cheek.

"What will heaven be like?" she murmured in his ear.

He closed his eyes and held her hand. "Imagine our valley without wind."

She had promised the geologists she'd come back within a

week; when she didn't show, Galina and Snow Crane came to her instead. The work camp had been packed up and the rest of the team had already departed, but Galina had stayed on under the guise of cleaning up. She and Snow Crane arrived with sacks of leftover provisions, to say good-bye for the winter, but they found the Kols desultory and forlorn.

"They're sick," Hugo told them.

The patriarch's presence was shrunken, as if the preternatural core of him, the molten thing that had powered him all these years, had suddenly dried up or drained out. He bowed to no one in particular and extended an arm toward the door.

The geologists entered the house. The interior was messier than usual, the dross Agafia constantly collected—twigs, moss, stones— accumulated in piles, giving the room the texture of a bird's nest. Galina and Snow Crane sat by the siblings, offered pills and shots, a helicopter to get them to a hospital for treatment.

"We are not allowed that," Dima mumbled from beneath his blankets. He lay calm now, legs straight and arms folded. His eyes had darkened into a muddy blue.

"Please," Galina said.

"It's suicide to refuse treatment when we can get you to a hospital," Snow Crane said.

"Just sit with us and pray."

In the bed next to Dima, Natalia drifted in and out of consciousness. Agafia and Hugo closed their eyes and their voices rose triumphant. *In the day of affliction which hath befallen us, we fall down before Thee, O Savior Christ, and beseech Thy mercy: Ease the suffering of Thy servant.* Hugo's low tone and Agafia's high cry wove through the thick air. *O merciful Lord, hearken to the supplication of Thy servants who pray to Thee.* They manifested their yearning, knitting their love with their song. Snow Crane stretched out on the floor and let the vibrations drape over him.

"Please," Galina said.

Amen.

For several days Snow Crane and Galina kept vigil. At night they walked to Dima's cabin and fell asleep confiding to each other in guilt-ridden pillow talk.

"Did we bring our germs to them?" Galina murmured. "Poison them with our modern pathogens?"

Snow Crane petted her back, to calm her and keep himself awake as she talked.

"First the germs, then the mine," she went on. "By the time we're done here, we'll kill off everything in the taiga."

Howls came from a distance.

"The wolves know."

Snow Crane pulled her to him and pressed his forehead to her flat back.

■ ■ ■

In the morning, Agafia's screams woke the valley. Galina and Snow Crane assumed Dima or Natalia had passed and ran, stumbling, hurrying, in the cries' direction. They found Agafia standing by the riverbank. She crossed herself.

"Look!"

The river ran red. Nothing else about it looked different—the same lazy curves and small rapids, the same familiar shoals and banks—but the water flowed as red as if the river had been transformed into a great open vein, bleeding out onto the taiga. Petrichor drifted from the water's surface though days had passed since the last rain.

"The end, it's really here," Agafia whimpered. "All at once."

It was a red not of painted fingernails but of fresh organs. It didn't stain Galina's fingers when she dipped them in the stream and it didn't color the pebbles on the shore. Galina had never concentrated on the colors of the landscape, hadn't registered how essential the sky's blue and the water's steely gray and the trees' green were to their substance and how one change could turn the world upside down. Years ago, at a gallery in Moscow, she'd seen photographs shot on infrared film. The film turned greens bright red, scrambling the natural color palette into a profusion of magentas, pinks, burgundies. A layer peeled back to reveal the brighter world below. A mystery.

How strange to see mysteries materialize.

"Is there a mine nearby?" Snow Crane asked.

Galina considered what she'd learned about this stretch of taiga. In her mind's map, she ran her finger up the river, slowly tracing in her memory the stream's winding line through nothingness. She remembered, many kilometers upstream, a nickel mine marked on the map. She hadn't known if it was operational but had noted it because it was the closest industrial site, with the accompanying rail lines and loading docks, to their camp.

"There must've been a spill," she said. "It's just a mine, they must've had a spill. It'll turn back to normal soon."

Hugo had joined them on the bank. Father and daughter

seemed not to hear her. They bent and crossed themselves, their singing uninterruptible.

"It's a mine spill!" Galina raised her voice, frantic. "Everything's going to be fine! Man did this, not God!"

"The end days," Hugo said, "they're really here, just like our books said."

Agafia and Hugo stayed on the riverbank all day. Galina and Snow Crane cleaned up the little cabin and visited the sick siblings, who lay sweating, waiting for their God to cure them or take them, content with whatever decision He made. Agafia and Hugo returned to the house late, drained. Galina cooked dinner, set a table. They'd brought so many supplies over the course of their summer visits that it almost felt like a normal meal.

"It'll pass, I promise," Galina told them.

"You told me you're here to make a mine," Agafia said. "That is your work?"

She hadn't fully considered what the geologists were doing there.

"An iron mine, yes."

"What will it be like?"

"A large hole, going deep into the ground. Giant machines will descend into it and dig. At first what they take out will look like rocks, but then it will be processed into metal."

"Where will the hole be?"

"That's what we're here trying to figure out."

Agafia squinted at her surroundings, picturing a large hole in their place and Galina, floating atop it, orchestrating its excavation. Agafia would sit on the crater's edge, whistling, and the dug ground would swallow the sound hungrily. The hut would still exist, somewhere, in her mind, standing in a parallel reality. She found it hard to imagine it all gone.

"Will it make our river red?" she asked.

Galina hadn't considered it. Hadn't asked if other mines she'd opened made rivers red.

"It shouldn't," Snow Crane said.

What is ungodly when one does not have a god? Galina thought as she drifted off to sleep that night. The god she was taught to love was progress. It was a god of absolutes, and she hadn't been taught to question its cost. It shaped the way she saw everything: she could enumerate a potential mine's worth but not a mountain's. She could follow a streak of ore hidden deep underground without seeing that it led to a *BOOM!* in the landscape. So much power in her fingertips that it blinded her. She thought about her mine, its purpose, and now Agafia rose as a counterweight to that purpose. Agafia's body, of indeterminate size and age, a blockade to progress or something worse. As Galina drifted off, they faced each other in a vacuum without terrain, Galina with her pickaxe, Agafia with wolf-hair tufts behind her ears and butterflies alighting on her crown. Agafia approached her, purring, and licked Galina's cheek.

The dampness on her face drew her into deep sleep, dissolved there into intangible discomfort.

When she woke, she ached with a soreness she couldn't place.

■　■　■

Natalia went first, relinquishing her miseries the same way she endured them, quietly.

Dima died a day after her.

"A man lives for howsoever long God grants," he told Agafia, just before he died.

She retrieved her texts, found the canons for the departed, which had gone, lately, mercifully unused.

Most pure Mother of God, beseech thy Son, Whom thou didst conceive without having known a man, she recited, *to grant rest to His servant who hath fallen asleep.*

Galina listened to Agafia's recitations, the cantillated verses that rolled off her tongue in nauseating endlessness. *Lord, have mercy. Lord, have mercy. Lord, have mercy.* Galina had never lost anyone, not even grandparents, and the grief's potency overwhelmed her. She shook and vomited all morning after Dima took his last breath. She derived an odd comfort in the certainty she'd done it, that she'd killed them in some way, whether with her microbes or her worldliness; the Kols were not inoculated against either. If she had done it, she could take responsibility, she could act somehow, and keep at bay the tsunami of powerlessness that death released on survivors. She could protect Agafia. She just needed to figure out how.

Agafia became a flurry of activity, preparing her siblings' bodies for burial, attending to prayers as if to business matters, and directing the others to what needed to be done. She sent Hugo to harvest the garden and told Snow Crane and Galina to dig the graves. The earth, summer-soft and pliant under their metal tools, opened up willingly to the sky. Galina stepped into the deepening hole with a shovel and scraped at the sides. This broaching of holes in the ground for strange purposes, it was her calling. To lay a body, to extract rock, to return, to empty, to bring peace, to seek progress.

Pits as takers, as givers. The soil descended in stripes, a thin black cap threaded with roots, underlined by a white-gray layer. Below that, an orange, iron-rich horizon sank into the perpetually frozen ground. Somewhere below that, her ore. She footed the shovel into increasingly hard dirt. The pit swallowed the shovel's dings.

"How deep should we go?" she shouted up.

"As deep as we can!" Snow Crane replied from the neighboring grave.

He gave her the pickaxe and took the shovel to remove the clods he'd hacked out of the grave's floor. Galina lifted the mattock above her head and let gravity sink it into the soil. The force of the impact vibrated up her arms. She'd managed to dig another meter before the land really resisted. The mine would descend hundreds, thousands of meters. Scraping with the side of the pickaxe, she evened out the walls and base and scrambled out. From above, it looked like the start of some bigger opening, a chasm. The grave and the mine suddenly conflated in her mind. Only their size separated them: a small hole for the dead, a large one for the living.

"Do you think the mine is going to ruin everything here?" she asked Snow Crane.

She'd hung her feet into the grave and sat watching him finish. Snow Crane had a way of avoiding her questions when they crept into the realm of the philosophical. It made him feel helpless, he'd told her once, to discuss things he couldn't do anything about. Sweat glistened on his forehead as he sent shovelfuls of rust-colored dirt flying from the hole. Galina rarely felt helpless because she'd always had the power to change things. Or maybe she'd just never set her sights on big enough obstacles. The mines, for example. She'd never considered anything beyond productivity, ease. Agafia's cries, the eerie red river, her own blooming affections for this stretch of unnamed territory. Lately she searched for a way out.

Snow Crane finished and climbed out of the grave. He jutted his chin, pointing toward Agafia, who approached carrying something. She laid the parcel gently on the ground. On a simple wooden cross, she'd carved: DIMA, FAVORITE BROTHER, SUNSHINE IN WINTER.

"You should go now," she told the geologists. The sun, somewhere behind the trees, was already fleeing for the season. An overnight wind had blown in a light snow. "You're already late. Fall is here."

They didn't wait for the burials, but left early the following morning. They'd return at the next thaw, when the ground would again shed its snow cover, allowing them to examine its surfaces and its nooks, the hardship of winter briefly paused. One more field season, and Galina would finish the mapping and sampling, would really know what lay beneath her feet.

"See you next summer," Agafia said as Galina and Snow Crane set off. They hugged good-bye and trekked back toward the empty camp, where the helicopter remained, waiting.

"I'm coming to Moscow," Snow Crane told Galina as they walked. "To you."

PART II
ЧАСТЬ II

PART II

CHAPTER 3
Глава 3

In Moscow, Galina waited for Snow Crane at her apartment with a spread of biscuits, homemade cakes, Turkish delight, sour cherries floating in crystal saucers, boxes of candy with roses painted on the rectangular lids, dried apricots, and nuts. As if she were welcoming a dignitary with unknown tastes. As if sweets could be a proxy for words. She steeped tea in time for his arrival.

When the doorbell finally rang, she ushered him into the small apartment, offered him a pair of her spare slippers, and sat him down at the table. She loaded a plate with the delicacies and pushed it toward him across the table. They'd barely said hello.

"At the orphanage, the boys dreamed of this," he said. "We were an imaginative bunch. We'd lie in our bunks and try to one-up each other, creating new types of cakes, creams, cookies and biscuits."

"I can imagine what the food in the cafeteria was like," Galina said.

"No, you can't. We'd pile the slop from the lunchroom into layered concoctions to make it seem more palatable, more cake-like. We called them turd pies. When I started studying geology, I thought of those disgusting mixtures during stratigraphy lessons. I came to see the cutaways we studied as petrified slices of multilayered slop cakes."

"I thought stratigraphy was magical," Galina said.

Snow Crane had set down his small bag on the table when he entered. He had come with few things—a small rock collection, some books, a journal, an address book, and several changes of clothes. Galina unpacked these and spread them on the table as Snow Crane cut into a cake with his fork. Like Agafia going through the camp's objects, Galina pointed at the rock collection.

"Tell me about that," she said.

"Everything goes back to the orphanage," Snow Crane said between bites.

"Start from the beginning."

"When I was there, all the boys my age slept in one big room," he started. "Rows of beds with low metal frames took up the entire space. The interiors were powder blue, and someone had painted plump clouds on the ceiling. On sunny mornings, with the curtains thrown back, the blue almost looked like real sky and I would lie in bed on my back, cradle my head in my arms, throw one leg over the other, and daydream like a boy at ease somewhere by a river.

"Every day I asked when my mother would return to take me home, and the nannies would act hurt.

"'Aren't we enough for you?' they asked.

"'It's like having five mothers!' one of the women told me. She stroked my head, kind-like. They were all young and some of them did act motherly toward the boys and girls, but I kept asking anyway.

"In the mornings, the nannies led the children in *physkultura*. They lined us up in our white underwear and white tank tops, too-big armholes and leg holes like hula-hoops around our thin limbs. Stretching our skinny arms out, we squatted, kneeled, jumped rope, and stretched each other. We took turns lifting the weights stacked in a corner of the room. I put effort into the exercises and my arms started to take on a muscular shape. I would admire myself in the full-length mirrors after class and think about how I would show off my new strength to my mother when she picked me up. How I could help her more around the house with my muscles, just like a real man. That's what the nannies said to me, 'You're a real little man.'

"After *physkultura* and a quick splash of cold water from a metal bucket, we went to school. My teacher was a good man who told me on my first day that he had been an orphan too, and that things would turn out all right. I sat in the back of the classroom, doodling in my checked notebook, deliberating how I'd become an orphan and what that meant. I didn't know!

"I remember once the teacher read a poem about Vladimir Ulyanov to the class, repeating the lines for the children to commit them to memory. At home my mother had read poetry too, and we'd studied verses together—poems about rivers and fields and animals. When the teacher called me to the front of the class to recite the poem about Lenin, I stood for a long time without speaking. I hadn't been paying attention. Finally I recited one of the poems I had memorized with my mother, about the river's shimmer in the sun and how it flowed through time like a road through a city. The teacher wrung his hands over and over, as if washing them, and they made a sound like pages turning in a book. He asked me to return to my seat before I could finish the poem.

"A boy named Marat started following me around. I was always distracted because I didn't understand why I was there, but Marat was distracted because he was made that way. He was like one of the unstable elements, always vibrating, slipping between states, alive with a dangerous energy. He stared out the windows during class and rambled aimlessly, arriving late to meals and activities.

"'I liked that poem you read,' he told me the day after the teacher had sent me back to my seat. I recited it to him all the way to the end, the lines I didn't get to say in class. Marat closed his eyes as he listened and swayed just barely side to side.

"'Beautiful,' Marat told me when I finished. He drifted in a trancelike state, his lips constantly moving with silent words and phrases.

"'I like to write poems,' he told me. I remember how he said it, so nonchalant.

"Marat's bed stood a few rows over from mine in the sleeping room maze and at night he'd crawl over with a flashlight and his blanket. We'd put my covers on the floor under my bed and hang Marat's over the edge, to make a fort, and sit inside it reading. Marat supplied the books. They looked like the mimeographed books my mother used to read. I didn't know where they came from but I didn't care because Marat had exceptional taste. He invited other boys to join us in the fort, but usually just the two of us spent evenings together, reading and gossiping about novels as if they were the news. Our favorite was *Moby-Dick*, which was lucky since it was so long.

"Some months after my arrival, I received a letter from my mother. It had many stamps on it, forwarded several times from one location to another. One stamp showed an airplane with a smiling pilot. Another had a Pioneer with a red kerchief tied around his neck. A third showed Lenin." He still remembered the letter and repeated it to Galina verbatim:

> *Dear son,*
>
> *How sorry I am to disappear from you like this. I promise you* ▮▮▮▮▮▮▮▮▮▮▮*. I am in a* ▮▮▮▮▮▮ *now. I live with other women who, like me, were* ▮▮▮▮▮▮▮▮▮ ▮▮▮▮*. We work the fields and some of us are sent to a furniture factory during the day to assemble armoires. At night* ▮▮▮▮ ▮▮▮▮▮▮▮▮▮▮▮ *tell each other about our children. I tell them about how smart you are and about the stories you'd write in school. I am in* ▮▮▮▮*, far far from Moscow. It is even colder here than in Moscow* ▮▮▮▮▮▮▮▮▮*.*
>
> *But do not worry, I am okay. I am looking forward to seeing you. Hope you are studying.*
>
> *Love, Mama.*

"After I grew exhausted reading the letter over and over to myself, Marat read it to me.

"When he came to the blacked-out sections he made things up. 'I promise you that I will bring you many books and toys and sweets,' he read. 'I am in a small hut on an island hunting for treasures now.' Then we improvised. 'Perhaps she is on the Galapagos Islands studying turtles and lizards and strange birds and left in the middle of the night because she knew she couldn't take you. That's why it took so long for her letter to arrive! It had to travel so far, all the way from an island. On the islands live turtles larger than you and me and you can approach them and stroke their hard shells. There are birds with strange beaks colored red and blue like the walls of our room, and black, and the yellow of Uzbek melons, and they come in all different shapes, some of them sharp like daggers, others curved like ladles, long and short and some are even not exotic at all.' You know, things like that. I understood it wasn't true because it's not colder than Moscow on the Galapagos Islands, but we would talk about the Galapagos Islands for hours, picking through the dusty yard of the orphanage, completely unaware of the games the other children played around us.

"Once, Marat and I walked off from the orphanage. As soon as we passed through the gate, I recognized the neighborhood—my mother had taught at a school around the corner and often brought me along. I wove through the crowds on the sidewalk toward the Children's World department store. Marat had never been there, and when we walked in he stopped in front of the escalators to take in the twinkling lights strung from one floor to the next. The bulbs' yellow glow landed golden on his olive skin so that he looked lit from within and the million little lanterns reflected in his eyes like constellations. We rode the escalator up and down, then chased each other to the toy section and ran our fingers over the Cheburashka figurines, boxes of modeling clay, and miniature red Malysh pianos. I remember I lifted a small wooden box, labeled ROCK COLLECTION, from a shelf. Inside, square compartments held small polished stones in different colors and shapes. I fingered the rocks, feeling their coolness on my fingertips. When a saleswoman asked where our mother was, we sprinted out of the store and down the cobbled street to Alexander Garden.

"Snow still covered the gardens and the fountains stood empty, but we strolled the pathways toward the eternal flame. Marat wanted to warm by it but we could not approach because men in uniform, stiff as pencils sticking out of the granite plaza, stood guard. I realized I was still holding the box of rocks in my hand and tucked it deep into my jacket. I stole this box. It was an accident, but I stole it. I've switched out the rocks over the years, now it's a personal collection, but I couldn't bear to get rid of the box because it reminds me of Marat."

"Did you get in trouble?" Galina asked.

"We watched the flame at the plaza dance for a long time. It took on an extra-saturated color. Dusk was settling in around us so we walked back toward our room with the clouds painted on its ceiling, where it was always daytime. When we came in our cheeks were cold and flushed. The nannies knew we'd been gone. They rushed toward us talking all at once.

"'Where have you been?' they said. 'If you keep acting up this way your mother will never come get you.' The nannies could be cruel that way.

"The cook made cabbage soup for dinner that night, with borodinsky bread. I remember because the nannies wouldn't allow us to come to the cafeteria. Our friends marched into the bedroom, each producing a crust of bread, sacred offerings tucked into their undershirts."

Snow Crane dug the fork into another cake without slicing it, eating right from the plate, and grinned at the memory. He had reintroduced the intimacy of the helicopter rides without the helicopter. A clock tick-tocked on the wall.

"I bought all this stuff," Galina said. "Except the cakes. I made them." A confession.

When they finished eating, they slid the chairs close to the table and walked over to the made-up bed in the corner of the room. They took turns undressing each other.

■ ■ ■

Snow Crane's few belongings blended easily into Galina's apartment. He never told Galina where he lived before he appeared on her doorstep that fall and he expressed no desire to return to that place. But he freely shared stories from his more distant past. They spent the winter getting to know each other.

When the weather allowed it, they passed evenings on the Lenin Hills looking at the city below. In the snow, Moscow's dull glow looked like someone had balled up a piece of aluminum and then smoothed it back out on the horizon. Light fell unevenly throughout the capital, buildings and chimney smoke rose into the low sky and dissipated into it, and the frozen river below ran toward the crinkled sheet of metropolis like unspooled white yarn. When the cold overwhelmed their lungs, they stayed indoors, talking, confiding the strange outlines of their lives, as if picking through coded documents to figure out how they'd managed to cross paths so unexpectedly.

There was the work too. Snow Crane dusted off his geology degree and became a full member of the team analyzing ores, rather than a seasonal pilot in the field. They established a routine: a simple breakfast with the poppy-flower curtains thrown open to let in the gray winter light, a record playing as they spooned sugar into tea. Galina leafed through newspapers. Snow Crane read novels. A mutt living in their courtyard met them as they emerged from the darkened stairwell and accompanied them to the metro. The dog took up two seats if the car was empty, one if crowded.

The dog reminded Snow Crane of his thirteenth birthday, and he told Galina about it. Marat had given him a copy of *The Call of the Wild*. They read it together in the fort that same morning, cheering for Buck, the mutt blessed with otherworldly power, to not succumb to the man in the red sweater, who beat him, and to overtake the mush team's lead dog, Spitz, and assume his position. Snow Crane identified with Buck: the dog had been thrust into a harsh new reality after being abducted from a loving home. His plight spoke to Snow Crane. Tucked into his sheets and blankets, he read how Buck had to learn to dig a bed of snow to stay warm and how he ate quickly so that the others wouldn't steal his food. He read how Buck would pull the mail to mining camps in Alaska. Snow Crane imagined his mother's letters packed between the parcels that Buck hauled across white plains and frozen lakes.

Stray dogs hung around the orphanage, and the boys tried to hitch them together in complicated rope harnesses. One by one Marat looped the rope around their bodies, tying bulky knots at their chests, then around their legs and out on their backs. Six dogs, which the boys had fed scraps, allowed themselves to be strung together in this way to a rusty-railed sled. The animals were of all different sizes and temperaments. Marat's one-rope harness didn't allow the dogs to move in their straps without pulling on the others. Marat and Snow Crane sat on the sled, legs tucked close to their bodies.

"Mush!" Marat commanded.

Some of the dogs lay down and others tried to run, but even the ones that moved pointed their snouts in different directions, so the sled remained in its place. The dogs bared their teeth at each other and tangled in the ropes yelping and biting until Snow Crane finally stood up and untied their harness.

"They're too spoiled by the city!" Marat said.

The mutt that followed Snow Crane and Galina around wasn't spoiled, though. He was savvy. An urban denizen. He exited with them at the Universitet Station and walked to the geology building on campus. The geologists worked in an old building with drafty rooms, but their lab benefited from large windows that let the city in.

They analyzed the samples they'd brought back from the taiga, checking if each had iron, correlating its origin to the map. The rocks lay stacked in boxes and scattered around like hard cookies on the counters of their workspace. They peered at the stones through microscopes, made notations in busy notebooks. They drew colorful maps delineating how far the deposits extended, as well as what kinds of rock surrounded and overlay them. They marked it all with patterns—pinks, yellows, and blues with hashmarks, plus signs, and polka-dotted arrays—like light spring blankets upon the range.

When Snow Crane came across particularly pleasing cross sections, where the minerals' colors shone unusually radiant or the stripes produced especially pretty, singular worlds, he slipped them into his bag and took them home. He worked them into bevels and presented them to Galina as jewelry. The first time he fashioned a pendant from a piece of rock; he hung it on a long chain and slipped it around Galina's neck over breakfast, and she never took it off.

After work, they reunited with the mutt and returned home,

buying sweets at the government store with Galina's ID. They cooked dinner, read, walked the yellow-lit streets talking to dogs that crossed their path. They almost never made the bed and would take their sweets into the nest of covers, curling into each other, picking crumbs from sheets stamped with tractors.

"What happened to Marat?" Galina asked. They were lying with the lights off.

"No one knew who sorted the boys and girls, but some godlike finger pointed at each of us and around the age of sixteen we peeled away to our separate destinies," Snow Crane said. "Many of the girls were sent to factories outside the city. Some stayed on at the orphanage, as nannies. Instead of sleeping in the communal room, they slept in a smaller room with the other nannies. Others volunteered to ship off to the north, to work on hydroelectric dams, roads to nowhere, construction boondoggles. Many big projects slowed after the war, yet they weren't altogether closed. I used to imagine my mother was somewhere up there, hammering spikes into baseplates, stitching wood into latticed bridges, pouring her energy, like cement, into something that might last forever. I never received any more letters from her.

"The boys also shipped off to factories, to building sites. Many volunteered or were volunteered for the military. They showed up in ill-fitting uniforms to say good-bye and sat on the creaky metal springs of too-short beds and promised each other to write. Marat decided he'd go north, help build something. He told me the experience would be good for his poetry.

"'Maybe I'll meet a nice village girl,' Marat told me dreamily, 'one of those with the wheat-colored hair and milky chalcedony eyes.'

"By then, I'd become obsessed with my stolen rock collection. Over the years I'd added pebbles and stone chunks from the street. I carried around a stack of waterlogged geology books I found in one of the classrooms. Marat was constantly asking me to describe rocks so he could incorporate them into his verses.

"'They sound so exotic, like the names of French princesses,' he used to say.

"The government had provided Marat with a train ticket to one of the construction villages. The nannies who raised him found a long military wool coat, gloves, and boots, probably from some dead soldier. He looked theatrical, a handsome hobo playing a general. When the train departed Leningradsky Station, he stood in the open doorway, that long coat blown open by the wind, his brown eyes tearing up. I stood on the platform, waving to my friend.

"'Send me poems!' I yelled after him. The train jolted and rolled out of the station.

"That's the last time I saw him."

Galina cried at his stories.

"How can you stand it all?" she asked. His losses seemed to mount without reprieve compared to her safe childhood.

"How about you?" he'd ask. "Who was your first friend?"

"Her name was Sasha," Galina said. "There was something about her of the unkempt; she had wild hair and mismatched socks and was always biting her nails. She had freckles all over her face, long-fingered hands, and a pronounced lisp. She wore shirts with too-long sleeves, probably pass-me-downs from her older sister. She let them hang down over her knuckles, as if trying to hide them.

"She was my neighbor at our first apartment. She was much

tougher than me. One year my parents gave me a red tricycle for the New Year. The very next day I went out to play with it and some boys stole it at the playground. Sasha found out who stole it, beat him up, and brought my bike back.

"I didn't realize then, but her family was much poorer than mine. When she came over to my house she'd want to eat or try on my mother's clothes. We'd put on my mom's silk dresses and paint our faces with her makeup. Sasha had a record of Cuban salsa songs—I don't know where she got it—but she didn't have a record player. She brought it over every time she came and we played it on my father's turntable.

"She would take my hands in hers and lead me around. She knew how to move to the music, her feet bobbing on the floor, like fishing floats. I couldn't keep up. She'd say, 'Galya, just listen, listen to the rhythm!' and throw her head back, joyful.

"Then one day she came without the record. Her father had broken it, splintered it into a dozen pieces against the wall. She flipped through our stack of vinyl but all we had was old marching band compilations and Tchaikovsky.

"Something changed after that. She couldn't get a break in school either. The teachers smacked her beautiful hands with pencils because her cuticles were always bloody. The kids started to tease her for never having the right notebooks or getting her homework done. One year she got lice and the school made her mother shave her head. I hadn't realized how sad she'd become because she kept her hair over her face. She had well eyes, dark, deep, lightless. I think her father beat her.

"We moved when I was in fifth grade, into a building for the government class. My father had gotten some sort of promotion. Sasha didn't have a telephone at her house and my father wouldn't let me go visit her in the old neighborhood. I never saw her again."

Snow Crane sighed, looked around the room, as if searching for their lost friends. In falling in love, they first had to share their past loves with each other.

■ ■ ■

In the apartment, on wallpapered walls, hung mountain portraits, panoramas Galina had stitched together from multiple photographs. Yellowing glue exposed the seams between black-and-white mountain passes and appeared in the middle of fine-grained stretches of snowfields, like crevasses. After dinner, they'd sit and admire the photographs, pointing out especially pretty expanses, snow piles shaped like animals, and the bare jagged spines flexing toward summits. Their admiration for the mountains was mutual and fetishistic.

Galina had come to it through geology. She studied orogeny, the processes of mountain building that set all of geology in motion. By understanding the mechanics of the massifs, she could appreciate their loveliness. It was backward, like a doctor who grows to care for a person only because he knows the workings of his body: *I know how your heart beats so I can see your soul.* On assignments, she mapped and analyzed a landscape before she ever looked around. She took aerial photos in the beginning of a job but shot the pretty panoramas at the end, once she could admire a site with greater understanding.

For Snow Crane, despite his early thieved rock collection and the geology books he carried around, it had been an opposite infatuation. First the mountains, then the science. The orphanage had enlisted him in the army without his knowing. The nannies told him a few weeks before he was due at the barracks. With Marat gone, he spent more time with his other friends, who liked to drink. The night before boot camp began, the boys drifted around the city. One of them had an uncle who let them come over and perch like a murder of crows on stools in his kitchen. The tiny space closed in around them like a dollhouse. Stained wallpaper covered the apartment walls. They played illicit records that had been etched onto the X-rays of tubercular patients. Summer skies squeezed through the grimy windows and woke a destructive streak in them. They poured out of the kitchen, into the hall, down the stairs, into the building's yard. A woman sweeping the dust off the sidewalk glared at them and raised her corn broom at the boys, threatening them. They laughed at the old lady, lit cigarettes, leaning on the playground's metal bones.

Girls from the neighborhood strolled by in dresses sewn from old drapes, long hair hanging over smooth backs. Everything about them was curtain-like—the way they sashayed into each other as they walked, how the boys' words sent ripples through their group, gently parting them like a breeze. Some of the girls approached. Forward, fantastic creatures, they asked for cigarettes. The orphanage separated the girls and the boys, and although they reunited for meals and classes, outside of those situations the presence of girls made Snow Crane quiet. Quieter than usual. A girl walked over, eyes the color of glaciers, legs bruised, fine cuts on her hands.

"You climb trees or something?" Snow Crane asked when she introduced herself. Her name was Valentina.

"Yeah," she said. "And mountains."

"Mountains? For what?" he asked.

Her front two teeth grew in one over the other, like two crossed fingers.

"For fun," she said. "They send you to the country to train. You sleep outside in tents and walk around in the mountains and have campfires with your friends. When you're ready, you attempt to summit peaks. I haven't climbed any big ones yet. But I will. I'm going to be a Snow Leopard."

"What's that?"

"It's the title you get when you climb all of the peaks higher than seven thousand meters in our territory. Communism Peak, Victory Peak, Lenin Peak, Korjenevskoy Peak, Khan Tengri. That's the five."

How did she know all this? Someone had brought down the moonshine and they passed around metal mugs of it, flirting.

"I'm going to the army tomorrow," he told her.

"My father told me the army has a mountain division," she said.

Everybody got very drunk that night. A guitar appeared, with thick plastic strings and a small body. The boys strummed it and sang Aleksandr Galich songs. Everyone knew the words and sang along and rocked against each other. Stalin was dead and for these drunk orphaned kids that meant they could sing Galich's songs in public. Marat had introduced Snow Crane to Galich—he'd introduced him to everything—and he missed reading Galich's poems with his friend when they sneaked out of the home. He would've liked this, Snow Crane realized, a bunch of unshaved, handsome boys and girls who dreamed of mountains singing protest poetry under open skies.

The next morning he showed up at army headquarters, received his uniform, and sat with a general to fill out questionnaires. The general asked him what he had to offer.

"I climb mountains, sir," Snow Crane lied, and saluted him.

The general raised an eyebrow. "Aren't you from the orphanage?" he asked.

"Yes, sir."

The man closed his bloodshot eyes and rubbed his temples. Snow Crane suspected the general was as hungover as he was.

"Would you like to serve in the mountain division?" the man asked.

"Yes, sir," Snow Crane answered, too loud. He saluted once more. The man laughed.

His first encounter with mountains: the sharp ridgelines of the Caucasus range split him open. For the first several days in training camp he walked around wobbly on his feet and with a headache equal parts altitude sickness and awe. The barracks stood on a high plateau, perfectly level, as if someone had taken a sword to a mountaintop. Snowy peaks ringed the encampment on all sides. Jeeps had delivered the boys, with supplies, to the barracks along a path carved into the mountain and driven off. Everywhere they went, they went on foot.

In the mornings, they rose from their A-frame canvas tents, double flaps to seal in warmth, and lined up in a meadow. *Physkultura* had followed him here, but he didn't mind. Stretching and pumping their muscles in drills led by a barking general was re-freshing under an alpine sky. Skin prickled and pinked by the dawn cold, nostrils cleared by fresh air, toes dew-wet, he operated in a state of elevated wakefulness.

After the morning exercises, they cooked breakfast—millet and canned meat—then hiked down off the plateau. Some days they walked through the valley; others they switchbacked up a neighboring mountain. Instructors led courses on rope work, how to tie harnesses, how to belay each other down a rock face, medical essentials like making casts and tying tourniquets. Mountaineers, not military people, taught the classes. Who knew where the generals had found them or how they'd convinced these semi-anarchist loners to share their skills with the military. Lacking the military's code of conduct, the instructors imparted their own alpinist code. A Russian mountaineer never leaves a comrade behind, they said. They taught their charges how to get an immobilized person down a mountain, how to check for frostbite and keep a shocked body warm.

The generals didn't come along for these instructional outings. Then one morning they did, leaving the camp empty. The group marched into the valley, then spread out along the mountains, seeking high ground above the unnamed stream below.

"Ambush!" one general yelled. "This is an exercise about learning to ambush the enemy." The enemy were the Chechen rebels, crossing the whitewater, headed north to Moscow. Some of the soldiers had to play the Chechens, milling by the water, waiting to get besieged. The alpinists showed them all how to disappear into rock folds while keeping sights open on their fellow troops. Then the generals took over, demonstrating how to kill the Chechens from their hiding spots. One of the mountaineering instructors, Misha, was Chechen and told the generals they shouldn't teach them to just shoot Chechens.

"It's just an exercise, don't take it so personal," one general said, and slapped him on the back.

One by one the pretend-Chechens went down. They lay by the river, spread out on rounded pebbles, looking up at fast-moving clouds, shot by silent bullets. Blanks were too expensive to waste on this exercise, so everyone had to pretend to hear the echoes of gunfire flying through the valley, assume the rounds reached their comrades' hearts. When they defeated the enemy to the generals' satisfaction, the rest of the boys hiked off the mountains and the platoon practiced crossing the whitewater with ropes. The water ran the color of melted turquoise.

Snow Crane had packed his old geology textbooks from the orphanage and when he had time to himself he brought them along to examine outcrops. He sketched the rock's layers, measured the odd angles of the lines, and traced the folds of stone, like kneaded dough, in his notebook. Sometimes he left the notebooks behind and just walked, arms clasped behind his back over an ice pick, steady deliberative steps forward. On one outing he met a toothless sheepherder who had recently returned from the Far East to his homeland and grinned at his flock as at children. On another he saw a mouflon grazing by itself, as if it too was just out on a pleasure hike. How could he thank Valentina for this, for the world?

Toward the end of their time in boot camp, the general gathered the boys and told them they had to prove themselves with a summit.

"Elbrus!" the general said.

Snow Crane had read about Elbrus, the highest mountain in the Caucasus, the highest in all of Europe. In his books, Snow Crane read that it was a dormant volcano, its top a big crater from where it blew out its peak during the last eruption. The next morning, they packed their camp and started moving toward Elbrus. For a week, they traversed emerald-green valleys and filled their flasks from cold streams. They sang songs as they marched, boots tied tight around thin ankles, pots and pans clanging on external-frame backpacks, stubble on tanned chins. When they arrived at base camp, Snow Crane laid his head on the ground. Deep below the grass and granite, he heard the slow churning of melted lava, the sleeping volcano's gentle snores.

For a few days, the platoon lazed about camp resting and acclimating. The general told them that four hundred people had recently summited Elbrus all at once. It was supposed to serve as motivation. The country's penchant for *massovost* had made it to the mountains. Snow Crane talked to the peaks as he strolled, introducing himself on his own terms.

On summit day, the group rose at two in the morning, the stars shining like high-powered flashlights as they cooked breakfast. After they ate, Snow Crane lined up behind the instructors and led the pack out of base camp. Slow, steady, up. Long breaths in. Out. He exhaled frost clouds and broke through them as if through finish lines. He felt powerful. The rest of the platoon stretched behind him in single file, their breathing and the crunch of snow amplified by crystalline cold and silence. Snow Crane could feel his blood circulating within him, as if the temperature turned it viscous and slowed its movement. Somewhere below him, Elbrus's magma. His lifeblood and the mountain's, keeping time.

The snow grew thicker with every step. The ice fields groaned and whined and sang. Snow Crane's breathing was labored and wheezy. The boys picked their way through a crevasse field, then rested and drank water before the final summit push. The sun had come up. Snow Crane put on dark goggles and looked out on the white fields in search of shadows. In the goggles he resembled a spy from World War II, maybe from one of the airborne divisions.

"Let's go!" Misha signaled.

The instructors trod a path and Snow Crane followed. He walked right to the top until there was nowhere else to step. From the south summit, the ground dipped before rising to the northern peak; the smooth saddle sparkled in the morning light. Below and all around, the crinkled Caucasus's myriad points rose from fog and shadow. He stood in a bowl of peaked meringue.

When everyone had made it up, the instructors showed them to a metal box chained to a post.

"You have to leave a note or a memento when you summit," Misha said in his thick molasses accent. "Every single summit."

To demonstrate, from his inner pocket he produced a photo of his little house, a young girl posed in front of it, his daughter. He'd scribbled something on the back. He held it up to the sun, kissed it, and dropped it in the metal box.

"Your turn," he said.

The general took out a tattered notebook, ripped out a sheet of paper, and started listing their names. At the bottom, he put the date and the division's name, Seventh Guards Mountain Air Division, and drew a pair of wings with a conical mountain growing between them. He dropped it in the box and passed the notebook to Snow Crane. He wrote, *From here I can almost see my mama*, and placed it in the box.

On the descent, the boys put on their military green ponchos, all mismatched, recycled from the war, and buttoned them between their legs. When they spread their limbs, they looked like flying squirrels. Tucking the ice pick to his chest so as not to stab himself, the general dropped on his behind, and demonstrated how to slide down the mountain. The boys ran, propelling themselves down the snowy hill, yelping.

"I know you're military men," Misha said when everyone reached the river, "but now that you've summited Elbrus, you're also alpinists. And every alpinist must get an alpinist's christening."

Some of the boys had already taken off their shirts in the sun's warmth. They gathered around their instructor, leaning into the mustiness of their gathered bodies. The trainer prayed:

If your job gets in the way of your climbing, quit your job!
If your wife gets in the way of your climbing, leave your wife!

To each line they answered in chorus, voices rising. They memorized the prayer and recited it together, laughing, their arms around each other. Misha told them to strip down and jump in the river. Rushing toward the valleys, the icy water tumbled over rocks and spit up white foam. Two of the coaches secured a rope across the stream, for the boys to catch themselves on if the rapids grew too strong. One by one they jumped in.

When Snow Crane's turn came, the coldness of the water

shocked him, lungs recoiling into hard walnuts inside his chest. Rapids churned around him and held him—he relaxed into them, legs straight in front of his body, arms out to the sides for balance, as if in a chair. Rays of light bounced off the cascades' white foam and hit his eyes. Blinding him. Releasing him. The cold became a part of him, the river a feather duvet, the sky a canopy, the valley walls witnesses to his transformation. He caught the rope, climbed out of the river, sat on the pebbles, and smoked a cigarette.

It took years before he could finally enter the university to study. He'd served his time in the army, then flew missions after he was recruited for pilot school. He was an older student, but an enthusiastic one. In a dorm room that smelled of feet, he dyed ropes for climbing and read geology texts and poetry collections, smiling at both as if they were one and the same. That was a happy time, he told Galina, when he could study without application. He never aspired to be a geologist, he said, just to know geology, the earth's work.

"I was the opposite," she told him. "I wanted to mine mine mine. To move mountains." Together, they would look up at the walls in her apartment, hung with alpine panoramas, the gods of the peaks watching over them.

■ ■ ■

Galina's mother, Lida, sensed a change in her daughter, figured out a new person in her life was behind the smile in her voice.

"Why don't you two come for dinner?" she suggested over the phone.

Galina didn't want to go, didn't want to subject Snow Crane to the stifled interiors of her childhood, where her father ruled with his severe stare, the firm silence of his expectations. But Lida insisted.

They arrived on time. Polished surfaces and stiff furniture, small and straight-backed, filled the apartment where she grew up. Clean mirrors covered tall, fold-out closet doors. Hardback books with uncracked spines lined glassed shelves. The apartment a trap fortified with sharp corners and hard surfaces. It had been a brutalist prison for a child. The table was set with fine crystal and the good china. Growing up, Galina had been used to big-foreheaded men assembling around the long table and staying for hours, settling into their chairs like Easter Island statues. She used to hide behind the stiff curtains, sleepy on her feet, and look out at the street through the ninth-floor window to the drone of conversation and clinking glasses, the scrape of forks on china, the labored breathing. She hadn't sat at the table in years, since she stopped celebrating birthdays at home.

Lida had prepared plov and samsa from her Uzbek cookbook, an attempt to impress her guests, and they sat immediately to eat, without extended pleasantries or greetings. Galina had told Snow Crane not to feel pressured to make conversation—either they'd dine quietly or her mother would set the tone—so he forked at the rice politely and refilled everyone's glasses.

It was the first time Galina had brought someone home. Her father had fussed at her to marry immediately after university. When she was in her midtwenties, he started to tell her she was losing her looks and would never marry if she didn't do so soon. He'd tried introducing her to colleagues' sons, but she refused to meet them. By her late twenties he asked, repeatedly, if she had medical issues of which he was unaware. When she turned thirty, he dropped the subject entirely and encouraged her to focus on her career. Now he eyed Snow Crane across the table, unsure where to start his assessment of this new development.

"And your parents?" Lida asked. "Are they alive?"

"No." Snow Crane shook his head. He tried to do it merrily, to maintain a sense of normalcy at the table, but Galina's father pushed for more information.

"Oh?" he asked. "What happened to them?"

Snow Crane chewed a mouthful of chickpea and sipped at the Georgian wine. Galina had told him that her father was an economist but served in the state's shadowy echelons doing who knew what, that she herself mistrusted him, that he was a machine. Snow Crane considered lying, but Galina pinched him lightly on the thigh, reassuring him.

"I never met my father," he said. "My mother was a teacher, she was disappeared when I was a child."

"Oh?" her father said, this time with interest.

Lida scooped fresh plov onto the serving plate from the iron pot.

"Eat, eat," she urged them all. The rice was dry, but they piled spoonfuls onto their plates. Snow Crane picked at the steamed garlic bulb, pushing soft flesh out of each aromatic clove with his fork and mixing it in the rice.

"What was she detained for?" Galina's father asked.

For living a worthwhile life, for loving poetry and laughter, for being, Snow Crane thought. He looked up from his plate, for a moment forgetting where he was.

"You'll have to ask someone else about that," Snow Crane answered. "I don't know."

"Come help me get the dessert." Lida motioned to Snow Crane, and he followed her into the kitchen. "Don't pay attention to him, he's harmless. He just can't help himself," she said, and handed him creamed delicacies from the refrigerator. She patted him on the shoulder kindly. "I'm certainly glad you're here."

They paraded the sweets to the dining room, and Galina cleared the table of dinner. Lida took control. She put on a record, some irrelevant background noise that would make her husband clam up, and opened the curtains to allow the room to breathe. "Has Galina told you about my amber collection?"

Snow Crane shook his head.

"Shame on her!" Lida exclaimed, grinning. She took him by the elbow and led him to a corner with a squat chest of shallow drawers. When she opened one of the drawers, it dripped with amber—raw, polished, in jewelry, figurines, inlays, embedded in miniature paintings, pinned in rows on beige backing that allowed the yellow-orange orbs to shine from within.

"I know my collection isn't scientific, but I don't care!" Lida said. "I find beauty in the preservation of something so ephemeral. Imagine!" She held up a smooth oval of amber with a bug trapped inside, threadlike legs splayed in all directions so that it looked like it was slipping and falling at the moment of capture.

"My mom's been collecting these since before I was born," Galina said. "Her first one was a gift from her first boyfriend!"

"This one"—Lida picked up a teardrop of amber dangling from a hatpin—"I didn't have a nice hat, but I loved it anyway."

"She's got a bigger rock collection than either of us," Snow Crane said approvingly. Gold reflected on Galina's face and in her hair, flitting like gilded butterflies as Lida moved the specimens around.

They spent the evening admiring Lida's things—the amber collection, a stack of hand-painted Uzbek plates in blues and greens, a small pile of poetry books she kept dust-free and creaseless. They inspected the apartment's contents as if at a museum. Galina's father followed them at first, trying to preserve the conversation and the sentiment of the gathering. But the more they uncentered him from their attention the more bored he grew, then audibly unimpressed with what he called his wife's "baubles," and finally he receded to his reading chair with a paper. He served himself tea, sipping it loudly in the corner of the room as they laughed at the table.

On the way home, Galina finally relaxed. "My mother," she said, "is a savior." Her mother, with the shiny hair, breath that smelled of yeast and cherries, wildflower meadow heart stomped flat by her husband's austereness. He the house, the cage. She the rare bird trapped inside it. Galina had been a miracle baby, born late, and an only child. She'd always harbored a sense of guilt over it, intuiting that maybe Lida would've left her husband if it hadn't been for Galina.

"I never want to be like them," she told Snow Crane as they walked.

"That's what everyone says about their parents," Snow Crane said. He took her hand and folded it into the warmth of his pocket.

■ ■ ■

The listlessness toward her work had followed Galina home from the field. Months now she hadn't had her heart in the assignment.

Perhaps Agafia had stolen her attention then, Snow Crane now. She couldn't help but be distracted by the two of them. But a larger shift mired her, an apathy unfamiliar to her. *Who cares if the mine ever opens?* she thought on more than one occasion. Maybe it was the monotony of her duties—survey, map, sample, *boom*. Perhaps the mounting guilt from easy promotions, how she'd climbed the ranks by her father's hand rather than her own. Or maybe she saw the mountains for the first time—really saw them—how they rose defiantly to the sky and curved their skirts around green coves. Their particular smell, holy and clean.

She was a decent geologist, good enough at her job. She tried, certainly. But for the first time in her life the title tasted lackluster on her tongue. The red river flashed sometimes behind her eyes like a flare, faded, lingered. The walks she had taken with Snow Crane lingered too, but differently, like a cigarette's pleasant numbness.

"You've got field season fever!" her colleagues told her when she confided in them over spirits.

But she wasn't a romantic, not prone to such easy agitations of the mind. This state, which so bewildered her, came naturally to Snow Crane, and he held her hand as she tried to articulate her newfound lostness, the suddenly blurred boundaries of her self. "Galochka!" he'd say, smiling. "Is this really your first crisis of the soul?"

"It's not funny." She pouted and grew pensive, faraway.

She decided to tackle the problem head-on, to convince herself of the goodness of her work. Of her duty to complete it. A friend of hers ran the magazine *Da!*'s editorial department, and she asked if she could write an essay about the work of mineral exploration. She imagined a love letter to the process of discovery, an insider's look at the day-to-day miracles of walking the terrain, of making it yield its riches. She wanted to summon the awe of her student days, convey the responsibility of her craft. She would not write about numbers or five-year plans. Her only graphic would chart where vistas and pig iron met, the geologist at the crossroads, a rail switch operator.

She labored over the essay for several nights, choosing her words carefully and reading sections of it aloud to Snow Crane. It focused on camp life, on the wall of trees that enclosed the little settlement, filtering the noisy rush of the river; the routines of canned breakfasts out of metal kitchenware; the helicopter outings and hikes; the ding of hammers and the backpacks weighed down by rocks. She endeavored to deliver to the Moscow urbane the doing of geology, how discovery happened in the remote corners of their country. She transformed the static steel rails the city dwellers rode into a process, which human geologists like her drove. She sought to capture the labor of geology, not the accomplishment, and submitted a stack of portraits of the mountains and rivers she'd come to love.

"Already I am being restored," she told Snow Crane.

He patted her hand, returned to his novels. Her struggle was so unfamiliar to him. He worked to eat, to avoid arrest for vagrancy. He had no loyalties to the state, no civic calling, no debt to industry or even to the steppe. He loved the mountains but felt no particular need to exploit or protect them. He liked them, in other words, on their own terms. He accepted his own time there under this paradigm, and knew that the mountain could eat him, could reward him, ignore him. He'd take whatever the land gave. It had become his way.

But Galina labored over her manifesto as if it would justify her to the mountains and the smelters, as if there was some rightness in any of it. When she submitted it, they celebrated with ice cream. A photographer arrived to take photos of her at a nearby park.

"Is your soul calmed?" Snow Crane asked.

"I don't know," she admitted.

The piece ran unexpectedly on a cold January day. She walked in to work to find red roses crowding a crystal vase on her desk.

"Congratulations!" her colleagues said.

A stack of *Da!* sat by the roses. Inside, her article on the expedition. A photo of her, hair backlit and ablaze, forming a halo around her face, took up the entire first page. A *Soviet woman, both beautiful and smart, leads an expedition to mine iron*, the caption read. Galina's face filled the magazine. Photos of her, as if she did the work entirely alone, crowded out the text. They looked enhanced, like someone had added eyeliner and blush on the negative before sending it to print. She didn't remember posing for so many pictures. *She may not have a manicure, but she'll carve out the next great mine out of the taiga with her hands*, it read. *Millions of tons of ore will soon be shaken loose out of the frozen ground as the Soviet Union overtakes America in steel production.*

"Wonderful," her boss said.

The piece had been edited down to a few unimaginative paragraphs. Instead of transporting readers to walk alongside Galina as she worked, all they could do was gaze at her. Rather than process, it peddled false promises. *I will help beat the Americans if it's the last thing I do,* it quoted her. Her father, she thought, must finally be proud.

Snow Crane invited her for a walk. They found their mutt waiting by the entry and together the three of them strolled circles around the geology building in silence. Women passed them wearing fur hats that shifted in the wind, the animals rearranging themselves on their heads. The snow had settled into hard banks along the sidewalk and its brightness lit up the exhaust-darkened buildings' pastel walls. Passersby lowered their heads. Ladas slid across the slick road and hit the sidewalk, frightening pedestrians. Snow Crane led her into a shop and purchased two ice creams in paper bundles. They ate the sweet cream packed in its sodden cones in the freezing cold before Galina finally agreed to go back.

"My soul," she told Snow Crane, "is not calmed."

When they returned to the office, a man in uniform sat straight-backed on one of the desks, swinging his legs. He fingered the samples laid out on the table over a map and picked his teeth with a torn photo negative. When Galina and Snow Crane walked in, he raised his head just slightly and handed her a well-thumbed copy of the USSR economic outlook, Bible-thin pages etched with columns and rows of numbers, a tangible incarnation of the nightly TV newscasts that featured a mustached bureaucrat droning out production numbers: *In the past year the USSR produced 300 million tons of coal, 10 million tons of cotton, 3 million tons of beef, 20 million tons of milk,* an eternal stack of reading sheets barely off-screen to assure viewers of this man's enduring work.

The official motioned for the book and flipped to the section on mining and extraction. He licked his thumb, turning pages with it in calibrated speediness, the wetness of his finger leaving the corners of the pages slightly translucent. He stopped at the section titled IRON ORE and handed the book back to Galina. The historic summary showed the numbers slowly rising year by year.

"Not everything is doing so well," the official said.

She flipped to other pages. Graphs for wheat, oil, lumber showed thin, jagged lines pointed down, like arrows that hit an impenetrable target and kinked upon impact. The official carried himself like a bureaucrat but when he spoke he betrayed an academic past, which tempered him in Galina's eyes.

"We are hoping for a successful season for you this summer," he said. He rose from the table he'd been sitting on and stood in front of Galina. "I just stopped by to wish you luck."

He straightened his coat and laid a clammy hand on Galina's shoulder, dampening her shirt, like the pages of the book he'd leafed through. He removed an envelope from his bag and handed it to her before he left.

"This weekend, there's a gathering. A perk of your new position. We'll pick you up, the details are in the envelope. And I'm sorry, but please come alone."

She opened the envelope. The note inside said to dress for a party.

■ ■ ■

On Friday after work, she took her best dress off a hanger in the closet and ironed it by the window. Her grandmother had sewn the dress for her out of twisted silk patterned with blocks in shades of ochre. The design made Galina think of tectonics, a new theory going around that the earth's crust was made up of plates grinding and crashing into each other, their cataclysmic physicality the cause of earthquakes and mountains and seas. The fine fabric lessened the effect, transforming the blocks into soft dunes when she moved. She slipped the necklace Snow Crane had made around her neck and dabbed perfume behind her ears.

The car came on time. She sat in the back, the driver polite but quiet, glancing at her in the mirror as he drove out of the city along a rutted road increasingly lined with snow-heavy trees. It was already dark. The driver caught glimpses of the countryside in weak headlights. When they arrived at an opulent dacha, the driver pointed the car at the shoveled entrance of the house and clicked on his brights to light the way for Galina. She stepped into the beam and walked up a swept path toward the chatter of the party.

Inside, she spotted the bureaucrat who had invited her, and he smiled broadly at her across the room. He greeted her with a flute of champagne and led her by the elbow to a table heavy with plates and bottles. She hadn't seen this type or quality of food in her adult life. The crispy white bread spread with dewy caviar beads, smoked meats and fish laid on large plates in fractal patterns, each slice of salami a synchronized swimmer frozen mid-routine, dark chocolates in wafery gold foil wrappings, Napoleon cake so thick with flaky layers of pastry that it looked like a well-thumbed tome at its edges. Wedged between the plates stood bottles, all open, of vodkas and whiskeys and cognacs and wines with baroque labels and real corks. The bureaucrat promenaded her around the table, filling her plate with sandwiches, spears of fresh cucumbers, and tiny pieces of cake.

All around her milled well-dressed, intelligent-looking men. The bureaucrat introduced her to people. A doctor studying cancer. A physicist on a very important project. A chemist who'd discovered a new compound that was stronger than steel. A mathematician working on artificial intelligence. A botanist who made the cotton crop in the East heartier and richer. She was the geologist opening the next great iron mine, the woman who'd eliminate the Union's need to import steel and drive the construction of new homes, the building of new tractors, the resurgence of the sluggish manufacturing sector.

"She's more important than any of you men!" he joked with each new introduction, his cheeks now puffier and redder, as if he'd covered them with two leaves of purple cabbage.

A motorcade arrived outside and a parade of women sashayed through the front door. They were otherworldly, perfumed Martians with long limbs and smooth hair and clothing so beautifully cut that they seemed another species entirely. Galina realized then that she had been the only woman at the party before the group arrived. The bureaucrat released her elbow and drifted toward the newcomers, until one of the women took him by the arm and led him to a corner. His cabbage cheeks blushed a deeper red. The women spilled through the door of the house and dispersed in the crowd like an overturned vial of mercury beads, lustrous droplets of something dangerous gliding along the floors. The scientists approached them, surrounded them, leaned into them with their eyeglasses and champagne flutes. Somewhere in the house a band began to play.

Galina sat down by the table and considered wrapping some of the delicacies to bring home to Snow Crane. She poured red wine into a cut crystal goblet and moved a plate of cheese closer to her. The physicist she'd met now resembled a cooked noodle trying to stand, tall and unreinforced, his body a tottering threat over the woman he had claimed. She sat watching the others, the women handling the clumsy scientists with practiced professionalism. A man approached Galina at the table and picked a cheese sandwich from the plate.

"Looks like they didn't plan the entertainment with you in mind," he said to her, and pulled up a chair.

"Don't let me keep you," she said. "I'm just as happy with the sandwiches."

She'd always been a good eater, not a person one had to convince to finish a plate of food. The bacchanal before her, which she had to herself, made her ravenous. She reached for plates: meringue reclining in glasses of cream, buttery croissants spooning on a long oval platter, Hungarian salamis shimmering like fish scales on a smooth cutting board, skewers of mutton festooned with lightly pickled onions, Georgian bread with melted cheese oozing through slits in the dough, an intricate serving bowl heaped with Olivier salad, then another with deep purple vinaigrette salad, and another with julienned carrots polka-dotted with garlic and red pepper. She reached for a plate of herring layered with hard-boiled eggs, potatoes, and beets—a *herring in a fur coat* that she remembered from her grandmother's cooking. In the middle of this spread lay an entire pig, apple in its mouth, currants in its eyes, ears crisped. Parts of it had been sliced, but she dug the tines of her fork into the unsliced side, twisting it until clumps of meat peeled off, and she placed piles of the pork on her plate, along with everything else.

Growing up with the privileges of her father's position in government, she'd seen this all before. She'd attended parties like this, eaten from spreads like this, been showed around and presented like this. But after school, she'd left these dispensations behind like an uncoupled train car. Now she was encountering it all as if for the first time.

Galina did not abide by courses. The sugar juices of the sweets bled into the servings of meat, over the cold cuts stuck to the porcelain, and the lumps of salad blended on the crowded plate. She took bites of the food and placed more little sandwiches on top of it as she chewed. She did not eat fast—she stayed measured, polite—but she could not stop her eyes from roving over the table as cooks from somewhere in the back of the house continued to bring out more plates and placed them on polished silver stands with legs. The table's offerings grew upward, the dishes like buildings in a city, casting shadows and forming horizons along the table's length.

The man watched her eat, then picked up a meringue bowl and scooped it with a spoon.

"This is your first party, I gather," he said. He spoke in a slow, measured Russian, with an accent that made her language sound soft. "I'm David, I'm also a geologist."

Where David's eyebrows should have been, bushy caterpillars

approached each other from opposite sides of his face. He had large, hooded eyes the color of sunlit honey, amber disks that he seemed shy to show off to unsuspecting interlocutors.

"I work in M. Ever hear of it?"

Galina nodded. "Of course."

She had never visited because it had been a closed city for so long, but she'd read books about the solid iron mountain that had once stood there and the steelworks that now dominated the settlement and covered the snow in soot.

"I hear you're the one that's going to find the new pile of iron to feed our factory."

Galina chewed on a piece of salty meat.

"Don't work too hard," he said.

The band upped the tempo, and he asked her to dance.

"I thought I was here for work," she said.

They wove between other couples. The women were leading, their partners asleep nestled in their breasts. The singer of the band was dressed like Edith Piaf and sang her songs in Russian-accented French, infusing the notes with a heavy Slavic dolor.

"She doesn't seem sad enough," David joked.

He spun Galina along a wall and into another room, and although the voice of the singer started to fade he held on to her and danced her into yet another room, and another, until they came to a door. He let go of her and invited her for a smoke outside.

"They throw these parties several times a year, invite all the depressed scientists to gorge themselves on imported salamis."

His Russian was decent, but his accent relaxed the words in his mouth, as if he chewed before letting them out.

"Who gets to come?"

"Bosses. And all the scientists whose phones they've tapped."

Bare bulbs on the roof shone a perimeter around the back of the house. A crème brûlée cap of snow coated the yard. They watched a man walk the line of lights, weaving in and out of darkness, each step punching through the crust, until he fell down, his body in the black, his legs in the light.

"You're not from here," Galina said.

"I'm a consultant. From America."

Galina panicked, her body trained by years of her father's dinner conversation to recoil from foreigners as if from fire. She took a step toward David, to physically counteract her reflexes.

"They even watch the foreigners?"

"They especially watch us." He winked. "I'm supposed to clean up the steel mill, the air. It's not a popular mission."

When David finished his cigarette, they dragged the man who had fallen in the snow into the house, slumped him against a wall, and rejoined the party. Galina sat next to one of the women hired to entertain at the table. She angled a salami into her purse and zipped it shut. The bureaucrat who had invited Galina picked up a glass and hit the rim with a butter knife until people quieted.

"We are very proud of the work you are doing," he said. "The masses may be the heart, but you are the brains behind our Union."

He hiccupped. Edith Piaf was also stuffing something into her purse. The bureaucrat rubbed his belly. Before he wrapped up his speech, people had already resumed singing ballads at the scattered tables. Galina wrote down her address on a piece of graph notebook paper and handed it to David.

"I'd like to come see M.," she said.

"You're not a spy, are you?" David grinned at her as she headed toward the door to look for her driver. She'd heard about Americans' teeth, how straight and white they could be, how they were always flashing them.

Her chauffeur sat perched on the hood of the car, smoking. The drivers had sneaked a few bottles of vodka, which lay empty in the snow.

Snow Crane was still up when Galina walked in. She pulled out napkins full of sweating delicacies from her bag.

"Courtesy of our government!" she said.

The last bundle she took out contained chocolate-dusted truffles she'd found in a box with French lettering.

"These are for you, these are for you," she repeated over and over, as if she could never give him enough.

■ ■ ■

Some weeks after the party, Galina received a note from David. Scribbled in barely legible, tiny lettering, it invited her to M. He wrote that he'd secured the permissions from his superiors for her and an assistant, but to come soon in case they changed their minds. In the postscript, he wrote: *After you left, we went night skiing. We raced each other through the wood as if salami lay over the finish line. Good thing I won, because salami did lie over the finish line. I'm saving it for your visit.*

She showed it to Snow Crane. "Want to go?"

Their department head approved the trip, Galina as project

lead, Snow Crane as assistant geologist. Their superiors stamped sheet after sheet of paperwork lined with purple-inked signatures. Within days, they were making their way through the airport. Encampments of passengers waiting for flights crowded the halls. The terminal smelled like the entryway to the sauna, where everyone takes off their shoes and undresses before entering. No commercial flights serviced M., but the pilot of a cargo plane had promised to make a stop to drop them off. They sat in the cabin with the pilot, perched on narrow seats and tucking their elbow to avoid hitting any buttons or switches. It reminded her of the summer's helicopter flights, and a warm flood washed under her skin. When they approached, M. sparkled like a Kremlin New Year tree out the main windshield. Orange lights drew neighborhoods and streets and, almost in the middle of the settlement, a giant, glittering ornament.

"That's the steelworks," the pilot said.

"There are more lights in this town than in Moscow," Snow Crane said.

The airport was empty when they landed. The pilot pointed in the direction of town and returned to the skies without guidance from airport staff. Galina and Snow Crane walked along the tarmac toward the city. The air hung thick and stung at the soft tissue in their throats.

"Shouldn't it be daytime?" Snow Crane asked.

Passing cars flashed their brights in the sooty haze. They didn't see any cabs, so they asked passersby for directions and arrived on foot at the address David had provided. They found David in their hotel room, reading a newspaper on one of the beds. Heat rolled into the room from every surface, as if it were some sort of conductive chamber. Hot waves emanated from the geometric-patterned wallpaper, the faux wooden wardrobe doors, the bare lightbulb dangling from the ceiling, the ironed sheets and woolen blankets on the narrow beds. David had opened the window to let out some of the heat but sweat still poured down his face.

"You won't get cold in here!" he said. "Let's go."

A car stood parked outside the hotel lobby. David sat in front, directing the driver on a tour of the city.

"I'm sorry, you missed daytime by a couple of decades," David said. "We have a bit of a pollution problem here."

He kept a handkerchief over his nose as he instructed the driver where to go.

"This town was supposed to be like an American city, laid out in a grid, rational, organized, primed for industrial production. They even hired a German to do the urban plans, you know, to keep the lines straight," David said.

"It's all just ideas here," the driver said. He lifted his eyes off the road for a moment, checked out the two passengers in the back. "These friends of yours, maestro?" he asked David.

David nodded, and to reassure him told the visitors, "This is a neighbor. We make vodka in my apartment together. Really good stuff."

"Refined." The driver grinned, lifting his fingers to his mouth and kissing them.

"Anyway, the German quit because nobody listened to him. In fact, they threw up half the city before he arrived. Put all the wrong things in all the wrong places. They put the housing blocks downwind of the mill and the water treatment plant intake downstream from it."

"The German never stood a chance," the driver lamented.

He turned off the boulevard and wound down a narrow path, the car pointed toward a far-off light. He slowed, picking his way on the unpaved road, sliding on the pressed tire tracks in the snow. They caught glimpses of the mill through the gauzy air and ice-encrusted thickets. Finally the driver steered to the bank of the river. It stood frozen, creaking its whale call cries in the still evening. Its surface glowed pale blue, a nightlight for the perpetually dimmed city. People ice skated on the river and sat fishing in holes drilled into the surface. A bright red line painted on the surface cut the ice in two.

"Why the border?"

"Can't go beyond it, it's dangerous," David said. "The mill lets out hot water on that side of the river, the ice is too thin."

On the opposite bank, the mill's buildings and smokestacks competed for height on the horizon. Beyond the mill, nothing. Smog smeared the outlines of the hills around them.

The driver turned the car around and they drove back to David's house in silence. They settled in David's kitchen, crammed on stools between the stove and a tiny table. He brought out the vodka and poured.

"To steel!"

Glasses clinked. He poured another.

"To your mine."

The driver poured more.

"To friendship."

They drank late into the night. Every interior in the town

seemed overheated, as if each room was directly plugged into the mill's furnaces. The warmth nourished the intimacy in the kitchen. The strangers leaned in a little too close, asked questions a little too frankly, laughed a little too loudly. The American's influence. The driver sat back rubbing his great, pregnant belly in tipsy amusement, red-faced and jolly.

"This man is a Russian at heart." The driver slapped David on the back. Again, he kissed his fingers and flung them at the ceiling.

"What are you actually supposed to be doing here?" asked Snow Crane.

David became very serious, as if the time had come to explain himself. From the open window, snow swirled into the kitchen, settling on the table's colorful oilcloth.

"I'm supposed to clean up this mess. I'm supposed to help write policies to protect the environment. I'm supposed to paint the Soviet Union green."

The kitchen quieted. "Instead, I'm making vodka."

■ ■ ■

David's father, Jon, worked the overnight shift in Pittsburgh's largest mill. In the mornings he returned home covered in a fine gray dust that transformed him into a monochrome photograph. Only his eyes, shiny, a warm and inviting brown, made him three-dimensional. He used the cellar door and took his clothes off in the unfinished basement before clomping up the stairs and emerging in the kitchen in only his underwear, somehow preserved an almost bluish white beneath the dusty clothes. David and his siblings, eating breakfast, would greet him with cereal spoons in hand and talk at him with milk sloshing out of their mouths.

On weekdays, he drove the children to school. On weekends, he handed out small paintbrushes, and they spent mornings dusting that same gray patina off the roses he planted around the home's perimeter. In the evenings, David liked to lie in his father's lap and mindlessly twirl his wedding ring round and round while the man read to him. With time, his father's fingers thickened, gnarling around his wedding band until he could no longer take it off and David became too old to twirl it.

Jon and his oldest son found new ways to be with each other. Jon took him riding in a square-nosed white Ford truck. Often they'd go out in the mornings, when everything was still a little sleepy, and drive slowly, waving to neighbors and extending their time together. Jon would set the truck in neutral and let it cruise down the steep hill until they reached the neighborhood's main street. Then he'd shift into a low gear and crawl past the clapboard butcher shop with the hand-painted sign; the Hungarian church, all round windows and ochre brick; the Polish restaurant that shook when the trains rumbled past; the bakery; the grocery. At the end stood the mill, and Jon would lift one of his fattening fingers and point at the flames escaping from the square holes of the otherwise windowless blue façade. "Kind of looks pretty from a distance," he'd say, and either reverse course back to the house or make a loop through town where they'd pick up produce from the Strip District's outdoor market, an almond cake or a box of cookies for the family from Bloomfield, the Italian neighborhood.

People lost limbs and eyesight, and all manner of disfigurations mangled the men who spent precious hours in the mill's maw. But year after year Jon came home safe each day, sustaining his height and his pride and all of his digits so he could return to the mill the next night to labor. And the next. And the next.

One morning, when David was already in high school, smoking joints as he walked through the woods and thinking about dropping out so he could protest the war or scribble full-time in his notebooks or go live in a commune somewhere in California, far, far away from Pittsburgh, his father came home early. Dewy nighttime blues still colored the morning even as daylight sucked them from the horizon. He walked up from the basement in his underwear and sat down at the kitchen table. David poured him coffee. No one else had come downstairs yet.

"Don't be fucking up in school," the man said.

Steam from the coffee wetted the dust he still hadn't wiped from his face, darkening it. His voice sounded like a bunch of rusty pinballs rattling in a box.

"Yes, sir," David said.

His father cleared his throat, but the effort made him hack. Jon lifted a hand to his mouth and coughed into it. A mass of bloody phlegm filled his hand. Jon closed his hand around it and stepped toward the sink.

"What the hell, Dad."

"Take the day off school," Jon said.

"You told me not to fuck up," David said, grinning.

They drove across town in the white truck and ate breakfast at a diner with chartreuse plastic booths. Each ordered a piece of pie and watched the other eat, mistrusting the day ahead. After, they parked in a church lot and David rolled his eyes but Jon told him not to be an asshole and that he had something to show him. Dim bulbs lit the small interior.

"Let your eyes adjust," Jon said.

Out of the blackness shapes swam to the surface. Murals covered every inch of wall, the dark paint one with a bigger darkness. Large bodies appeared, in overalls and carrying metal lunch buckets, atop small hills. In the background, the familiar lines of mines and mills, the dips and rises of the Allegheny Valley framing the saintly men. The scale of men versus mountains, the large hands versus the small buildings made the human figures feel lordly, significant.

In one painting a group of women in gowns the color of deep blue ocean stood around the laid-out body of a man with a good, square rib cage and sinewy, strong arms. Peachy, light paint separated him from the grays, mossy greens, and ultramarines, all underwater colors, of the rest of the tableau. He lay on sheets of newspaper, which protected him from the indignity of the bare ground below. The women looked at him without looking, mouths turned down, eyes turned up. Great, voluptuous clouds billowed from smokestacks to the heavens. Across from that painting, another showed Mary grieving Jesus.

"The painter, he was a Croatian," Jon said.

"Stay still," David told him.

He took out the camera he carried and let the flash charge.

"Ready?"

He snapped one photo of his father, hat in hand, the dead man behind him glowing in the bulb's glare. David still carried that photo with him in his notebook. In it, Jon held a stoic half-smile, brows straight and thick like David's, biceps still hulking in the cloth of his shirt.

Jon shrank so fast after that. His clothes drooped from his frame and he had to roll the sleeves of his shirts so they would not hang over his hands. The wedding ring began, again, to spin round and round on his finger. Eventually he took it off and placed it in a small saucer by his bedside, so as to not lose it.

David graduated from high school, got into Berkeley. California bound, just like he'd dreamed. He packed the picture of his father, the camera, a few books, a typewriter. Jon gave him the white truck. He drove it across the country, elbow propped on the open window, thin T-shirt flapping against his chest, the country opening up as he clicked off miles along I-80. It was his first time leaving Pittsburgh and the air tasted different and his life looked real.

By the end of the first semester, his father had died. He didn't have enough money to travel home for the funeral.

"He said he loved you," his mother told him when he called home from the dorm telephone. "And to not fuck up in school."

"What's the cause of death?"

"The doctor would not say."

David signed up for six courses for the next semester. He sat in the eucalyptus grove between classes, reading novels for his literature class and studying formulas for the chemistry lab and solving physics equations. *Don't fuck up in school.* He went to special topics lectures in the evenings and did all of his homework and passed all of his exams. He made friends. He did not declare a major. He thought about his father and the blood he coughed up, tucking each gob of bright-red phlegm into napkins, hiding them in his large hands and smiling after each fit to reassure his family.

In the spring semester he went to a concert with a friend. It was in a small room and the drummer beat out rhythms that quickened his heart. The loudness hugged him, sound waves holding him up from every direction like so many hands. The singer's gritty voice unleashed in the tiny venue, bounced off the walls, and crashed into David, over and over, waves pummeling him. He allowed himself to cry. Sweat and tears poured down his face. He stepped up to the stage, closed his eyes, and floated, as if in a sensory deprivation tank.

He started attending shows every weekend. It was the sixties and there was an edge to the music, the bands not afraid of playing loud or dirty, which suited his state of mind. He liked to scream in the presence of other people, to sweat, to raise his arms as if in surrender. He figured out he was angry. During phone calls, his mother told him his younger brother had secured a position at the mill, and that the neighbor was sick, coughing up blood, and the school principal had died, and she herself wasn't feeling well, it would pass, oh well. He turned up his records and, transported, fell asleep with ringing in his ears.

At one show, a woman got onstage to introduce the band. Yellow hair lit up her face as if she stood blocking the sun and the audience turned to her as if tugged by a string. She had a high-pitched voice, but she spoke forcefully into the microphone. She invited those present to join her to protest a pharmaceutical company dumping chemical waste into a nearby stream where people liked to swim.

Someone threw a bottle at her on the stage. David drew a poster and attended along with a small group of people. They chanted into a gray sky that hung over them like a great, sound-dampening pillow. A man came out of a side door, smoked a cigarette, showed them his middle finger, and went back into the building.

Something sped up in David's psyche. A rage spread within him like a wildfire. In one class he learned that scientists hypothesized that polluted air could cause cancer. David ran his finger along a list of US cities with the worst air quality, starting at the bottom of the list and clicking off cities, up up up, until he came to Pittsburgh, nearly number one. This shocked him. Why wouldn't the doctor say? He asked the teacher a lot of questions, and the woman tried to answer them. Often she'd reply, "It's hard to say, we just don't know yet." He signed up for more chemistry classes, geology, public health. David finally declared a major. He graduated at the top of his class.

By day, he worked as a consultant for energy companies and factories to prepare their facilities and operations for the slate of federal laws that they expected would soon roll out on air and water quality standards. In reports, he enveloped each set of recommendations in the guise of friendly advice and thanked his clients for their work.

By night, he organized campaigns targeting polluters and gave depositions to lawyers preparing environmental lawsuits. He worked nonstop, in the background, assuming pseudonyms so his two lives would not cross.

Somehow he'd avoided notoriety or recognition for the protests, lawsuits, and unflattering news stories he helped orchestrate.

Maybe the FBI had a file on him, a manila folder with black-and-white photographs of him marching, or transcribed phone conversations of him dictating letter writing campaigns. But if they did, they did not share it with the Russians when they issued a visa for him to travel to the Soviet Union. David wanted to do more.

A colleague had shown him photographs of Russian cities where flowers bloomed in great Persian gardens. Intrigued, David found an Intourist pamphlet, printed by a Soviet tour operator, in a local travel agency and marveled at the pictures of the wide, tree-lined boulevards of Kiev, Sevastopol, Chernovtsy. He read that planners quarantined industry away from population centers to keep cities clean. People gulped up the air like fresh mother's milk. No one coughed up blood into crumpled tissues. A new policy of détente had been announced between the US and the USSR, and through his alma mater he found a job that would allow him to travel to Russia. It was similar to his work at home, a consultant position advising the state on best practices for fewer, cleaner emissions. He wanted adventure, yes, but also to shame his countrymen. As if they'd care about their enemy's cleaner skies. He didn't know much about Russia or M. before arriving.

He disembarked with preternatural enthusiasm. He studied Russian for hours each day, scheduled meetings with anyone who'd give him one, and deliberated the town's infrastructure. But it didn't take long for disillusionment to grow like a great thicket of bamboo in his mind, impossible to beat back. How could a city so defiantly turn its back on its residents? It was Pittsburgh magnified, Pittsburgh concentrated. Still, he advised the relevant parties as best he could: scrubbers on the stacks, purer coal, move the residential quarters from the mill's immediate vicinity. They wrote down his suggestions and made him sign off on them on page after page of official documents. They said thank you.

At the party where he met Galina, something snapped. A spillway that had held back his bitterness unlatched, flooding him. All of his efforts futile, his mind a swamp; his father's death was pointless, his own life's work ultimately in vain. After Galina left he got very drunk. He approached the other scientists, and mumbled in their ears about his frustrations in M. Maybe they could help him? The scientists slapped him on the shoulder and asked him to teach them American curse words. He obliged. Late into the night, they sat in a circle, cursing.

When he returned to M., David spent evenings reading with the windows shut. A small fan shuffled stale air around the apartment. He glued sheets of plastic over the window frames so the studio acquired the feel of a conspiracy theorist's headquarters, sealed and sour. David visualized the various organic and inorganic particles in the outside air burrowing into the lining of his lungs like maggots into flesh. He'd knead at his chest, trying to rid his mind of the images, and when that didn't work he'd do sit-ups and push-ups on the floor until he couldn't lift his body.

He thought about Galina, the hesitant quiver in her voice that suggested she knew how to listen. He inquired about her, learned she had connections through her father, a reputation for being honest. He invited her to visit. And here she was sitting in his kitchen. What did he think she could do for him? He didn't know. But he told her everything: about his dad, how the light never penetrated the smog, how his neighbor's children were all sick with rare illnesses, how his own lungs failed him when he walked too briskly. She listened, conspiratorial in her concentration, but said very little.

Galina and Snow Crane took a taxi back to the hotel. The room hadn't cooled any so they slept on separate beds. They hung their arms off, intertwining just two fingers, a fragile bridge between bodies.

Galina woke up gasping. Outside the window, snow still swirled on treeless streets. She stuck her head out to refresh her lungs, but the air entered her body like cement.

She thought about her father. He didn't like to leave Moscow and had sold off the family's dacha without her mother's permission. It wasn't efficient to grow their own vegetables if they didn't have to, he said. When he finally came around to Galina's profession, he congratulated her on the contributions she would make to the state's industry. Uncomplex, was how she described him to friends. As if he'd figured out the world a long time ago and it really was a very simple place.

He'd never pass as a believable villain in a book, she used to tell people, because he was too flat.

She wondered if he'd ever made it to this town in his many trips around the Union, if he'd ever had to breathe this air.

Snow Crane rolled over and beckoned to her. Pressed her to his sweaty chest, held her.

Lips against lips. Legs intertwined.

"It's awful here," he said, coughing.

In the morning David picked them up in his car and drove them around a different part of town. Each of them nursed a hangover, and an awkwardness crept into the vehicle. On the sidewalks, women pushed strollers wrapped in fabric, as if cotton could protect young lungs from the air's munitions. Children skipped to school in surgical masks. From mountain to crushed and sorted ore, to blast furnaces to this. Galina fingered the polished stone that hung around her neck. She had helped create this.

"What can I do?" she asked David.

"Anything."

PART III
ЧАСТЬ III

CHAPTER 4
Глава 4

It was the winter of visitors. Decades they had managed the whiteness without company, but now guests materialized almost daily in front of the Kols' hut.

First came the animals. Agafia knew, of course, that they were out there, had seen them from a distance, but they had rarely approached the homestead. The Kols and the beasts inhabited different planes of the same place for their survival, acknowledging each other only when necessary. But one dusky afternoon Agafia watched a wolf slink toward the homestead from the tree line. He had eyes the color of runny egg yolk and a winter coat so thick it looked like a borrowed fur draped over his own generous hide. He curled up in front of the door like a house cat, and on the other side of it Agafia could feel his warmth. For a week, he returned every night before disappearing.

Another day a moose approached and pressed his nose to the tiny window, filling the whole of it with his face. Ice grew thick over the panes, and from inside Agafia saw just a shadow of its knotty snout. She wished Dima were not dead and he would come and kill the moose and she would say a prayer and they would cook the meat for supper. The animal loped off, Agafia watching him through a crack in the door.

About a week after the moose, Agafia watched a man materialize, the shape of him growing larger as he slowly made his way toward the hut across moonlit meadows. At first it appeared that two wolves trailed him as he walked, but Hugo realized they were dogs, and when the Kols came out to greet the trio, the animals cocked their heads to the side, questioning. The man told Agafia and Hugo he was a hunter exploring new terrain for ermine and sable. He'd made camps like beads strung the length of river south from his homestead, but he'd never ventured north before.

"May I come in to warm for a bit?" he asked.

Hugo had already stoked the fire in the hut as they watched the man approach.

"I didn't know there was a settlement here," the hunter said.

"There isn't," Hugo told him. "This is it."

He explained their situation, the same story they'd told the geologists. The man, who called himself Pavel, seemed unsurprised.

"Ah," he said, "we get all sorts out here."

His village, he explained, lay about a hundred kilometers east of the river.

"We're practically neighbors."

"And your village," Hugo said, "are there any Old Believers?"

For decades, Hugo had suspected that they had stopped just short of Belovod'e, some short distance this way or that from the utopia they had sought when they set out all those years ago. For a while he had said so to his family, who had suffered on their long journey, but as they settled he brought it up less and less. Instead, he took long walks, searching, hoping still to stumble upon this paradise, which he had failed to reach.

Pavel shook his head. There weren't, he explained, but close to one of his camps downstream, right on the riverbank, stood a monastery of Old Believer nuns. It was the closest settlement he knew of in his range. Hugo's brows arched over his small eyes. He thought, once again, that he hadn't walked far enough.

"Practically neighbors," Agafia marveled.

Agafia had let Pavel's dogs inside despite Hugo's and their master's protests and they curled at her feet, their spines crescent moons, snouts tucked and eyes upturned. Agafia had never stared into an animal's eyes before, not up close, and an instant and disorienting affection coursed through her. She sensed a godliness in the dogs, a goodness she'd never registered when she'd glimpsed the wolves with whom they shared their valley.

Pavel said the dogs were siblings. He'd picked them out as puppies from a neighbor's litter. The one named Maniac, orange like wet pine with black paws, was the most boisterous in the brood, and the one named Bird, with a thick salt-and-pepper coat, quiet but self-assured. Together they would make a good team, he figured, and had paid for them with three jars of his best clear liquor and a clutch of furs.

"Now they're my family!" he said with a laugh, and patted them on matching black spots on their rumps.

Pavel's ease reminded Agafia of her brother, and that night he slept in Dima's bed. Maniac pressed his body to the stove but Bird sat by Agafia's bed. He placed his pointed head on the mattress and let her caress his nose with a firm, rough finger. Pavel called Bird off, but Agafia clicked her tongue defensively and Bird slumped on the floor beside her and slept there all night.

Over tea the next morning, Pavel had a proposal. He wanted to spend the winter in this stretch of taiga but didn't yet have camps to shelter him there. He wanted to use the Kols' homestead as a base while he explored. He offered a share of the furs as payment, but Hugo waved the idea off.

"What will we do with these small furs here?" he said.

He tangled his fingers into his beard and fell into thought. Pavel could stay, he finally said, but he would have to live in the small hut that had been intended for Dima and help around the homestead when he wasn't away. To celebrate, Agafia opened a small jar of honeycomb, a gift from the geologists, and broke off chunks for each of them, sharing her portion with Bird.

* * *

The next morning, Pavel gathered his belongings and broke trail to Dima's cabin. It had stood empty since summer and he had to chisel his way in, chipping away the ice that had sealed the door to the frame. Snow shrouded the bottom of the exterior wall, but animal relief carvings on the walls peeked out from the snowdrift. Pavel stopped to look at them: a pig, a rooster, a heron. The heron retained its proper proportions and grace, but the others looked off. The rooster's head sat directly on the body, neckless, so that it resembled a fluffed chickadee. The hog's ears pointed like a wolf's, furry. *They probably haven't seen a pig in forty years*, Pavel thought. The dogs dug holes in the snow by the door, and curled to protect themselves from the elements.

Inside, the floor was frozen. Firewood lay stacked floor to ceiling, overwhelming the tiny space. Dima had prepared everything for winter. Agafia and Hugo had told Pavel about the others the previous night, their quick demise, the cemetery that now grew along their garden wall, the way death smarted in the summer when everything was alive. Pavel unpacked his bag—clothes, food, some notebooks, pens, his gun—in the dead man's cabin, organizing everything in sorted piles on a table he arranged out of logs. The hut warmed and he lay down on the oven.

Pavel had intended to wander with the dogs in widening circles around the taiga, looping mountain ranges and rivers with his tracks. It was true that he wanted to explore this new tract of land north of his customary hunting grounds, but he wasn't looking for animals, which his range supplied in abundance. His wife, Masha, had died at the opening of the season, bled out like a sacrifice while giving birth. The baby, too, had perished. Pavel had stayed by her bedside long after she stopped moaning, after the defeated midwife abandoned her in a chaotic array of blood-soaked sheets and echoes. The velocity of his loss stunned him, how quickly he emptied out, like a reservoir streaming out of a broken dam. And now here he was, living in another dead man's cabin, seeking to refill himself.

He rose from the oven, threw in fresh wood, and watched it catch before climbing back on the hulking furnace and into his sleeping bag. The tiny cabin didn't have any windows so it made no difference whether it was day or night, summer or winter outside. A pleasant darkness had rushed in as soon as he closed the door and hung in the air like some sort of talisman, bringing on sleep and protecting him from his thoughts. He drifted off, warm and lost, and slept until the oven had chilled and cold seeped into his slumber.

When he woke he heard the dogs whining and threw them handfuls of jerky from his stash. He'd have to procure more meat for them soon. *At least I can keep them alive*, he thought. His wife's face flashed in his mind, dulled. The dogs had known when she passed and howled mournful songs for hours, as if kindly but diligently escorting her out of a place where she preferred to linger. Pavel lay back down and massaged his temples. Since he needed to support only himself now, there was no need to bring back so many skins. He decided he'd hang around the homestead for a while before heading out.

■ ■ ■

The Kols and Pavel spent their days attending to their singular survival and reunited for meals. Sometimes he'd join Agafia on an errand, to check her traps for animals or haul clean ice to the hut, but mostly he preferred long hours in the solitude of his own room. The distance that separated the homesteads kept Pavel's legs strong as he walked back and forth in the snowdrifts. The spoils of the heavy pack he'd carried and the supplies the geologists had brought diversified the Kols' meals. Pavel didn't pray with them. When it came time for that, he returned to his cabin and climbed up on the oven. He figured his grief was like a long hangover he just needed to sleep off. He'd tuck in and drift off, not waking until the cold grew too sharp to ignore.

With nothing to do the dogs grew restless and started to stay with Agafia when Pavel loped off to his quarters. She brought them along on her outings and they pulled her on her hide skis through fresh snow, relieved to be of use. Bird in particular stayed close to Agafia, training his wide eyes on her with hypnotic concentration and smiling with his black-whiskered lips. Agafia slipped Bird scraps from the table, unthinkable in the household, and fell asleep each night with her hand resting on the dog's scruff. They had chosen each other so obviously and completely that Maniac and Hugo, who'd each lost a companion to the budding friendship, didn't attempt to separate them for any reason. Even Pavel let the dog be, too distracted to register the betrayal.

Pavel found life with the Kols a kind of salvation. He projected his grief onto them and they absorbed it like dull kopeks, then beamed back an equilibrium undented by their own recent losses. They didn't ignore Dima and Natalia's absence, but simply incorporated it into the doom and exaltation of a worldview that had thrummed steadily through untold miseries and churnings of history. This calmed him.

Pavel began to read to Agafia. He'd brought a copy of *The Arabian Nights* and, like Shahrazad telling stories night after night to keep the king from killing her, Pavel opened the book and read to keep the Kols' favor. Hugo dozed by the oven, but Agafia sat rapt, Bird by her side, and clucked at the magic spells and deceptions that bound the book's pages.

"What religion is this book for?" she asked, for the only books she knew were religious texts.

"No religion," he said. "It's just for entertainment."

He thought she would declare it worldly and reject this small nightly pleasure, but the next evening she invited him to stay after dinner and read some more.

"You can leave the book here for safekeeping, if you'd like," she said, when he set off for his cabin at bedtime. She kept it with her own books, reverently retrieving it when she wanted him to read.

Pavel gave Agafia a small mirror. She gazed into it, moving the small square of glass around to assess each centimeter of her face. Though she thought often of time, its passage inherent in the rhythm of her prayers and the very seasons of her existence, she somehow had never placed herself *within* time. But her face was carved by it, and she traced the lines with a tentative, frightened finger. She brought the mirror close to her mouth and reflected her teeth into it. When the piece of glass fogged with her breath, it amused her. The next day, while they were eating lunch, the mirror caught a ray of sunshine that had broken through the woolly cloud cover and reflected bright specks on the cabin walls. That became a favorite pastime in the short winter daytime hours, catching light with the silver square, tossing it back out on surfaces like water out of a bucket.

Pavel sought counsel from Hugo and Agafia. He hadn't been a spiritual man, trusted more the physical world around him. But with his wife's absence, the mystical drew him. He had tried going to a church in a neighboring village and swayed under the spell of yellow candles and prayers. When he heard vespers sung in a cupola filled with golden iconography, he believed, briefly, in heaven's loveliness and his wife's presence there. But it didn't stick, perhaps because he was too eager for an explanation. How did she get there? And would he take the same road?

He asked the Kols this, for something to guide him, but they just shrugged.

■ ■ ■

Several weeks into Pavel's stay with the Kols, Agafia knocked on his door.

"Would you check the traps for an elk?" she asked him. "God willing, we will have some meat to ride out this winter."

She had the dogs with her and Pavel whistled for them to join him, but when they refused he put on deer gloves, loaded his gun, and took the Kols' sled. The sled was made of metal and he wondered where the Kols had acquired the materials, but it slid easily on the snow and soon he forgot about it and was making good time to the first trap. Nothing.

He trudged on, glad of a reason to walk beyond the path he'd flattened between his hut and the Kols'. The grief hangover persisted, and though he had loved his wife, the tenacity of the pain surprised him. His people, rural Russian stock, were accustomed to grief, it was their great inheritance, so that real grieving seemed at times superfluous. The midwife never came back to the house, never explained what had happened. Pavel never sought her out to ask. That too was a special inheritance, the capacity to live on without asking too many questions after tragedy. Pavel's sister had brought him warm bread in the aftermath and that was good enough.

He approached the third trap. Fresh tracks surrounded the hole's perimeter. When he drew closer he saw first a tuft of brown, the rack, the rounded torso, a tangle of limbs. The animal had landed without grace. It breathed in long, labored gulps. Still alive but just barely, impaled on the spikes Dima had sharpened.

"Poor thing," Pavel muttered.

He raised his gun and fired a shot at the elk's heart. The animal slumped over, a trickle of blood painting a pocket of snow red. The cold seeped into his coat and his fingers stiffened in his gloves. He lowered the ladder Agafia kept leaned against a nearby tree into the trap and took out his knife. He'd never be able to drag the whole animal back to the cabin. It was enormous. He carved the meaty hindquarters, the ribs, the shoulders. The elk had suffered, had flooded with adrenaline as he stumbled into the trap, lay there pierced by the crude spikes, and this would not make for good eating, Pavel thought, but he cut into the flesh, peeled away the skin, pared meat from bone, slicing his way through the elk's anatomy. He threw each slab of meat onto the snow. Sweat dampened his underlayers, chilled him. Pavel climbed out of the hole and packed the meat. So much more lay wasted in the trap, but there was nothing to do about it. Maybe he could come back tomorrow. He climbed back down and covered the animal with snow, entombing it for safekeeping.

Dragging the loaded sled behind him, he turned back toward the hut. The wolves had by now smelled the catch, he feared, and trained their ochre eyes on him from the woods. *If they come, they'll take the fresh meat and spare me,* he assured himself. He kept his eyes peeled and gun cocked. The snow lay thick and Pavel made slow progress.

When she was alive, Masha had accompanied him on

expeditions. She spent the long days by his side, checking traps, skinning animals, tending fires for tea. "Otherwise I'd never see you," she told him. He'd worried she hadn't conceived because of this work but didn't say anything. They talked little, but each body was a comfort to the other, a bulwark against the cold and the storminess of their thoughts and moods. When she did conceive, it was on the trail. They'd taken a day off to mend gear in camp. The sun melted the icicles that hung from the hut's roof. It had felt like spring and they made love.

A far-off wolf howl wrinkled the still air. Pavel checked his gun and quickened his step. The sled's weight, its load of resplendent red meat leaving a trail of blood in the snow, pulled on his arm. He'd always sensed a protective force around him, and since Masha's passing that force had materialized into almost solid form, as if she still walked by his side, silent but present. He took one of the smaller hunks of meat from the sled and dropped it on the ground, wiping his hands in the snow around it. Maybe they would be satisfied with a small serving. When he looked up he glimpsed a lone wolf loping toward him from the north, still far enough that its shape smeared in Pavel's vision. He hurried on, past the second trap, now almost back to the first trap. Hard breathing had frozen his beard solid and made his face heavy. He jutted out his chin like the hull of an icebreaker ship, to lead him back toward the cabin.

At the first trap, he noticed tracks in the snow. The wolves had been there; they'd been stalking him since he started his trip, maybe even from the cabin, watching him. He stopped, looked around. Another howl reached him, closer now. Pavel threw his head back and released his own howl, mournful, confident. When he and

Masha lay in the quiet in camp they often heard the wolves going, their cries carrying across great distances. Sometimes the song was exuberant. Other times a lonesomeness pierced the air and they held each other tighter against its chill. "He's lost," Masha would tell him, "he's looking for his pack." New voices would respond across the way, as if to lead the lost one back. Pavel gathered his breath, cupped his hands around his mouth, and released another howl. It took off, swooped to the trees. He couldn't see the wolves anywhere, but he knew they had eyes on him. He started walking again, this time without quickening his step.

Pavel made it to the family cabin without seeing the wolf. His own dogs greeted him, barking and wagging their tails, oblivious. Agafia and Hugo were sweeping the floors with bunched pine branches, shedding needles more than cleaning. The needles scattered on the floor freshened the room. Lately all the women in his village wore piney perfume, a concoction one of the elders brewed and traded for various goods. They all smelled the same. On the road when he walked by a group of women, it was like a breeze stirring a stand of pines. Agafia spied the meat on the sled and bustled toward it to help unload.

"Oh!" she said. "Oh!" She showed brown teeth and ushered Pavel to the fire.

Hugo salted and strung a leg on a string over the stove, to smoke. Agafia packed the rest into a leaning shed that looked like an outhouse, but served as their pantry. That evening they feasted—Pavel cooked buckwheat and stewed a hunk of elk meat with salt and some dried apricots he found in his pack. For dessert, he stabbed open a can of condensed milk and poured it into a bowl of freshly gathered snow. Pavel mixed until the snow became creamy, and Agafia carried a small mound of the ice cream to her mouth in a wooden spoon and closed her eyes. The cold clump slithered down her throat, coated her belly. Was ecstasy a sign of worldliness? Agafia took another spoonful, then backed away from the bowl, and sat watching Pavel eat it alone.

■ ■ ■

Agafia kept a log clean of snow outside of the hut to sit, even in the winter. Often Peter reclined on the log whittling figurines out of branches and whistling, looking himself like a rustic statuette in repose. If she spied him in her spot, Agafia usually stayed indoors. When she peeked out on an unusually cold afternoon, she instead found Pavel. The dogs saw him too, and barked at their owner's appearance.

She and Hugo came out with wooden cups of tea. The wood didn't keep her hands warm, but she liked to lower her face into the steam until condensation covered it, dewy drops on her lashes and a rawness on her cheeks. If she didn't wipe it away, the droplets crystallized into a wafer of delicate armor. When she moved her face, the ice cracked, and she'd repeat the ritual until the tea cooled and the steam failed to rise.

Hugo grumbled about the cold, rubbing his hands together and stomping his feet. When the air is always cold, degrees of misery barely register, but this evening the air itself crystallized into needles and froze their nose hairs. Each inhale stunning, sharp.

"Let's make snow!" Pavel said. He was in unusually good spirits.

"As if there were a shortage," Hugo cackled.

Pavel went inside and put a pot of water to boil on the stove. When the surface broke with bubbles, he carried the pot outside.

"One, two, three," he counted.

He thrust the pot up, sending hot water into the air.

"Poof!"

The droplets candied in the icy air and drifted back down to the ground in a gossamer mist.

"Magic," Agafia mouthed. The night was otherwise clear, and she stepped into the cloud and let the crystals settle on her.

"It's early afternoon but already it's so dark," Pavel said when all the snow had fallen.

Hugo looked around, as if to confirm the darkness.

"What'd you dream about last night?" Agafia asked.

To pass the time, the family recounted their dreams. She and Hugo had stopped when Dima and Natalia died because they were each dreaming of the others.

"In my dream we lived in a village, in a house with a goat tied out front, a bearded fellow with yellow eyes that bleated when we came in from working in our fields," Hugo said. "He came in from the forest one day, all white with black ears and a black spot around his eye. At first, I thought it was the devil come to warm himself by our fire. But in time I came to trust this goat, even to love him, in my dream. When I came in from the fields I was glad to see him at the hut waiting for me. In the old life I had a dog like this, that came and went with me everywhere and waited for me outside of church, but in my dream it was a goat, which is just as well.

"The village—it was Belovod'e. We had finally made it there

and it was as glorious as I knew it would be. Bells from one hundred forty churches rang out in unison so that the town pulsed with holiness. Great earthquakes shook the settlement, but the bells never cracked and the churches never fell. We grew rice in vast, wet fields and grapevines on dry, hot hillsides. I dreamt we'd made it there after all and the priests welcomed us."

He shut his eyes, to return to the dream. Agafia didn't mind him talking about the place the way her siblings had. She still believed in it, its elusive coordinates evidence of its worthiness rather than frustrating make-belief. She reached out to pat her father's knee. Hugo awakened.

"And then one day I came home and the goat wasn't there. His post and his length of rope were gone too. He had taken them with him, as if in his travel satchel, and had set off away from us. The fields dried up, the grapes, everything. I tried to follow him but I became lost."

"Lost again," Agafia sighed, and patted him once more.

"I dreamt of Masha," Pavel said. "It was warm and she came to me. She held our child, all dimples and rolls, like some Madonna, beatific. She did not say anything, but the way she stood there, straight-backed and strong, I knew she was all right. She held out the baby, who cried, and I wanted to touch him but feared him, his saintliness. I think he knew I didn't want him, that I blamed him somehow for what had transpired. But Masha didn't care. She just stood there smiling, looking at me, letting me look at her, like we had done here on earth. I guess we all dream of our own paradise," he concluded. "What about you?"

"I had a dream that was just a feeling," Agafia said.

Usually her dreams came to her in a rush of images—giant pinecones she had to climb as if upon the scaffolding of rising churches, tiny elk that galloped about her body like fleas, piles of snow she peeled apart like a stack of waterlogged pages to reveal the lush gardens beneath—but lately her dreams vibrated through her as wordless premonitions. She didn't understand them.

"What did it feel like?" Pavel asked.

"It felt like my dreams knew better than me."

Hugo let out a thoughtful "Hmm."

"Often I dream of large things or small things, but lately I just feel that things are at the same time large and small, they surround me and I surround them simultaneously. I too feel large and small. It's not a dream but a visitation to other bodies, other forces. Like I am gravity itself and the thing that resists gravity also."

They sat in silence, feeling the forces of their own bodies pressed close on the small bench. The stars, lint on a black sheet of sky, pilled into a streak of Milky Way. The snow glowed blue and trees swaying in the forest radiated a creaky melody. Above a tree in the distance, an orange light pulsed. Agafia put down her cup and pointed. The orange grew, enlarging as it hurtled toward them, taking over the horizon. For a silent moment, everything flushed orange, the world a flaming maw, a split-second opening into a snowless world. Then the portal snapped shut and a burning mass landed in front of the hut, sending tremors through the ground. The hot object sizzled in the snow, melting a ditch around its perimeter and sending up a curtain of thick steam.

"A gift!" Agafia clapped.

A metal capsule lay before them, dented from its fall and still hissing in the snow as it cooled. Agafia took a stick and tapped on all its sides. The capsule answered with a low-pitched *thunk-thunk*.

"God watches over us," Agafia said.

Pavel searched the sky.

"They only come one at a time," Hugo said. "They come as blessings, irregular."

The steam thinned out and all three of them approached the pod. Along a metal seam, Pavel found the initials of the space program stenciled in thick black letters.

"Oh," he said. "Space trash."

He'd heard from his neighbors how it rained down in the taiga, the vast land a repository for wild dreams, but had never seen any himself.

"Trash!" Agafia scoffed. She pointed to the sled parked by the hut. "What do you think we made that sled from?"

Other objects came to Pavel's mind. The metal belly of the oven in his hut. The small flat-bottomed boat under the house's eave. The strange, twisted scraps of metal and bent screws they kept lined up like figurines in their icon's corner.

"We've never had one fall so close," Agafia said. "Usually we have to go looking for them."

"We've never had one so big," Hugo marveled.

For days, no one touched the object. They met around it, discussed it, incorporated it into their triad. For the New Year, Agafia wove a wreath out of pine branches and secured it to the nose of the capsule.

Eventually Hugo began to undo the thing. Using tools the geologists had brought, he unscrewed fasteners and peeled metal sheets in layers so the capsule opened into a ragged, sharp bloom. Wires sprang out like stamens. Agafia plucked them and twisted them into rings, bracelets, brooches with which she adorned herself. Hugo piled the useful metal by the hut and cleared it daily of snow.

"Maybe we will make a steam house," Hugo said. "Dima would've liked that."

Planning projects helped the long winter days pass more quickly. Hugo scribbled designs for the sauna they'd build and they sat around talking about future winter nights spent in its steamy comfort. Their ideas warmed them practically enough to avoid building the thing, and soon they moved on to other ideas. Agafia sketched hanging reflective chimes to keep animals out of their garden and drew complex medieval snares to trap ungulates.

"How lucky," Agafia said, "how lucky we are God loves us so."

■ ■ ■

The pattern of fir needles like quilt stitches in the snow, the wind-twisted ice cap on the small roof, the scratch of the forest in the wind. Each morning Agafia swept ash from the stove into a bucket and dumped it outside before bringing the fire back to life. It burned like some inextinguishable eternal flame in the oven's belly, keeping watch over the long dark hours. Agafia grew restless in this stretch of winter, when spring seemed finally fathomable and yet no sign of it emerged. A limbo of workless days, too cold to daydream, when there was nothing to do but exist. She'd taken to daily washing, rubbing snow on her face, under her arms, and between her legs until her skin grew prickly with cold. She acquired other new routines to fill in the hours. Rebraid her hair, recite her prayers, retie her shoes, repeat. It was the first winter without her siblings, and their absence intensified the dreariness. Hugo spent more and more time sheltered in his own head. Pavel, when he showed up in a decent mood, helped. But more than anything she relied on Bird to brighten her days. She'd started allowing the dog into her bed, and they lounged, her belly pressed to Bird's spine, whole afternoons under their blankets. The men disapproved of her coddling, but Agafia paid them no mind. Bird would throw his head back and Agafia would find the velvet of his snout with her lips and she'd pull the covers farther over their heads and they would relax into the mattress, heavy with contentment.

On nicer days, they'd crawl out of their den-like cot and walk. At first they'd move reluctantly, suddenly frozen, but soon they'd loosen, revitalized by the fresh air coursing through their limber bodies. With Bird by her side, Agafia hiked farther, filling the few light hours of the day with excursions. Bird would break trail, leaping through deep snow and sticking his nose into snowdrifts. Agafia would follow, stepping and sinking despite her snowshoes. Bird would run ahead and return to check on her, before rushing off once again. Agafia gave no commands and pursued no particular task. At first this aimlessness confused the dog, who was trained to sniff out and retrieve his master's prey. He would wait for her instructions, but Agafia would contemplate the middle distance, then pat him on the head and whistle for him to go, incomprehensibly, onward.

When Peter joined them on their walks, Bird seemed to sense his presence. He'd lope sideways away from where Peter stood, cutting his eyes in his general direction, untrusting. Agafia liked that the dog appeared to see Peter when no one else could, and Peter liked the animal, which reminded him of his own dogs, the grace with which they'd hunted and their eyes. He told Agafia how he felt the presence of God when the sun hit their irises and instead of closing their lids, the dogs stared straight ahead, sun-bathed and re-splendent. Before Bird, Agafia might have shunned his sinful words, but now she knew them to be true, had observed the same phenom-enon in her Bird, had admired his steady gaze. Peter told her about his favorite dog, a greyhound named Lisette, whom he'd allowed to lounge on the fine furniture like a court aristocrat. "My shadow," he told Agafia. "Her bones," he said proudly, "are preserved in the natural history museum in Leningrad." Agafia had never been to a museum and she imagined a fine cemetery for dogs, which in her mind was proper and right.

One afternoon the three of them walked a new path to a neigh-boring cirque Agafia had never visited. The snow still lay thick, leav-ing little on the ground to look at, flattening distances. She was out of breath, legs burning. She hadn't planned to be gone so long, but each time she thought to turn around the lake at the center of the cirque appeared so close and she wanted to reach it. Soon, though, the sun settled behind the hill, coloring the land blue, and the temperature grew steadily colder, as if she were descending deeper and deeper into a cool sea. Agafia whistled for Bird, but he trotted ahead. She quick-ened her pace to catch up and had almost reached him when some-thing flashed over her shoulder. In the unreliable dusky light, the streak of brown cut across the snow like an apparition and was gone. Bird had seen it too and stood, his tail erect. "Bird!" Agafia called.

Peter squatted by her, squinting at the animal. Bird paused, pointing with his nose. He glanced back at Agafia, who called to him once again; then he turned and began to run in the opposite direction. He ran *on* the snow, rather than through it, his paws floating on the ice cap as if he were made of the same substance, blown this way and that by the wind. The dark blur of his body flickered lower in the bowl of rock they'd entered, weaving in and out of view between the snow's undulations and the mountain's folds. He ran fast, naturally, destined for this very thing and finally unleashed to do it, his legs folding and unfolding in long, fluid strides. Agafia yelled for the dog to return, raising her voice in panic. It bounced back to her in scattered echoes. The fading light swallowed the shape of Bird as he receded farther and farther, racing toward the lake that stared out of the cirque like an unblinking eye.

"Must have been a sable," Peter said. "He's chasing it."

Agafia hiked up her skirts and retied her snowshoes. They were hours from home.

"You can't go after him!" Peter said.

But Agafia was moving slowly in Bird's tracks, calling his name in a steady rhythm and clapping her hands. She'd lost sight of him but aimed toward the water, the only clearly visible landmark. The mountains had transformed into inky silhouettes and stars packed the sky.

Agafia thought of the summer nights she'd bedded down on riverbanks and flattened meadows into beds, but to spend the night outside in the winter was surely insane. She placed one foot in front of the other, fighting off fear and cold with movement.

"To sleep outside in the summer is to be one with the elements," she told Peter, "but to do so in the winter is to survive the elements."

"It's a fine distinction in the taiga," Peter said, chuckling.

He trotted after her, pulling at her sleeve to turn around. Somewhere they heard Bird's excited yip, then a silence, another bark, this time in a lower register, and silence. She tripped in the dark and landed with her face in the snow, shocked. Peter helped her up and tried once more to redirect her homeward.

"No," she said, and stood gazing at the stars. The snow creaked, as if they were all, the mountains and Agafia and Peter and somewhere Bird, sliding downward together, the ground beneath them straining like a great tide. Galina had talked to her about how somewhere deep below the ground, a molten ocean churned, moving the very land around, which Agafia found ridiculous and enticing, like she was spring melt floating down a river, like she was going somewhere. The stars multiplied around her, each light divided over and over into several, spilling over into the sky.

She didn't remember what happened next, but she woke in the morning in a snow cave. Milky light streamed in through the white ceiling, like a fog. Her cheek, pressed to an icy wall, was numb, but the rest of her tingled familiarly, nipped but not frozen. Peter sat across from her, humming quietly some old hymn she hadn't heard since her mother's passing.

"Good morning! The cave kept you pretty warm, didn't it?" he asked cheerily.

Agafia crossed herself and climbed out of the hole.

"Bird!" she called.

She was close to the tarn now, could see the gray slush that filled it. How odd that it was not frozen solid. Her toes and fingers stung as she unstiffened her body, taking small steps. On the opposite bank a dark figure bent to the water to drink.

"There!" Peter cried.

"Bird!" Agafia yelled out.

The dog raised his head, looked around, and ran toward them. His heavy panting reached them first, then the dog himself, tongue lolling, waving his tail at Agafia.

Blood stained his snout and pink icicles hung from his whiskers.

"Where have you been?" Agafia scolded him. Bird jumped on his hind legs and licked at Agafia's face, his breath putrid and warm. The sun was high, but already counting down to the next cycle of darkness.

■ ■ ■

The changing of the seasons accelerated after her night away from home, as if the taiga was hurrying its thaw to avoid a repeat. Snow piles relaxed into pillowy mounds and icicles started to drip from the hut roof. Daylight grew brighter, stretched into hours. Tentative spring blooms pushed through the snow crust, adding color to the insistently monochrome landscape.

Hugo and Pavel followed Agafia around, fearing fragility in her psyche. She'd told them about the trench, how she'd slept soundly all night, how she woke in it without any explanation, as if she'd dug it bewitched. The tips of her fingers retained a shiny burgundy sheen and a deep blush of frostnip stained her cheek. Bird stuck closer to her even than before, whether from a renewed sense of loyalty or from concern, and Agafia watched him anxiously, awake to a wildness she hadn't known he possessed.

"He's just a work dog!" Pavel told her. "You could've frozen to death out there!"

Bird lay by her and she placed a hand on him.

"I couldn't abandon him," she said.

They left it at that, all of them thankful to have avoided another disaster.

When nerves calmed, camaraderie rekindled in the household, the three of them cleaning together to welcome the new season and drinking cups of tea on the wooden bench by the entrance. On a sheet of paper from a notebook Pavel carried, Hugo renewed plans for the banya, promising to start construction as soon as wood became more accessible. They sketched the summer garden and patched the homesteads. Pavel told Agafia about his home in the village, how he could hear his neighbors quarreling next door and how pigs escaped their enclosures and tracked mud on hung laundry and rugs. She laughed at his stories, eyes pinched shut when she let out her guttural hoots, sealing each surge of glee with a huff before she resumed listening.

Agafia visited him in his hut too. She fretted at its austerity, which amused Pavel, considering her own. She brought gifts—a wooden mug, an elk hide Dima had prepared to serve as a blanket, a shawl for a pillow. Once she brought a small stack of colorful hard candy wrappers she'd collected from the geologists' camp and pasted them on the wood walls with sap, like shreds of wallpaper.

"Pretty," she said once they were all up, admiring her handiwork.

Aside from that, she rarely entered, just stood on the threshold giggling. He thought of Masha standing at the doorway of one of his camp cabins on their first trip together, the same way she leaned and blocked the light, which pooled around her fuzzy hat like a halo. Her birthday was the night Agafia disappeared and he had prayed for Masha to protect her.

■ ■ ■

There were the seasons, which revealed themselves in myriad ways. With each winter, each summer, each spring, they counted also the years. But to keep track of the days—the religious holidays, the daily readings and prayers, the complicated rituals they protected, all that had driven them there—Dima had been in charge. He had started each morning with a complex calculus, tabulating the cycles of the moon and the previous days' liturgies to triangulate the date. Without knowing their place in the religious calendar, they'd be no better than the heathens, unable to uphold the rituals that kept them true. The family entrusted Dima as timekeeper the same way they delegated Agafia as a priestess of the garden. Together the two of them maintained the Kols' spiritual and material survival.

When Dima passed, Agafia had taken on his load. She knew by then how to count time, had practiced for years by her brother's side. After burying him, she determined the date and engraved it on the cross marking his headstone, in homage.

With inks he mixed out of wood ash, Dima had written down special dates. They served as anchors in the wide-open sea of the expanding universe. He stored daily dates wholly in his memory. Agafia endeavored to do the same. But when she skipped her counting the morning of her outing with Bird, it threw her off for days to come, so that one afternoon Pavel walked up to the Kols' hut and found Agafia and Hugo in a panic.

"We have lost track of time!" Hugo told Pavel.

Agafia had opened the books in the house, running her fingers along the pencil markings that crowded the front and back pages.

"She must go back to Dima's last annotations!"

Pavel carried a small calendar, and before bed each evening, out of habit, he crossed out the day. There was never anything to schedule, so the two thin lines he drew over each day blocked out weeks of nothingness. He would gaze at the long rows of Xs, eyes crossing and vision clouding, the passage of his life an optical blur. Pavel had sought out the loss of time, its annihilation. It had rushed forward day by day without Masha, and he had wanted to pause, to compress a world without her, by getting lost. Offhand, he also didn't know what day it was—didn't care to know—and barely what month. But he could know.

"Do you want me to check my calendar?" he asked.

Agafia shook her head, but her face brightened.

"I will use Pavel's arrival!" she said.

She found Pavel's entrance into their lives, which she had marked in her book. It was the Week of Holy Forefathers, when they had read the story of Abraham and his faithfulness in the Book of Genesis. It had been a new moon.

"We have had five new moons," she counted, pressing down one by one the fingers on her left hand until she made a fist. She clenched her hand, holding tight each of the five months of Pavel's presence in their lives. *Has it been that long?* he thought. Then she returned to the book, consulting the list of Christian holy days which ran for pages, to refine her timeline.

"John the Theologian, Prophet Isaiah, Apostle Simon the

Zealot, Hieromartyr Mocius, the Georgian Martyrs of Persia . . . Glyceria!" Agafia looked up at her father.

"Virgin-martyr Glyceria," she said triumphantly.

"Are you sure?" Hugo asked. She flipped through her antique Bible until she landed on the correct reading for the day.

"I'm positive," she said. She grinned, satisfied. "May thirteenth," she said.

That evening Pavel took out his calendar, flipped through the book of Xs until he came to the first unmarked page. He crossed out the completed day: May 13. Half a year without Masha. Their child would have been crawling soon, would have been babbling in an elfin tongue, would have smiled at him by now. He curled up on the oven and went to sleep.

The Kols, for days after, reminisced about how Agafia almost lost track of time. It entered into their personal canon. They talked about their dreams, about the good years when they had procured meat, the summer the geologists arrived, and the day Agafia almost lost track of time. They built their own mythology as they had their huts, log by log, story by story, constructing a carapace in which to feel real, present. They knew how the story ended—the Last Judgment, chaos, darkness—but until then there was time here on earth, some days resplendent.

■ ■ ■

Spring wrestled out the last liminal winter chill. Light and birds returned. At dawn the three of them drank minty herb tea and ate cold kasha. Birds rehearsed for their sunrise crescendo, tuning their beaks and clearing their voices like an orchestra before a performance. They heard the high-pitched *chirp chirp* of the rubythroat, warm one-syllable bursts from the jays, the back-and-forth rusty trombone slide that signaled far-off cranes, the thrush's whistle and trill call like a checkmark. Sometimes wolves joined in the choir. Once they heard the screams of an elk laboring somewhere in the woods. In his village, Pavel had listened to the radio as he prepared for his day; this was just like that, the forest radio, clicking on to announce the day.

By early June, pastel green sprouts pushed out of the ground in neat rows. During long winter idleness, Agafia had recalled for him their barren years, when the entire crop had failed. Now she made her way along the rows, kneeling with tall woven socks over her knees, whispering to the plants and patting the soil around their fine roots with maternal tenderness.

Pavel followed suit, giving himself to the soil, blowing spider-webs off the shoots' leaves as if they were errant eyelashes and pluck-ing weeds from their perimeter with his fingers. Tools brought in by the geologists lay by the plots but went unused once the potato and buckwheat seedlings sprouted, as if to care for them with anything but the most delicate of touches would make them wither and die.

In the afternoon, they rested by the river. The rush of water pulled with it the air and the mosquitos, so they could sit without swatting at the thick clouds of insects that followed them every-where. Agafia collected wild strawberries and guelder rose in birch boxes, the former to gorge on, the latter to cook down into med-icine. Pavel thought of the little red berries Masha used to stitch onto his shirts and how he'd compared her rosy cheeks to bunches of guelder rose, as in fairy tales. It was the imagery of all Russia here, as if he were witnessing the origin of these familiarities. Red dresses and embroidered kaftans came from afternoons picking berries on the river—when one circle of workers set to canning them for the winter, another sketched them into the folklore. It was just like that in his village, which he suddenly missed. The spring was awakening him from his long sleep.

Pavel had grown to care for Agafia. Hugo never accompanied them to the riverbank and so they talked freely, like children daydreaming. She'd hike up her skirt just high enough to let the dirt-caked knees of her socks dry out from her morning's crouching. Pavel averted his eyes from the strip of pale skin she exposed to the sun. It was the whitest flesh he'd ever seen, as translucent and sallow as the rootlets they pulled from the ground while weeding.

On a sunny afternoon, after hours in the garden and by the river, he shuffled happily toward his hut. It was like a summer evening in his youth, when he strolled the village tipsy with friends, greeting passersby with their hats. He dragged his feet through the grass, blades sticking between his toes. His innards twisted inside him, the slightest pull on his sex, which he hadn't felt in months. Agafia walked behind him in her own world, humming a hymn under her even breath. Bird stayed close to her, as if to protect her during this state of reverie. Dima's hut flushed picturesque in the oncoming dusk, its faded wood glowing against the forest's velvety darkness, wildflowers framing its perimeter. Pavel invited Agafia inside. Bird lay down and crossed his paws on the threshold. Pavel made a fire, poured tea. He'd swept his dirt floor and had taken to keeping a blanket spread out on it, like a rug. Agafia sat on the blanket, quiet, lost in thought. Pavel sat next to her.

He leaned toward Agafia and ran a finger along her face. She crab-crawled from him off the blanket, onto the earth floor. Her eyes grew wide, like when she'd recounted her dream of the house-sized pinecone, but she stayed quiet.

"This is not worldly," Pavel said into her ear. "This is human."

Wetness between her legs. Bird growled softly from his place by the door. Agafia stuck a hand into her gown to check whether she had relieved herself. Shivers shook her body and sweat damp-ened her hair so it stuck to her scalp and neck. When she tried to speak, her voice failed her, mouth dry. An animal fear, all body, rose within her, vibrating her organs and warming her skin.

Corporeal senses firing until her mind sharpened too, aware of some large danger in the vicinity—more poisonous gas than phys-ical force.

Pavel crawled toward her and sat close. When she didn't move, he gently pushed her skirts up, uncovering first the whiteness of her knees, then the creped surface of her thighs.

Hugo had once told her that if Dima ever tried to reach under her skirts, she should stop him and tell Hugo right away. But this wasn't Dima. She looked to Bird, and the dog stood up and faced her, whimpering.

A peaty bog smell came at Pavel as he rolled her skirts higher. She wore no underwear. The smell was earthy like a deer's, not pu-trid, as if her body, lacking human comforts, had found some cervid equilibrium. He pulled her from the corner and stretched her out on the ground. Bird barked once, but Pavel clicked his tongue at him and the dog settled. Agafia did not resist, but under her breath, she recited prayers.

"This is human," he insisted in her ear.

He took off his bottoms, releasing his own winter smell, reeking of pickled dill and old sweat, and climbed on top of her. Veins on his arms rose to the surface, like rivers swollen by a flash flood. At the sight of them he paused for a moment, feeling crazed, were-wolfish, then resumed. He lost his way in the many layers she wore. It wasn't that he wanted to hurt her; he just attended more to the buds of wakefulness stirring in him from the sun, she the only one there to witness his rebirth.

Agafia lay still, head turned toward the wall of the hut her brother had built. A spider crawled along the bottom log, dipping a leg into the blackness of a crack in the wood, feeling for danger before it stepped deeper. Her body morphed around her—she was big and she was small like the spider, she was an ether expanding and shrinking at the same time. A sharp pain jolted her out of her daze and spread from her inside outward, glazing her. She willed herself back into a trance. Pavel grunted on top of her, his belly pressed to hers, his sex a foreign object inside her, his eyes boring into her face.

"Look at me," he said.

But she was the particle and the cloud, everywhere and no-where, and she controlled herself as long as she concentrated on the spider that inched closer to her face. She thought if this was truly bad, as she thought it must be, Bird would have protected her. The dog looked attentively at her but did not move.

Pavel arched his back and threw his head toward the door, and then he rolled off of her onto the blanket. He laid his head right on the spider, which disappeared under his hair. Agafia remained still, muscles tensed to not break her invisibility, give herself away. Some-where between her legs something stirred, a primordial shapeless sin climbing out of her. She put her fingers to where the thing slith-ered along her leg and found a bloody mucus, the thing's tracks.

She waited until Pavel drifted off to sleep. She wiped herself with his sleeping bag, fixed her clothes, and retied the shawl on her head. She stepped back out into the sunshine feeling suddenly sore and tired, a waterlogged tree trunk, sinking. When she called for Bird, he rose and followed her, tail wagging, panting with happiness.

■   ■   ■

Agafia didn't tell Hugo about her encounter. She intuited the sin of it. She climbed the rocks that weighed down her mother in the meadow and slept there for several nights, under an elk hide. Raw-ness weighed her body down and her insides stretched until her skin glowed thin and rupturable. That afternoon stayed with her as an undefined mystery; though something physical had happened, only fleeting impressions flashed behind her eyes, snippets of in-tangible fear and fervor. As if she could only pull up the memory through slatted windows, looking in and seeing the bits of the events in thin shards of light. The incompleteness of her recall made the whole thing more confusing, as if it had happened to someone else entirely while she, half-blind, watched.

She avoided Pavel, avoided going down to Dima's hut. The act of having to circumvent him enclosed the vast taiga around her, trapping her. She prayed for hours, singing her sincerest supplica-tion to a Lord that, too, felt distant and foreign. *This is all my fault,* she said to herself, before returning to prayer. Hugo commented on her sullenness and attempted to cheer her, but she remained quiet and aloof. Her one comfort, the dog Bird, stayed away. Agafia blamed herself for that too, and ached for Bird's company.

She started to think again of the Old Believer monastery Pavel had mentioned when he first arrived. Perhaps it was Belovod'e, that lost utopia. It stood not too far downriver, he'd said. She began to dream of a new home at the monastery and to conjure the feelings of freedom and fellowship that she'd find there. Her home in the taiga had grown stale before, but this time, she thought, it wouldn't pass. Not even with the coming summer. Would the women have her, such a sinner, in their midst? she wondered. She feared they would sniff out her wickedness. She obsessed over the monastery, though she didn't dare to ask Pavel more about it. In this theoretical place, she constructed a new life for herself.

One afternoon Hugo found her on the riverbank examining their worthless boat, built years ago from another fallen space object.

"Where would you like to take that thing?"

Agafia stayed quiet for a long time but decided to speak honestly.

"Do you think we could visit the monastery downriver? Visit with our people for a while?"

Each winter aged Hugo a full decade, it seemed, and the skin on his face sagged. His fingers gnarled around a walking stick, a constant companion of late. Agafia worried she'd hurt him with her inquiry, vocalized for the first time his failure to reach Belovod'e. He worried, she knew, that he hadn't made a life on earth worth living while he waited to get to heaven. Hugo cleared his throat and returned to momentary silence before answering.

"Yes," he said. "It is a good idea."

He leaned into the boat and flipped it over. A spit of gravel in the river shallows formed a still pool. Hugo dragged the metal tub into the water and stood back to evaluate how it floated. The vessel teetered from side to side before sinking deeply on its right flank. Just the lip remained above the surface while its other edge soared high into the air. Hugo pushed on the tall edge, trying to straighten the boat in the water, but when he removed his arm the vessel swung back into lopsided repose.

He heaved it out of the water and brought down tools and sheets of the metal he'd rescued from the space trash. The sun hunkered over him, reflecting piercing beams of light off the silvered metal. Sweat rolled down his forehead as he hammered at the boat's haunches. He peeled off a metal layer on the sinking side and with a dull wooden hammer punched out the canoe's flanks. Its belly bulged broader than its nose so that it looked like a pregnant heifer head-on. Satisfied, he scraped it toward the water. The boat nodded before settling deep in the pool, still leaning, though less. Hugo pushed on the bottom to see if the thing would float with weight in it, and water rushed in as the vessel dipped.

There are ways to show your love to a beloved that require much less and simultaneously much more than words. With every leaf of metal Hugo added and subtracted from the stubbornly drowning vessel, with every nail he counted out from a small pouch tied around his waist and every smear of sap he pressed into the leaking pits that riddled the carapace of his daughter's hopes, he showed her. This life in the taiga, that too was a way of showing his earthly love for his family, to protect them from the many sins that could undo them before they reached paradise. Perhaps he had loved them too much. Agafia watched him work, handing him tools and metal scraps like a surgeon's assistant and bringing him water when he stopped to rest.

"Do you think it'll work?" she asked.

Hugo hammered without answering, dragging the boat back into the water and watching the new ways it failed. He labored on the premise that some perfect amalgamation of patches would make the thing sail and he only had to discover the pattern to make it all work.

Peter stood next to Agafia and groaned. He'd apprenticed in a shipyard in the Netherlands, disguising himself as a regular worker in order to learn every aspect of shipbuilding. The czar's insistence on performing even the most menial tasks involved in ship construction stressed his hosts, but it taught him how ships work, the physics that made them float, and the craft that made them beautiful. This was no ship—but he stood by itching his hands at Hugo's unskilled guessing game.

"He'll never get it symmetrical swinging that hammer around randomly," he told Agafia.

"Hush," she murmured.

"The bow needs more lift in this fast-moving water," he said.

He held out his hands for her to examine. Thick calluses covered the skin. "I built my boats with my own hands," he told her. "I could teach you. Look at all the wood around here!"

"You just don't want me to find my sisters," she hissed to him. Then, to her father, "Do you think we can make the nose higher?"

"You'll drown," Peter sneered.

Hugo entered the water with the canoe. It bobbed under his grip, but sat relatively high on the water. He lifted a leg, then his whole body into the belly of the boat, his arms shaking as he tried to stabilize the unsteady vessel.

"Agafia!" he called to her on the riverbank. She squinted at him as he lifted an arm to wave. The movement upset his fragile balance and sent the metal bowl swinging wildly until it dumped him in the water.

"Oh!" Agafia gasped. She crossed herself and ran to him.

"Tomorrow," he said when she reached him. "Tomorrow, we will try again."

■　■　■

Pavel craved to go to Agafia but stayed out of her way. Hadn't she been curious? Hadn't she sought human contact, something both normal and divine? But no, he knew he'd hurt her. Scared her. He'd never touched Masha with such viciousness. He got out of bed and did push-ups on the floor in the dark, until he couldn't lift himself. He was a pulsing mass, lost in his own body. He'd betrayed both Masha and Agafia. At dawn, he swept out the hut and dusted. He'd wanted to cleanse and instead he dirtied everything around him, inside him. The sun rose early, dragging in another day.

Agafia had told him about the geologists when he first came; by his calculations, they were due to return soon. They would take up their work, inspecting the ground with their tools and keen eyes. If he stayed long enough, he'd see this still pocket of land slough off pristine blankness and give up its deep, hidden ore. He pictured the mountain as human, then opened it. The brutality of the images in his imagination startled him. He thought of the splayed arrangement of Masha's body after everything was over, how ravaged she had looked. The midwife had cut her trying to get the baby out. He'd gagged at the sight of it, the fleshy vulnerable fact of her body. Visions of mountain innards, ore twisted like intestine.

He sat outside Dima's hut taking in the warm spring day. Whiteness still covered the mountains, though snowmelt swelled the river. Blades of grass sliced through the ground, reaching for sunlight. Birdsong burst forth from every trembling tree branch and windblown ghost trunk. Nothing was what it was, it was all landscape. Beautiful, frightful, overwhelming panoramas overfilled with peaks and flora, which he'd been taught to think of as emptiness. His village was surrounded by similar vistas but they'd been blocked by the teeming humanity of the settlement, small though it was. He'd have to return to it soon.

He never had gone trapping, had spent the whole winter holed up with the Kols and napping on the oven. Without the furs' income, he'd have to find work for the year. There was the town's collective farm, where village residents picked perfunctorily at long tracts of frozen land.

Plaques congratulating them for settling the agricultural frontier hung in every kitchen. Like the Kols, they grew potatoes. Some wheat. The crops came up like hopeful stray hairs on a balding head, thin, kinked, and ultimately not enough. He'd hated that farm, had turned to trapping to avoid it, so that Masha wouldn't have to tie that faded floral kerchief around her hair and set off in the morning with that unliftable fatigue on her shoulders. There was always next year for trapping. The dogs would be a year older and so would he. Perhaps they would all be a little wiser. Or not—he hadn't worked on the dogs' training in months. No surprise Bird had run off on Agafia.

Pavel took his gun and drew a bead on Maniac. Both dogs slept in the sun at the door, so rare lately since Bird had become Agafia's mostly. He'd never hurt his animals before, not in a cruel way, but felt a sudden urge to shoot them both. One time he'd killed a mauled dog that had limped out of the forest in terrible shape, because Pavel did not think it would survive, and he'd wept over its limp body. He'd been a kind master; it was one of the things Masha had loved about him. He'd shared meat with the dogs and bathed them in the river and talked to them softly and deliberately, as if to children. He and Masha had maintained a humanity in the house that differed from the weary rage that simmered outside of it, and that had extended to the dogs too.

He unloaded the gun and cleaned it.

In the afternoon he walked to the garden and, finding it empty, lowered himself to his knees and began to weed. The dogs had followed him and bedded down nearby as he worked. In the village everyone maintained their own garden and they grew lush and green. People cajoled cucumbers and tomatoes out of the ice-latticed soil while potatoes failed to thrive on the state farm. If only he had tomato seeds to leave Agafia, who'd never tasted such a fruit. As penance.

He cleared a full row, lightening Agafia's load for the next day. He hoped that she would notice.

A dull ache throbbed in his back. Pavel rose, stretched, and called the dogs to head home. Maniac and Bird trotted ahead of him, following their noses, weaving on and off the path, through tall grass, to the hem of wood, back.

Maniac spotted him first. His antlers glowed like illuminated branches amid the forest's darker wood. He was young, not paying attention, scratching his nose on a patch of tree lichen. For some reason he was alone, maybe lost. Maniac signaled to Bird, and the two of them lowered themselves into the grass slowly as they stared. Pavel noticed him last, then saw the dogs, the playful abandon with which they'd pinned him as a target. Pure hunt bred out of them all those thousands of years ago, but somehow the need to chase remained, a lupine vestige in their domesticated bones. Maniac rose carefully, as if to creep, then burst from the grass in a long leap. The elk startled and took off, knees still knobby, but strong enough to run. Bird followed. There was an instant, a fraction of a second, when both dogs froze and turned back to Pavel, to hear his command, which would assure them what they already knew, that they would have to stop, come back. They gazed at each other, the moment weirdly stretching in the dusk light. Finally Pavel raised an arm, just barely switched his wrist, as if to say, *Go*.

The elk was long gone out of sight and now the dogs took off after him at full speed, barking and yapping to warn the elk that they were coming, to let each other know just how fast to run. Pavel watched them disappear into the woods, stood and waited to see if they would return, listened to their cries until he heard them only in his head. *Good*, he thought, *now we're all free, Maniac, Bird, Agafia, and me.*

He returned to the hut, lit a fire, and sat at the open door ushering in the night. When the light had gone fully out he began to pack. There wasn't much, but he took his time, folding and stacking and gathering his things into little piles before stuffing them into the bag with which he'd arrived. He left only his calendar, for Agafia. In the morning he set off, not toward his village, but onward, to some new place he hoped would be less forgiving.

CHAPTER 5
Глава 5

The first night Bird didn't show up for bedtime, Agafia ignored the pinch of betrayal in her chest. It simmered all the next day, and through the night, and by the following morning it boiled over into rage. She stomped to the cabin to reclaim the dog, face hardened to not show her upset, only to find the hut empty and cleaned out.

"Bird!" she called out anyway. "Bird! Bird!"

She yelled his name frantically, to bring him back from the place Pavel had taken him, to reconstitute him in her arms. Bird had been hers and Pavel had stolen him. Agafia hadn't understood the thing Pavel did to her, though a real fear had grown out of that, but she'd understood her love for Bird, and the cruelty of Pavel fleeing with him set off a loud ringing in her ears. She wondered if Bird had gone willingly.

"A devil he was," Agafia told Hugo, "came here in disguise."

"It was his work dog," Hugo reasoned. "Though it's strange that he didn't say good-bye."

They stored Pavel away with all the other things they rarely talked about, or acknowledged to each other only sparingly.

The geologists returned just as the fireweed blooms began to stain the meadows purple. Agafia and Hugo came to greet them as they approached along the previous year's path from their camp to the huts, a fog of mosquitos announcing their arrival. The women touched each other's faces, stroked each other's hair.

"What a winter we've had!" Agafia told them.

She led Snow Crane and Galina toward the riverbank, and the four of them settled on a log. The warm sun softened them into each other's presence. Snow Crane's eyes drifted to the unhemmed fringe of forest in the near distance. How good to be back. He thought about Buck and how the primordial pull of Alaska's wilderness manifested as a force inside his bones, strengthening them to withstand the tundra. In his mind, Snow Crane tore off his boots, shirt, and backpack and, transformed into a centaur, galloped into the wood. He rubbed against the trees and rolled in the woodland litter to take on a sharp musk. His body relaxed, shoulders sloping visibly and releasing his neck. When he refocused his eyes, Hugo nodded at him, as if he understood.

"Tell us about it," Snow Crane said.

Agafia had been saving up the winter's happenings to relay to the geologists. The news came fast, without context, a stream of disparate musings so incoherently assembled that Galina and Snow Crane lost their grip on her world. It was always hard to follow her stories. They straddled unfamiliar universes; to decipher them was to extricate solid threads from tangled dark matter. Slowly, with questions, they spun understanding: Pavel, the hunter; his dog Bird, whose absence made Agafia weep; the strange gifts falling from the sky; how she'd tamed time. It had been an eventful winter. Hugo was disappointed at the hunter's sudden disappearance, but Agafia returned again and again to the dog, whose loss loomed as large as her siblings'.

"Sometimes I hear him barking in the wood, my mind playing tricks on me," Agafia said. She folded her arms in her lap, subdued by loss, then motioned to Galina. "I want to show you something."

She pointed toward the boat, stationed behind a mane of tall grass. It was misshapen and pocked, as if hail-pummeled.

"We've been working on it," she said. "With your tools. It's not perfect, but I want to take it downriver."

"To where?" Snow Crane asked.

"There's a monastery."

Snow Crane touched the vessel. Warmed river water thick with dead bugs sparkled on the bottom.

"Does it leak?"

Agafia shrugged.

"I worry," Hugo said, barely audible.

"We just have to carve good, sturdy paddles."

"I don't know," Hugo said. "I don't know."

"What monastery?" Galina asked. She didn't remember seeing it on her maps.

"Old Believers, like us."

Agafia wrapped her arms around herself, fingers grabbing at her sides, hugging. Maybe the sisters would embrace her like this, gather her skin into their strong arms and hold her up without judgment to the sun. They'd never found Belovod'e with its priests, but this would be even better, perhaps.

Agafia walked over to the boat and started to skim water out with a birch box. She dipped and swung it out too quickly, spilling water. She slowed herself, cradled the bottom of the box with her palm, measured. But with each dip the papery birch stretched and unraveled at the seam, until the box split.

Galina watched Agafia struggle with the water. She was agitated, coming to terms with the boat's unviability. She stopped scooping, muttered something, and let the birch fall in the river, where the current swallowed it. Agafia climbed into the boat and lay down, stretched along its still-wet metal bottom. She lay there, staring at the clouds above. The heavy cotton bolls stood still in the unmoving air. When the sun peeked out between clumps of cloud, the dimpled sides of the canoe refracted a smattering of light onto Agafia, so that she shone like a speckled fish.

"I missed you," Galina said.

Agafia sat up lazily, dazed and wet all over. "Do you think the boat will make it?"

Galina toed it with her foot until it began to rock. "You know, we have a small, inflatable catamaran. It'd probably be more stable."

"Can we take it?" Agafia asked. "To the monastery?" She was out of the boat and bouncing on her feet. "I want to see it."

Agafia insisted that the geologists return to camp the same day and accompanied them on the familiar path that she had walked the previous season. Fluorescent white moonlight lit the final dusky kilometers, brighter than streetlights on a Moscow boulevard. Agafia talked the entire way, for hours.

At the camp, she demanded to see the boat. It sat under a canvas tarp by the mess tent. Galina called over some of the workers to uncover it. Underneath lay the catamaran, its deflated rubber hulls two wrinkled raisins.

"You blow those up," Galina told her. "It's good for balance on the rapids."

Agafia convinced them to inflate the hulls so she could see it. Someone brought a foot pump and hooked it up to the first rubber casing in the halo of a kerosene lamp. They took turns, forcing the pump up and down, first fast, then slowing like a clockwork toy with an unwound mainspring. Agafia lasted the longest, a steady derrick pushing air into the rising vessel, grinning from under her scarf, pleased. Eventually the catamaran widened; its hulls unwrinkled and took on the shape of torpedoes, lashed together by a straight metal bridge. Galina cut open cans of braised meat and warmed them on a fire. The three of them sat on the catamaran, passing around the canned meat wrapped in a towel, sharing a fork. Agafia spent the night on the boat, on land.

In the morning the whole camp, the same faces Agafia remembered from the previous summer, gathered to carry the boat to the water. The rapids ran gently around the bend the camp occupied. A few of the geologists boarded for a test run, paddling into the river, nosing their way around jutting, sloped boulders. The cold water contracted the air in the hulls so they loosened. But the geologists steered the vessel through clear water to a sandy shoal and triumphantly raised the wooden paddles in the air. Agafia jumped up and down on shore. They filled the rubber hulls with more air until they bulged, then did another test run. Then another. And another. Agafia came with them on the fifth run. She sat on the little metal bridge like a monk, her skirts tucked close around her to leave room for the others, steady and radiant as they bumped along the gentle whitecaps. On the sixth run she took a paddle, and her strength on the right side of the vessel overwhelmed her companions so the boat veered left. They flew onto the bank with a thump, landing almost completely on dry land to cheers.

"Can we go?" she pleaded. "To the monastery?"

They decided to set off in a couple of weeks. Galina had packed extra food for the season for Agafia, and now she filled sacks for the trip: buckwheat, rice, canned meats and sausages, bags of tea, dried apricots and almonds from Uzbekistan, a can of condensed milk. She couldn't join the expedition because she had to supervise the camp and the core drillers, but she assigned Snow Crane, who was splitting his time as scientist and pilot, and another geologist, Ivan, to Agafia, counting on several weeks of their absence to deliver her to the monastery. Nobody knew where it was located, how long it might really take. Galina had doubts it even existed, but her maps had failed her before.

The night before the departure, Galina and Snow Crane closed the flaps of their tent and lay down to face each other.

"I'd like to sail you on that catamaran to Shangri-la," Snow Crane spoke into her ear.

"What does it look like there?"

"The snow is made of sugar, the sun is alpine but does not burn, the trails circle the summits in endless loops. You can stroll through the clouds without losing your breath."

"Are there rivers?"

"They are turquoise with glacier melt but warm like the Mediterranean, and the fish that live in their currents jump into your net and forgive you."

Agafia had gone back to her hut to make her own preparations.

She packed a Bible and some shawls, boiled a birch box full of young potatoes from the garden and tucked them into an old handkerchief. In the purple light of the evening, she made her way through the fields, caressing the plants and talking to them.

"Grow big and handsome," she babbled. "Grow for me while I am gone, I will return to you."

Agafia tried to pack Hugo's things, but he stopped her.

"I'm too old," he said. "Go without me."

She kissed him on the forehead and he kissed her on each cheek.

"You can stay there if you like," Hugo said. "Do not worry about me."

If Bird were still there, or her brother, she'd never contemplate it; but with everyone gone she had, secretly, considered not returning. She *tsk-tsked* with her mouth.

"I'll return soon," she said.

She hoisted her bundle on her back and set off. The farther she got, the faster she walked. Peter accompanied her, bounding alongside. His long stride outpaced her and he slowed to wait for her to catch up, just like Bird had done.

"Finally, a journey!" he said.

■　■　■

Everything was ready, the boat perched at the water's edge, packed with sacks of provisions, rolls of canvas to pitch the tents, a patch kit, the pump. Galina saw them off, waving from the shore with the other geologists. They set off just as the sun broached the eastern mountains, a ray of orange light tracing the peaks that hugged the river valley. For the first time in her life Galina prayed, for their safe passage and return, to her.

Agafia had spent her life on the bank of that same river, drawing from it her drinking water and her bath. She'd become accustomed to its edges, dipping her toes, entering only in her and Dima's swimming hole. Always the river had roared too loudly for her to approach it directly, as if walking into a lion's open maw. But here she was, floating in the middle of the stream, navigating it. She sat in the middle, with Snow Crane and Ivan at the paddles, but she the one steering the vessel, with her mind. *Faster, go around the boulder*, she would think, and the catamaran quickened and swerved. Then she'd straighten it out, onward, downriver. When they needed to slow, she'd lean back as if tugging on the reins of a horse or a donkey, and the boat's nose would rise and the water itself slowed, and they'd float gently, looking around at the wildflowers on shore and the banks brightening under the rising sun.

Around noon they found a landing spot and lunched. Agafia pulled out the boiled potatoes and dabbed them with salt. She dipped a wooden cup into the stream and washed down the dry potato with the river water. She chewed with her mouth open and talked about how Dima used to swim in the river in the summers, entering it in his white long sleeping gown as if for baptism, and how she'd worried he would tangle in his dress trying to swim to safety.

"I don't know how he kept the thing so white," she said.

Even his underwear reflected his unearthliness. Dima was gone, yet still she worried, as if he were in heaven struggling with the wet cloth even now. Ivan turned out to be the quiet, serious type. He had an immovable furrowed brow, but he was also attentive, nodding his concern along with Agafia's, ready to rescue Dima from drowning in his heavenly seas.

They got off the river before nightfall and made camp in tall grass. The men set up Agafia in her own tent, a ways from them, and she sat behind it praying as they prepared dinner.

They insisted they didn't need her help. She took this as an insult at first, but then decided she didn't want to help anyway. They hadn't gone too far downriver—she'd walked this far, at least, gathering berries and herbs—but already it had the markings of a true voyage. In the tent, her body shaking slightly, she thought up ways this could all go wrong, and then how she would right them.

The stretch of river they traveled the next day tumbled roughly so that the boat lurched up and down over the rapids like a bucking bronco and made them all sick. When they regained the land, they flattened themselves on the hard, steady ground on their backs. The day's travel had so shaken them that the drifting clouds and even the movement of the earth itself, spinning and wobbling around its axis, nauseated them. They lay with eyes closed for an hour to regain their composure, and when they finally came to they were starving. Snow Crane announced that for this day's work they deserved better than kasha, and he set off into the nearby woods.

He walked barefoot, regretting it when mosquitos chewed on his feet. He didn't have anything to hunt with or the time to make a trap, but he heard the birds singing all around him and looked up for nests. They were everywhere. He climbed the first promising tree he saw, toward a low crotch in the branches where a messy nest without guardians perched. In it, three perfect speckled eggs. He candled the eggs, shining his flashlight against the shell to check if there was a chick inside, and let out a yelp when they shone clear. He made a hammock of his shirt and walked as fast as he could back to camp. Ivan was already cooking kasha and meat. He cracked the eggs into the pan, and each of them received a runny yolk on their plate.

Agafia woke the next morning to something nudging her through the tent. It sniffed and pushed the canvas walls, and in her sleepiness she couldn't place its size. Bear, chipmunk, man. She couldn't tell. Ever since that afternoon with Pavel, that feeling had been visiting her, of the simultaneous bigness and smallness within her and all around her. She was that atomized cloud, big enough to block the sun. She lay still, gathering herself into shape, like a tornado.

When she finally crawled out of the tent, she found Peter poking at it with his foot, exploratory little shoves with the leather of his shoe, as if he didn't want to get his hands dirty. "Pft," she said to him. "Why are you bothering me?"

"Sleeping in," he said.

Agafia looked up at the sun, which had already climbed high into the sky. A haze obscured it, hanging gray and heavy in the air. It smelled like fire and burned her nose. She looked for the geologists. They'd left her some breakfast in a pan, but she couldn't see them anywhere.

"That's a first for you, sister," Peter said.

Agafia wasn't feeling well, sluggish and queasy, as if she'd never recovered from the previous day's rough water, but she ignored Peter. She rolled up the tent and gathered her shawls. She sat down on the pile of stuff to pray. By the time the geologists returned, she'd eaten and was getting antsy. They came jogging up, faces covered with perspiration.

"Agafia!" they yelled to her. "The rapids are big down there! Bigger than yesterday's!"

They'd gone as far as they could on land, until the terrain grew swampy and they had to turn around, to see what they could expect. They'd found a rabid river, foaming. Peter paced back and forth behind them as they described the trap ahead, how tree trunks lay stripped of their bark at the river's banks, discarded there by the meat-grinder torrents. They'd planned to radio for a helicopter once they reached civilization, so there was nowhere to go but downriver, but the passage was perilous.

Agafia listened, watched Peter. He smirked, daring her to abort the mission, to doubt whether God could protect her in these wild waters. To doubt Him.

"The Lord will protect us," Agafia told the geologists. "We'll be fine."

She stood up, picked up a load of things, and headed to the bank to pack the boat. The geologists murmured as she went, but they didn't stop her. They stood for a while, watching, until Ivan dragged over the last of their camp supplies and tied it all down with elaborate knotwork. In the end, it turned out they too had a high tolerance for magic.

The rapids started about a mile downstream, rising first like hillocks, then growing into whitecapped mountains. They tore at the water's surface, splitting it into big, dramatic shreds. The cat-amaran dipped into and out of the rapids like a fish caught on a line, darting, diving, unspooling the reel. Agafia and the geologists were soaked, and even the high sun could not dry them because the boat would dip and wash them anew with cold. Agafia sat in the middle, praying through the onslaught and jerking side to side to help steer. Snow Crane and Ivan guided with their paddles, arms taut under sopping shirts, yelling instructions to each other over the river's roar.

A rapid washed them into a rock that split the river in two and the current pinned them.

Pushing off with their paddles only strained the metal of the shafts, so that they started to bend. They were stuck in the middle of the river and could not get out in the strong stream. The rubber, pressed against the rock, distended, creating a fold in the skin. Snow Crane eyed the bulge surreptitiously, anxious it would burst and send the vessel dancing through the rapids like a punctured balloon. They piled on one side and tried to shift the boat with their weight, then the other side, bouncing from left to right to free it from the current's clutches. When the vessel refused to move, all three sat still and rested. Rushing all around them, the water grew louder, faster, more fervent—a crescendo. A tree cracked into the water somewhere nearby. Peter walked from the bank to the vessel and pushed it back out into the stream. The little catamaran took off, bobbing.

"It's like God Himself pushed us out!" Ivan declared, grinning.

Agafia shook her head. "Not God," she said.

The air tarnished around them, turning darker gray and more opaque, as if someone were drawing the curtains on the sun.

"It smells like fire," Snow Crane said.

They grew quiet, anticipating the blaze.

"Early this year, isn't it?" Ivan said, though no one replied.

Agafia recalled her father's stories about the church burnings, the smell of flesh. She remembered battling their own small blazes to protect the homestead. The way they'd marched along smoldering lines in the meadows, one foot in front of the other stepping on the hot creeping flames, stopping the fire's advance with their own bodies.

"Bad omen," she said.

Specks of soot hung suspended midair, too light to fall through the viscous air. The catamaran floated into the static of a TV screen. Agafia drew a shawl over her nose and tied it at the back of her head. The river had grown calm, to allow them to take this in.

Red lines of heat climbed up distant hills, but around them everything had already burned. As they floated past the active fire, a breeze picked up and lifted the ashes from the ground. Burnt matter swirled in dense animated coils, then dissipated over the water into billowy, dark ether.

Giant black flakes waltzed through the air, settling to float on the water's surface. The river turned into an asphalt road cracked with white rapids. It took nearly an hour to pass the fire. The wind blew the last of the ashes behind them, upriver, and they floated on.

■ ■ ■

The three of them daydreamed on calm waters. Agafia thought about her garden, how her plants were faring without her. How the hollows in the windowsill, smoothed by her elbows when locked in prayer, fit her shape. There was the birdhouse Dima had built, and its summer chiffchaff tenants whose crystalline calls cheered up even the leaves. She knew how to make the fire go even with wet wood and where, each fall, to plug up the holes in the cabin walls. Winters were hard, and summers were hard, and falls and springs, but the worldly world didn't beckon to her.

Instead, sitting on the catamaran, she nurtured a longing for the homestead and for her beloved Dima and the dog Bird, tucking herself into it.

Snow Crane conjured Galina, that intense look on her face when she was thinking. Her brows flattened into overhangs above her eyes and her gaze turned inward, scanning some unseen blackboard for answers inside her head. When the messages appeared to her, her mouth parted slightly, a door unlatched, before she began to speak. He loved to hear her talk, her strange halting sentences, stories coalescing with every detail she pulled from faraway places in her mind, as if adding a section of hair to a braid.

Ivan replayed reels of his son in his mind, his tiny brows arched in bemusement, the way he uttered "Papa" when he rose in the mornings or when Ivan cradled him in his arms at night, his strong voice when he pointed to butterflies, worms, beetles, ladybugs and called out, "Name!" demanding to know the world. Ivan hated to be away so long, to lose the familiarity of the boy's small body and the joyful chaos of his companionship. He'd asked Galina to consider him for the trip because he wanted the chance to call home.

In the late morning, all quiet on the boat, they came around a twist in the river, the current swinging them to the right bank. The river spilled into a wide stretch. Across the way a small church rose on the left bank. Clouds rushed past a thrice-barred Old Believer cross on the roof. Several women stood in a garden that stretched in front of the church.

"We're here!" Agafia hollered.

She sat up straight, fingers gripping the catamaran's metal bridge. Snow Crane and Ivan counted out a rhythm to paddle across the river. One-two-three, one-two-three. Agafia adjusted her head scarf, tightening it so that its edge framed her face in a neat, stiff oval. The women in the garden noticed the boat and gathered on the bank to watch them come in. Before the catamaran even scraped the shore's pebbles, Agafia jumped out. Water lapped at her skirts to her knees, weighing her down as she fought her way to dry land. The women came to her, their own faces wreathed in white. Their first meeting was an impromptu baptism at the water's edge. Snow Crane and Ivan invisible to them as they struggled to pull in the vessel and tie it up.

The nuns' white scarves trailed down their backs and made a white wall as they surrounded Agafia. She was the planet and they her many moons, circling her, drawn to her by ecstatic gravity. They reached out, embraced each other, cooed. Agafia didn't explain anything, just stood there, and they surmised everything. As if in their very cells they carried the same acrid smell of fire that signified Peter, as if they walked on the same needled soles, eastward and northward, away from him. She was another sister, returned. She had wandered, but that mattered so little compared to the fact of her arrival. A quiet rustle grew among them and the circle grew smaller and smaller, until it was so tight that it couldn't contain their prayers and a jeremiad escaped from the scrum, like a bird.

Snow Crane loved it when people acted like animals. Marat had taught him it was poetry, when people abandoned themselves to pure instinct, to touch, to chemical attraction, to survival.

"You're an animal!" Marat once told him when he confessed to feeling trapped at the orphanage. "A caribou. They walk so many miles."

He'd run his hand over Snow Crane's closely cropped hair.

"See, your head is velvety just like their antlers."

Snow Crane stood by the boat and watched Agafia with the nuns. Elephants, he decided. They never forget.

The nuns invited everyone up to the house for lunch. Soon rounds of cool cucumber and wedges of salted tomato lined tea saucers spread down a long table. The sweetness in the tomatoes was as concentrated as a Siberian summer. Buckwheat simmered in a cast iron pot hung over a fire, the steam scenting the room with earthy notes. Pork dangled over the fire too, and dripped fat into the kasha. When it was time to eat, they sliced pieces of the haunch into a skillet, and the aroma made everyone's stomachs groan in unison from hunger. A nun named Anna led everyone in prayer before they finally dug into the food, which silenced them.

That evening Snow Crane and Ivan stayed outside in their own tents. Agafia went inside, assigned her own room. The nuns handed her freshly laundered clothes and escorted her to a candle-lined nook with a metal tub. Warm water filled the bath and a fresh bar of soap perched on a plate by its lip. Agafia peeled off layers of clothes, bunching each article into a growing pile on the floor. A nun carried off everything to clean. Stepping into the water, she let out a guttural sigh. It had been ages since warmth like this covered her body. It was freshly squeezed milk, the womb, her body entombed in candle wax, liquid sunshine.

In good years, her father had prepared baths for the children monthly. She was the youngest, and by the time she dipped her toe in the wooden tub, an oily film from her siblings covered the cooled water, so she washed with haste, not taking the time to scrub behind her ears or the divots of her body. In bed after her bath, she'd rub her skin, scouring off dirt the water hadn't dissolved. Now she soaped the washcloth and ran it vigorously all over her body. Her skin blushed pink as she sponged herself. Dirt, released from the wrinkles on her face, the folds of her neck, the pores of her legs, browned the water. She ran her fingers through her hair and lathered her scalp, then scratched at it until her fingernails came away clean. Sloughing off her protective shields made her body itch.

Clean clothes lay folded on a chair. She ran the towel over herself, lifting her breasts to pat the skin under them dry and wiping between her toes before wrapping her hair up. She pulled on a white undergown, the starch-stiffened cloth rough on her newly cleansed belly. Then came the dress, loose and luxurious, the bright fabric catching the candlelight. She spun. Anna came in, sat her on the chair, and combed her hair, from the tips to the roots, humming as she worked.

When she'd finished brushing, she tucked short tufts of hair behind Agafia's ears and braided the rest of it. She ran a silken ribbon through the long braid and tied it. Her braid was thin. Agafia placed the white shawl on her head and looped its ends into a knot.

A clear ringing broke through the walls, a deep mature sound like an ancient birdcall. A smaller trill followed, the rest of the fledgling flock raising its voice in a ladder. At first the noise was chaotic, but then it found its melody and filled the room with it.

"Bells?" Agafia asked.

"Let's go."

Agafia had never been inside a church. The family had prayed at home, folded into a corner of the hut. Her father told stories of the churches he'd once loved, how the liturgy and the incense smoke filled the cupolas and thickened the air so that it held the body upright, like God Himself. At times he even talked about building a little church for the family, so they could hang their icons in a permanent place and walk together from their home to the church for vespers. But he never did construct the thing, just like he never built a banya or a proper cemetery. Anyway, there wasn't a priest to guide them. Their home wasn't a real home, rather a temporary sanctuary that had become permanent.

Anna, singing, took Agafia's hand as they crossed the church's threshold and led her along. Darkness flooded the space. Agafia dragged her feet along the smooth stone floor in order not to trip. The other women trailed behind them, their voices rising to meet Anna's. Agafia's eyes swept along the walls, a checkerboard of gold-haloed icons, her own favorite Avvakum watching from the walls. Hugo had told Agafia that heaven would feel like coming home. Its brilliance would flood her, awe her, and sustain her. He said the church was supposed to feel like heaven until the time came to ascend, and described basilicas striving to attain the beauty of a kingdom of love. All those upturned eyes, gilded coronas, translucent skin surrounding the faithful, cupolas soaring, voices echoing like a choir of angels. She had lacked the imagination to picture the splendors he described. Instead, she'd made the taiga her place of worship, her heaven on earth, her shelter. But here she was, one step closer, overwhelmed, desperate to pray correctly, to make herself heard.

Since Natalia and Dima passed, she and Hugo had prayed quietly. She flipped to the passages in her books, turned the pages slowly, ran her fingers down familiar passages, and whisper-sang to herself. Hugo was barely audible in his grief and old age. Without other voices joining her own, the silence muted her. She hadn't stopped praying, but she did it so softly that sometimes she worried her god would not hear. Now the words vibrated in her throat again, joining the nuns' voices. The whole chamber quivered with their monophonic supplications. Agafia folded her arms and closed her eyes.

Still, that night she dreamt not of the thick-walled temple but of a more familiar paradise. Striped goats and brushed-out sheep grazed in large meadows of juicy grass. Milk sprang forth from a brook on one edge of the meadow, and on the other side ran a clear stream of glacier water, cool on her throat. The grass never browned and the sky never grayed. A wolf appeared at the meadow's edge. It stalked the edges of her consciousness, then loped off into the distance, toward a waiting pack. They rolled in the grass, tongues hanging and tails akimbo. Paradise could be an earthly place to live, too. She didn't recognize the valley in the dream—perhaps another hollow on her map to Belovod'e, a stepping-stone to the place her family had sought. When she woke she recounted the dream to herself to commit it to memory, but didn't tell anyone about it at breakfast.

■ ■ ■

The nuns incorporated Agafia into their daily routines as if she'd been there all along. In the morning, she ran up the steps to the bell tower and tugged the ropes to set the ringing in motion. She couldn't control the sounds she released, so the bells squalled rather than sang, but it made her happy. After breakfast, together they worked the garden, harvesting ripe vegetables, weeding and watering. Sunflowers stretched above the fence that shielded the bountiful rows from hungry ungulates, the flowers miniature umbrellas of shade. Agafia plucked dandelion shoots from the soil. Her own green rows were probably overrun with pretty, bolting weeds. One of the women started up a song, calling out to the others, and they responded in unison. Keeping time, some with their shovels, some with their arms as they reached for fruit, the women coalesced into a centipede, picking its way through the land.

Snow Crane and Ivan loafed by the riverbank. Anna had dismissed them from the garden. When he became restless, Snow Crane fiddled with the radio he'd brought, trying to find Galina on the airwaves, but she wasn't answering. Snow Crane leaned on a sleeping roll, laid his book across his chest, and closed his eyes.

Siberia. He carried the place inside of him. It had given him Galina, those free, wildflower afternoons that allowed their warmth to bud. It had stolen plenty before that. He'd worried about returning to the taiga, about how the rush of memories might overwhelm him, but the previous season Galina's presence had helped keep the recollections at bay. Without her at the monastery, without something to do, they pooled in his lungs, making it hard to breathe. His first trip to the taiga had been involuntary. It had started with a box of letters from his friend Marat.

Written on translucent pages in blue-purple ink, they revealed snippets of Marat's life. He'd ended up working on a dam in the Far East. In slanted cursive, the words all leaning evenly as if the wind had tried to blow them off the page, he described summer mosquitos and winter hunger. The work had broadened his shoulders but narrowed his optimism, he wrote. Many synonyms went toward describing the weather, as if Marat had challenged himself to do the cold, heat, and discomfort justice. Poems rarely made it to these letters, and there was never a return address for Snow Crane. He wrote back anyway, long stories about army food and the smell of men-filled dorm rooms and the way his plane could shoot into clouds in bursts of speed. One day he would send them. He stashed all the letters, his and Marat's, in a box he kept hidden among his few possessions.

After a run one morning he came back to his cubby to see that someone had gone through the letters, leaving them scattered on the floor. The men in the dorm sat around snickering. Snow Crane picked them up, smoothed the envelopes and pages, returned them to a small pile. He sat down on a bunk and lit a cigarette.

"Did you like reading my letters?" he asked the men between drags. "You could have just asked, I would've read them to you myself. He writes beautifully."

A man with flat fish eyes grinned across the room. "I bet he fucks beautifully too," he said.

Snow Crane took a long, indulgent drag off his cigarette, the smoke from it dropping down heavy into his lungs. He smoked so rarely that he became light-headed. He started to feel like he was floating. Smoke poured from his mouth and nostrils as he exhaled. He rose and flicked the cigarette at the man with the fish eyes. It landed on his hair, singed it. The man lunged at Snow Crane, coming at him slow as a tank accelerating. Snow Crane barely knew the man; he'd seen him around, usually sprawled gracelessly in a sunny spot in the barracks, an oversized cat washing himself, smoking and looking at magazines full of pictures of topless women. He'd assumed he flaunted his contraband because he was stupid, but now it occurred to him that it was because he was connected. The man's father must've been a colonel, or an apparatchik. As the man approached Snow Crane stepped aside, grabbed him by the collar, and swung him into the corner of the bunk frame. Blood gushed instantly from his head and he slumped against the bed, breathing labored and cursing. Snow Crane collected his box and a bag and walked out, unhurried.

No one spoke about the incident, and the man with the fish eyes ignored him in the mess hall. Snow Crane flew his planes, bored up in the clouds. On the headset, he heard the commands from the control center on the ground and the other pilots' jokes. He muted himself and instead carried on conversations in his head with Marat, with the nannies who'd raised him, with his mama, with other people he hoped to meet one day.

A month after the incident, a younger pilot approached him during breakfast and motioned for Snow Crane to rise. The man with the fish eyes saluted Snow Crane as the pilot escorted him from the mess hall to an office where a group of higher-ups waited in a semicircle.

His own superior wasn't present, but a man with sweat stains on his uniform stood waiting.

"Son, reports have come in that you've been reading and distributing dissident literature in the barracks. Inciting trouble," the man said. "Is that true?"

It was pointless to argue. *Yes*, he thought, *that man really was connected*. Casual violence was rarely punished unless inflicted on the wrong man. Snow Crane stood silently and waited.

"We heard you've inappropriately touched men in the barracks," another man said. He cleared his throat. "Is that true?"

With few exceptions, Snow Crane didn't make life happen, it happened to him. He cowered in his body, a stowaway on a ship that a foreign and malicious captain kept steering into stormy waters. Into enemy territory. Snow Crane stood in front of the officers, watched the captain spin the ship's wheel—was he drunk?—and heard the ship start to groan as he redirected it onto an uncharted course.

The generals looked sorry. Snow Crane tuned out their voices and concentrated on their faces—clean-shaven, blue Ryazan eyes, dry lips. Thick blond eyebrows glowed on one officer's forehead. Another tried to hide nicotine-yellowed teeth as he spoke. They placed their meaty hands on the desk, as if to display their hard-earned thickness. Some wore thin gold bands. Snow Crane stood on the bow of the ship, squinting into the darkness, trying to make out the obstacles in the water ahead. The one with the eyebrows told him to gather his things.

On the train, he looked for signs of his mama all around; this was the route she must have followed, he thought. Could the grease on the window he leaned on be from her cheek? A soldier met him at the station and drove him, far, to a smudge of huts on the plain.

"Welcome to Siberia," the driver announced when he dropped him off.

On the miniature buildings made of rough-hewn gray wood Snow Crane noticed embellishments—here and there an elegant trim above a door or window. Some had numbers by the doors, like addresses in a village. The old-timers told him that when the camp first opened to provide labor for the timber operations, the site was empty. The prisoners slept in tents and built their own prison on the snowy plain at the edge of a forest.

"It's almost cozy now," they joked. "Made it nice just for you young fellows."

He asked around for his mama by name, but no one had heard of her. She must be in another camp, they told him. There were others? The prisoners laughed at his question.

"Did you kill someone with your innocence?" a bunkmate asked. "Is that why you're here?"

There was nowhere to go from the camp and the camp minders knew it. Perhaps because of that, they never bothered to confine or punish the men. In this way, the prison resembled a remote but normal timber settlement, where people worked hard, aged quickly. Camaraderie seeped in anyway. Whenever a man received a letter, he held a public reading. *Dear Lager*, he'd read, replacing his own name with the camp's, *The children are doing well*. They wept together at the updates from home, wherever home happened to be that day. They internalized the news, replacing the names of their bunkmates' loved ones with their own. The storylines grew confused in their heads. Unmarried men wept to receive news that their wives had birthed healthy daughters, and old men grieved anew for their mothers' untimely passing.

Snow Crane received a letter from Marat. It had been forwarded along, a testament to the organization of the bureaucratic machine that tracked him from the military to the taiga. *Dear Lager*, he read to those gathered. *I have finally met a girl with hair the color of straw and eyes like chalcedony. She comes from the desert and fits against me as if molded to my body from a sun-warmed sand dune.* The men cheered for their new friend, whistling as Snow Crane read on. *She is also a poet and writes more beautifully than anyone I've ever read. She talks in verse, in a voice that has the clear ring of slate parting. (I thought you would appreciate the analogy.) We share our poems with each other by candlelight. I told her how we used to read in our fort and she said, "Boys have truer loves than men." She says things like that all the time.*

Snow Crane's bunkmates cheered. "We love her too!" they yelled out.

Every day Snow Crane and the other men at the camp went out and worked the timber. He learned their crimes—telling jokes, stealing supplies from the factories where they worked, crossing local politicians. Some of them didn't know what had landed them there. They were all like him, steered there unknowingly, unable to wrest the wheel from their own drunk captains. The nannies and schoolmasters had taught Snow Crane that the molding of a society into a deliberate force, all red, all worker, all together, would enable him to achieve anything he wanted, would lead him to live a rich life. He was raised on the utopian promise of togetherness. But in the camp, sawing giant Siberian pines and cedars by hand, Snow Crane watched his captain waving to him from the bow, a smirk on his face, a pipe, a plan to which Snow Crane wasn't privy.

He took it out on the trees. He sawed with fervor, muscles taut with purpose. In control. A Stakhanovite molded from windblown dust and refracted light. A man felling trees with his bare hands. A man surely possessed of his own will and the ability to impose it on the world.

He opened his eyes, back suddenly by the river, in a different part of Siberia, a different encampment, another settlement of unwanteds. Trees danced above him. Somewhere, women's voices rose and fell, a shifting high-noon sough. Was Siberia prison or liberation for these women? For him it had become both.

■ ■ ■

When it was time for a break, Anna led Agafia to an undercut, shaggy larch and sat her down in the shade. From somewhere in the folds of her dress she took out a dried, roasted sunflower head and they passed it back and forth, picking seeds out of the flower's pockets and cracking them between their teeth. A small pile of zebra-striped shells grew between the two women.

Agafia had planted sunflowers in the past, but they never made good seeds. They were too soft and too small. No good crack to them. She placed a seed between her teeth and bit down. It splintered in her mouth.

"Listen," Anna said.

Agafia stopped moving her jaw.

"Here, we wait for the apocalypse in peace. When it comes, greet it with your sisters."

Anna placed a hand on Agafia's leg, to still her. Agafia took up the seeds again, her brain's gears powering up her jaws once more.

"It is Christian to share the faith and to help each other sustain it. There are so few of us left," Anna said. "And I fear the faithless will seek you out, draw you to sins the sisters can protect you from."

Agafia hogged the sunflower. She tightened her head scarf under her chin. The sins piled up in her head—her walks with Peter, lying with Pavel, her mother's wickedness for ending her life, which she sometimes thought contagious, how she cut her prayers short to be with the summer sun. She laid her head on Anna's shoulder. The home place from that night's dream returned to her. This time she recognized the river that flanked the meadow in which the church perched, the grass a thick wool rug, the goats with opals for eyes.

■ ■ ■

The next day the women walked into the forest single file, each with a basket hanging from her arm. The morning was cool and thick fog topped the ground. Agafia and the nuns parted the vapor with their skirts and disappeared into the thicket's blue. They looked like witches in a dark wood.

Anna led the way, weaving between larches hung with cones like ornaments and rough-barked scotch pines. A small knife dangled from her fingertips. Agafia had ridden the last rains in on the river, but the past week had been dry and she questioned whether there'd be mushrooms. She scanned around her, peeking under the spread-out pines' skirts. Her family had stopped picking mushrooms many years ago after they all started to look alike. There was the scare with Dima, who languished in bed like a wilted pile of stinging nettle for almost a week after they ate mushrooms one night, though they never did know if it was the fungus that did it. They grew cautious, leaving fat-capped specimens standing to drop their spores, though for some years they still ate the most easily identifiable mushrooms—the chanterelles in their frilly orange skirts, the blushed berry tops of the *siraeshki*. Eventually they stopped that, too, passing on whole stands of mushrooms even in times of hunger. Just a couple of decades in, and the knowledge people had gathered, refined, and passed down over centuries started to dissipate like the morning's fog.

Anna stooped with the knife and cut at a mushroom's leg, tucking it in her basket where she'd laid out a bed of pine needles so as not to bruise her harvest. The other women had spread out on the forest floor and crouched, filling their baskets, looking themselves like bright mushrooms dotting the darkened wood. Agafia sidled up to Anna. Anna carried two baskets, a large one and a smaller one. Into the bigger one she piled yellow blobs as spongy as rising bread dough, thick-legged matronly mushrooms with tops that looked like neatly pinned hair buns, thin caps with crumbly gills, and fused bunches of cream-colored fungi.

The small basket remained empty as the larger one filled, until she came upon a patch of white-legged mushrooms with red caps sprinkled with white spots as if with flaky salt, ready to eat. Anna cleaned off the knife on her skirts and got on her hands and knees. Into the bare basket they went, a bouquet of all-alike amanitas, jostling for room to show off their brightest reds, their whitest polka dots.

"Do you eat those?" Agafia asked.

"Not for dinner," Anna said.

Some of the women had gone deeper into the wood and disappeared from sight. Agafia, always counting to avoid losing anyone, swiveled her head, searching for the bright flashes of their dresses between the trees. In the woods by her house she had learned every tree and the topography of the forest floor, anticipating the rises of long-dead trunks buried beneath mulchy soil and dips where an animal once dug or a fallen pine's roots excavated a hole. It had taken a lifetime to learn just that piece of land, and now she walked a whole new forest. She stood studying the ground, and when she looked up everyone was gone.

Panic rose up around her, pummeled her like a wave striking with such force that water reached long unthought-of corners of her body. Wetness clammed her hands and a droplet ran from the top of her neck down her back. Sound would not come from her throat. She lifted her skirts and ran, tripping over fallen branches and sinking into the moss underfoot.

When Agafia was a small child, she'd gotten lost. The others, walking and talking and foraging, hadn't noticed right away, and she'd spent what seemed like hours in search of her family.

Fear hadn't come then, perhaps because she was a child, or because she assumed she could find her way out of the forest, even without the others. But now panic disoriented her. She ran a little in one direction, then turned around and ran in the other, so that in the end she seemed to return over and over to the same place. Finally she stopped and lay down on the ground. The dirt gave around her. She sank into the soil as if into a feather bed. The trees' breathing canopies allowed glimpses of the washed-out blue sky as they parted, then closed again. A slight breeze made the leaves dance, and they sounded like the swishing of skirts. Agafia calmed and fell asleep listening to the forest's murmur. She dreamt of a million nuns, their long raiment rustling as they walked across Siberia.

When she woke the women were all sitting around her in a circle. Her shawl had slid off and Anna was caressing her head. Agafia's own sister had never touched her with such kindness, and although her father had been gentle, he seemed to fear her skin. The sisters were singing, about a Kazakh horseman riding all day and night to get to his sweetheart. Baskets full of mushrooms sat at their sides lacing the air with an antediluvian smell.

Anna reached into her frock and pulled out a lumpy canvas bag. The others settled in, resting on their haunches. Agafia sat up, brushing debris out of her hair. Someone produced a thermos, and Anna dropped several desiccated mushrooms from her bag into the hot water. The caps of the amanitas had turned brown and wrinkly, but they plumped up in the water, regaining their suppleness.

"I've never had mushroom tea," Agafia said.

"It may feel a little funny." Anna turned to face her. "An old lady taught us to make this tea many years ago. She lived down the river and told us about life before Nikon. This tea makes you like the animals. It lends you their eyes and their noses and their paws."

"Which animal?"

Anna paused. "It is like a wolf and a crane."

The tea tasted bitter and went down like a thick elixir, coating her throat. It settled into a warm bioluminescent puddle inside her, lighting up when she shifted where she lay. She listened to the women sing. They had taken off their scarves and their hair hung in thick ropy braids. Whiskered voles and charcoal-colored squirrels and a fox peeked out from behind trees to see the commotion. Agafia stayed still, eyes wide open but immovable, staring skyward.

It was then that the ground beneath her began to move. She sat up. Everything was beautiful. She had tried and tried to reach such ecstasy in her prayer and only rarely had achieved it. Once she'd prayed by herself by the river's edge and the stream had shifted around her recitations and grown still, its flow frozen like the lined-up crystals of a gemstone, so that she attempted to walk across it. But the cold had snapped her vision when she dipped her toes in, and she'd backed away from the water in fear. Ecstasy and God and fear came hand in hand, as if without the precipice there was no elation. As a young woman she'd had trouble surrendering to her faith, despite trying. It had seemed like some sort of abyss. Since the geologists came, the abyss of the worldly world also loomed. She curled inward, into the void of her own longing. Out there, possibilities.

"Do you want to walk with us?" Anna asked.

She took her by the arm and her warmth poured into Agafia. The leaves on the trees trembled like butterflies and when Anna led her past a low-hanging branch they took off into the air, ascending as a cloud. Mossy outcrops glowed fluorescent on the ground and golden threads unwound from the nests in the trees, the ends hanging loose. They walked to a meadow carved out of the forest, a circle of thick grass ringed by the woods. The breeze stirred the air. Agafia heard her mother's voice calling out something indecipherable to the women.

Maybe I want a daughter, Agafia said to herself. The idea had never crossed her mind before. *Where do I find one?*

Some of the women had hiked up their skirts and their bare legs rose from the ground like strong tree trunks, young firm birches reaching for the light. Her own mother and sister had been so meek. There was the geologist, yes, but she was different, worldly. These sisters braided the river current into their blond strands, cupped sky in their soil-covered hands, hearts flashing like lighting in their torsos.

One of the nuns began to run in circles around the women in the pasture. As she sprinted past, the ground shook below Agafia, the whole earth thrown off-orbit by her stomping. Agafia put her ear to the ground to listen as the woman looped back. Her feet thundered on the ground, which reverberated as if from a stampede. The other women got up and started to follow her, all of them running through the meadow, arched feet suddenly hooved, hair undone from braids into unkempt manes, bodies assured in their breathing, a harras of wild horses reveling in their perfect being.

CHAPTER 6
Глава 6

A few days after Agafia and Snow Crane had departed downriver, helicopters arrived. Drill rig parts bundled in giant nets hung suspended from cables. Galina watched them fly overhead like a flock of birds of prey carrying their catch, and touch down in a clearing between the geologists' camp and Agafia's homestead. Engineers, mud loggers, strong hands to assemble the machinery spilled out. They were equipped with Galina's maps, marked with points where they'd extract rock cores, which would show whether mineral lay underneath. From the cores Galina would refine the deposits' shape.

While they toiled, Galina pored over the plot drawings in the mornings and walked in the afternoons. Without Snow Crane around, she worked all day. The sun barely set and she, with it, stayed alert, her mind churning like a slow, steady drill through hard rock. The maps her team had drawn over the winter showed a blob of ore melting over the now-familiar territory. It spread over the land like a cracked egg, spilling into crevasses and filling nooks. She ran her finger along the map looking for the X that marked Agafia's house, a tiny yolk.

She pictured machines rolling toward the homestead, oversized wheels trampling the taiga garden and metal claws closing over the hut's time-smoothed wood boards. It would take so little work to annihilate this landscape's peopled blip and replace it with a bigger one. One human project, that of progress, winning out over another human project, that of survival. The wolves take down ungulates. It's just the way of things.

Assembled, the rig rose like a toy monument. It would drill first in the locus where the magnetometer showed the highest gamma readings, where the presence of iron was most definite. Then the drill would punch holes in a handful of sections with lesser readings that spread in concentric wrinkles from the center. It was a small rig, meant only to extract thin rock cores. If bedrock is a densely packed pencil box, each core would be a pencil, slid free by the borer.

The drill hands built a cocoon around the machine of plywood boards with book-sized netted windows. They drilled twenty-four hours a day, steady as time itself, and deep. The plywood carapace made life more bearable for the operators by keeping out the mosquitos, which would have consumed them whole. Galina visited the drill site, watching core sections emerge and glide down a ramp—100, 200, 500 feet deep—to line up in neat rows, as if on a production line.

"Hurry!" she urged the drillers. She wanted them to move on to the plots farther from the Kols' homestead, so Agafia wouldn't see them cut into the ground. She directed that everything be done and packed away before Agafia returned.

"Can't push the rocks," the men told her.

This would be her last summer in the taiga, a time to hone her sample collection, refine her maps. Over the coming winter, she'd hand in her findings, data, and notes, along with any recommendations, and someone would decide to go forward and the engineers and laborers would take over. They'd crack the surface, first carefully, almost tenderly, opening up the ground, airing it out from frozen, still millennia. Once the ground yielded, they'd let loose the dynamite. Galina would be sent to another far-flung mountain, to map its riches for the next wolfpack. The way of things.

The day before she departed Moscow, she'd received a letter in the mail. It came from David, a mysterious, vaguely worded missive written in his messy handwriting, so unlike the uniform, slanting script taught to every Russian child at school. Its message ran for just one page. *Do something real. What are we destroying in order to build? Look closely. You can do more. I can too. Your comrade, D.,* he signed it. She carried the note around with her in a notebook and whispered to herself as she read and reread it, "I don't know what you want from me." But even before the letter, her apprehension around her work had been slowly rising, like dough expanding in a bowl, filling it, overflowing, and she understood the meaning of his words in her gut. The project she was leading was problematic. David had brought her to M. to show how her work poisoned the people, the very air. The trip had underscored her unease. Now he asked her to act on it, to slow the ruin. But how? She a mere cog in a vast universe of forward movement.

In the evenings, she sat by the ham radio. Static hissed, an alternate frequency of the humming bugs, and hypnotized her. At times ham radio enthusiasts' transmissions would break through with secret messages, their serious, faraway voices lobbing words into the void.

Galina waited to hear Snow Crane's voice among them, and on some nights they'd catch each other.

"Snow Crane here," he'd say.

"I hear you loud and clear," Galina would respond. "Take flight."

Agafia had asked Snow Crane to stay ten days at the monastery. That's how long she needed to decide whether she'd return to her own homestead or make a life there, with the sisters. Snow Crane had hesitated, but she'd pleaded. If he left, she told him, she'd never get home, and she wanted to decide her fate, not let it be something that just happened. Snow Crane understood. Anna opened the library to the two men and they settled into a week of long, buggy days by the river. They swam, gathered berries, tanned themselves, and read, as if at a particularly remote and unsupervised summer camp.

In the monastery library Snow Crane gravitated to Avvakum's writings, mesmerized by descriptions of his banishment in Siberia. Avvakum had served as archpriest in a Moscow cathedral, until he was relieved of his duties for not following Nikon's reforms.

"He refused to use three fingers instead of two to cross himself," Snow Crane told Galina over the radio.

"That's all?" Galina asked.

"That was everything. Imagine if someone told you to discount the basic rules of geology. Told you that rock layers on top are older than the rocks below them."

"Everything else would fall apart," Galina said.

"Yes. So Avvakum and his family traveled east, sometimes by cart, sometimes on foot, to their own exile. It was slippery and his wife fell to the ground. When Avvakum approached her, she asked how long they had to suffer like this. And Avvakum said, 'Till death itself!' So she sighed and told him, 'Very well, let's be on our way then.' "

"Sounds like a Russian woman, all right."

During one of his periods of exile, while imprisoned, he'd shared quarters with other ousted Old Believer priests, and they wrote argumentative theological treatises. They had to defecate on a spade and toss it out the window, because their cell had so few amenities. But somehow the exiles managed to write their letters and sneak them out of the prison. They dispersed throughout all of Russia, to Old Believer communities and beyond. Their condemnations of the reforms were seen as blasphemous by the czar. Eventually Avvakum was burned at the stake.

"Did he see it coming?" Galina asked.

Snow Crane read to her from the book of letters. When Avvakum was a young man he'd had a vision of a ship

adorned not with gold, but with many colors—red, white, blue, black, and gray—the human mind cannot encompass how fair and sound it was. And a radiant youth sat at the stern steering it. . . . And I cried out: "Whose boat is this?" And the youth replied: "It is your boat! Go sail in it with your wife and children, if you so wish!" And I began to tremble and thought to myself: "What can this mean? And where shall I sail?"

"The stormy sea was his life, which he foresaw, and the ship his own destiny, which he steered into the storms," said Snow Crane.

"That's heavy," Galina said.

Snow Crane thought about Agafia's dreams and visions and how Galina had told him about her mother admiring paintings of stormy seas and how he, like Avvakum, had spent time in Siberia, banished. They were all more alike and more different than a mind could hold in one birch basket. His own ship, had he steered it, like Avvakum? Or had the waves tossed it around, a creaking, straining hull ignoring the captain's navigation? He laughed into the transmitter.

"Heavy," he said.

"How's Agafia?"

"Slipped right into this place," he told her. "Happy as can be."

"How are you?"

"Lonesome for sweets and our poppy curtains."

They talked in code and the shorthand of their love, in the vernacular of familiarity and gentleness. People who happened to tune in to their channel would stop transmitting to let them have their space, listening in as if to a nightly program.

CHAPTER 7
Глава 7

The women wove through the hushed forest back to the convent, mushroom baskets in hand. At dusk, it began to rain. First a drizzle, then the drops grew fatter. The nuns started work on the night's dinner without changing out of their wet clothes. Agafia didn't feel well and excused herself. She lay down on the narrow cot in her room and with a sleeve wiped cold sweat off her brow. Rain had dampened her frock, but her own sweat had soaked it. She prayed with her eyes to the high ceiling, unmoving, too weak to cross herself. When the dinner bell rang she stayed in bed and shooed off the sisters who came to fetch her. They brought hot tea and fresh robes and cocooned her in heavy blankets. Snow Crane tried to enter the room to see her, but the nuns left him in the hall, waiting.

"Must be the rain," Anna told him. "She'll be fine in the morning."

In the morning, Agafia lay balled up with tension, her face as white as beech wood and beaded with perspiration. Snow Crane said they needed to get her to the hospital, but Anna waved him off.

"The hospital is a couple of days of rough river travel away. She'll fall off your raft."

All day the monastery stayed on high alert, the sisters rotating between Agafia's room and the chapel. Snow Crane brought cold compresses for her forehead and warm ones for her stomach, which she clutched with unweakened force.

Whatever was happening inside her had the strength and purity of an exorcism, and Agafia's mind drifted to the stories of exorcisms her father had told. In them, tables danced and empty chasubles took shape in a breeze and candles flickered with the devil's breath. But prayer stilled everything in the stories, so she reasserted her efforts.

In the evening, wetness seeped out between her legs and she reached down to examine herself. Sticky blood coated her fingers. She had missed her bleeding time last month, unusual for her, and now it came, late and painful. When Anna returned, Agafia asked her for some cloth and explained that she had started bleeding. Anna shut the door behind her and knelt by Agafia.

"Did one of those men sin with you?" she asked Agafia. Anna wrinkled her smooth white forehead, her brows bare shadows on her pale skin.

"No, sister," Agafia said.

Anna sat. "Are you pregnant, sister?" she asked.

Agafia barely understood the meaning of the word. She was the youngest in her family and had never seen her mother pregnant. Nor her sister. She'd read about it in her books, how the rounding of women's bellies lent them a saintly glow and how they suffered to bring life to the world. But her belly had never rounded and she had not suffered, until now.

"Did you lie with a man?" Anna pressed her. Her voice so kind, despite the alarm in it.

"There are so many ways to sin without trying," Agafia said. The weight of it exhausting. Pain flowed out with the blood, bringing relief. Earlier that day, in fever, she had daydreamed of daughters, but she knew now that was a mistake.

"It was the winter visitor," Agafia said. "He lay on me when the spring came."

"Let me bring you some cloth." Anna sped through the halls to find the men, who nursed cups of tea in a corner of the kitchen. The sisters avoided them and the men had kept to themselves.

"Who is the winter visitor?" Anna asked. Like the Kols, the women spoke an old Russian, tucking extra vowels into words, their lexicon an antiquarian relic. Snow Crane wasn't accustomed to their version of this speech. Familiar words failed to bring meaning to sentences. The Kols' house, the convent, they resembled a very specialized science conference, where the unfamiliar terminology was a wall against intruders. And here was Anna, saying normal words that did not make sense.

"The winter visitor?" Snow Crane said.

"A winter visitor lay upon her, and she just lost a bean babe."

Snow Crane diagrammed the sentence in his head, pulling apart the subject, the verb, the noun as adjective.

"Please," he said, "please explain."

"She's pregnant?" Ivan asked. Meaning surfaced like a whale.

"That's impossible," Snow Crane said. "She's too old." At least she'd looked it to him.

"The body is never too old for miracles," Anna said.

"The hunter. A trapper stayed with them," Snow Crane said at last. "That's the winter visitor."

Snow Crane wished Galina were there to know what to do. He had no idea what should happen next.

"I think the babe is gone," Anna said. She crossed herself, and the men imitated her.

"The winter visitor is worldly," Snow Crane told her. "From a village not too far away."

Word spread, and the women gathered to pray. Incense drifted out of the chapel, into the halls, reentering the living quarters through the windows. Snow Crane went to see Agafia. She lay flat in the bed with her hands crossed over her belly, as if prepared for her funeral rites. But her face was more relaxed and she wasn't sweating.

"When I'm better, we'll go back," she told Snow Crane.

"I thought you might want to settle here with your sisters," he said.

A chorus of voices to pray with and a covey of hands to work the garden. Her people had always relied on community, yet she'd only known it theoretically, in her father's stories. There was her hut, the elk and moose that came to see her but refused to submit to her hunger, the river where the pebbles were as familiar as her own birthmarks. And there was Anna, the cloister.

"I have brought too much shame to the sisters," she said.

"Did you invite Pavel to touch you?" he asked.

She threw her hands up in the air, quiet.

A week and a half later, they loaded the boat with provisions from the sisters and prepared to leave.

"It's not too far to town," Anna told them.

The men stood by the boat waiting. Agafia passed through the arms of each sister, lined up and waiting to touch her. Anna kissed her on the forehead before Agafia stepped up on the catamaran. As they pushed off, the current caught them and slipped them down the river. They heard the women's voices rise up in a song of mourning, before they faded around the bend.

CHAPTER 8
Глава 8

Agafia's sense of self was rooted in remoteness. Her lifelong isolation had defined why she suffered, how she lived. Then the geologists found her, the river flushed red, Pavel arrived, she discovered neighbors downriver. She'd wondered, vaguely, how the sisters procured the luxuries she'd always done without—the salt, fresh cloth, metal candleholders and pots. She assumed their exile to be complete too. But when she reached a city just two days after leaving the nuns, her fundamental understanding of her story shifted. Her family hadn't walked very far at all.

Scum colored the boat's rubber sides brown and greasy. Cement banks encased the river, and Snow Crane searched both sides for an opening where they could tie up and climb out of the stream. People strolling by the water pointed at them and stopped to look, but no one answered when Snow Crane shouted asking about a dock. Finally they spotted a break in the bank, a ramp leading to a factory parking lot. Snow Crane secured the boat and they walked through the lot and out toward the bustling street. Agafia grabbed Snow Crane's sleeve. He narrated for her.

"That's a trolley, it carries people to and from work and around the city. This is a factory—I don't know what they make here.

Maybe paper. These are all apartment buildings—look at the curtains. Every time they change, it means it's a different family."

She gasped, gentle, horrified. "They must be sleepy all the time."

She pointed to the passing cars and asked if driving, all this sitting, made people shorter.

A girl on a tricycle made her clap her hands. She paused and stared at the women selling pirozhki on the street. One of the vendors threw back a towel covering her basket to show off the glossy browned turnovers lined up in neat rows.

"They look like the pebbles on our shore," Agafia marveled.

Snow Crane bought one for each of them, and handed Agafia the warm, heavy dough, wrapped in greasy newspaper. She took one careful bite, releasing hot steam, then another, then chewed quickly to finish it. She held her greasy fingers up to the sun.

"It must be hard to be clean here," said Agafia.

Snow Crane figured the technology would shock her, the passing trains and cars, the tall buildings—the city's infrastructure. Some of it did; she marveled at the glass windows of storefronts, the asphalt's hardness, which made her walk as if the ground burned her feet, the manicured gardens planted in the streets' medians. But she was drawn more to the human fabric of the town—her eyes lingered on women's summer dresses, and she remarked on their short bobs and men's bare faces. She listened intently to snatches of conversation and wrinkled her nose at the unfamiliar smells. At the sight of children, she stopped and stared, unabashed, until their mothers ushered them along. As the youngest in the family, she'd never seen young children, the odd smallness of their bodies, how they twisted and folded in their mothers' arms like putty, the coronas of fine hair that stood around their faces like icons' halos. A small boy called out to her like a bird and she responded, so that he broke into a joyful, gummy smile. Anna had explained what had happened to Agafia, that she had lost something that one day might have been a child, but wasn't yet. Anna had been kind and patient, describing to Agafia the great magic of the universe, and though Agafia had not completely understood, a sense of grief made her lose her balance as she walked.

The small regional city clasped a dreary grayness about its shoulders like a robe, despite the sunny summer day. Snow Crane, eager to cheer Agafia up, tried to imagine the town through her eyes. He tuned in to the bustle, until it grew into a revelation; if he squinted hard enough, he could transport them to anywhere. New York, Paris, Buenos Aires. He tightened his own hold on Agafia's sleeve.

"It's so hard to experience new things," he whispered to Ivan.

Snow Crane led them through the unremarkable city pretending to be tourists. The three of them pointed at ordinary, everyday things—buildings, cars, municipal trash cans, ice cream machines—and exclaimed in unison. Agafia let out bursts of hoarse laughter at the people they passed on the sidewalk, scaring them, and clicked her tongue at each intersection, as if admonishing herself for pushing on into this strange world. What an astounding place the world could be through the eyes of an extraterrestrial.

Snow Crane's narration kept up a certain energy in their group as they explored, but her focus began to drift. The sullen faces on the street worried Agafia, who saw a whole town trapped in a communal un-ecstasy. There was something about the mass of people—the swollen legs of the old women in their dresses, the boy with a bandaged head, the way the little girls hopped with their hands clasped, the police officer's blank stare, everyone walking somewhere, moving in unceasing fury through too-wide streets—that perturbed Agafia. All those unfamiliar problems and souls. She laughed louder, edging toward the maniacal. When they came to a fountain ringed with cherubic mermen, Agafia averted her eyes.

"I need to pray," she said.

Snow Crane pointed to a cross rising behind a row of squat buildings. "Do you want to see another church?"

They wove through traffic and speed-walked down an alley. A rusty metal gate surrounded the church. Agafia unlatched the entrance and pushed open the building's heavy wooden doors. Inside, darkness. A handful of women, heads covered, lit candles. Voices floated on incensed air. Aside from the monastery, she'd never been in an Old Believer church, but she realized this wasn't one. It was a newer church, one where the reforms had been accepted. Icons crowded the walls, gold glowing in the candlelight. The icons had white luminous skin and eyes with heavy downcast lids. Three smooth and jointless fingers, instead of two, met to make the sign of the cross. Everything a little off, a little new, a little different. But also, the same. Her role, she'd been taught, was not to question the texts she'd inherited, their teachings and practical instructions, but to maintain them at all costs. Here was the thing she had guarded against, this other vision of God, which suddenly looked so similar to hers. This sacrilege she'd been taught to fear. The gold framing every icon, which lined the walls from floor to ceiling, dizzied her. If the beauty here was not God-given, if this was not a piece of heaven, the waiting area for that radiant forever, she didn't know what else it could be. It was second only to her forest. Her neck constricted, too tight for air to pass. A heaviness pressed down on her chest. Blackness crept in from the periphery, then shut Agafia out from herself.

When she woke, she was in a hotel room, tucked into a bed. Ivan sat by her side and Snow Crane stood at the windowsill with the radio, clicking the static on and off.

"Snow Crane here," he said, and waited for Galina. Agafia closed her eyes.

The audio fuzz drifted about the room like falling snow, ashes from a fire, and Snow Crane grew sleepy leaning on the windowsill. He nodded off, still standing, and dreamt he was a giraffe whose legs were buckling under him. Galina's voice woke him.

"Snow Crane, are you there?" she asked. In their own homes, at their radios, people sat up, turned up the volume, settled in.

"She was pregnant," he said. "She lost it."

The audible creak of chairs echoed through the land as people leaned closer to their radios. Then static. Silence.

"He's a monster," Galina finally said.

Someone listening couldn't resist and clicked on. "Tell me who it is, I'll kill him," a man's voice said.

"You just tell us," another voice said.

"Poor babe," a woman said. "I know how that feels."

Galina heard others relaying messages back and forth whenever they talked. All the parallel conversations came through in code—sometimes intentional, sometimes not. Unfamiliar names and problems took shape in the radio wave ether. But the interlocutors made room for each other on air, like people politely passing on the side-walk, and Galina had forgotten that others were out there, listening. Now the eavesdroppers were a mob, interrupting Snow Crane and Galina from their own chairs, from their own lives, like people yelling at a television.

Agafia sat up in bed. "Snow Crane?" she said.

"I have to go," he told Galina.

"I'll send the helicopter tomorrow," she told him. "Meet him at the airport."

■ ■ ■

The helicopter arrived early and the three of them loaded the deflated catamaran and their bags. Ivan had procured a goat for Agafia, and they pushed the bleating animal aboard too. Agafia clutched the rope around the animal's neck and petted it with a strong palm. She'd also trapped a cat that morning and it mewled from a box at her feet. The domestic life would keep her company at the homestead. Snow Crane threw sacks of flour and rice into the cargo hold. They set off for camp, rising above the city, heading north. Below, the density tapered out into villages, rural homesteads; then the wilderness crept in and took over, the forest running unbroken below them so that it seemed they were hovering in place.

Agafia watched for something familiar beyond the thick glass. The helicopter lowered, the treetops flattening under the surge of air. Looking at her home from this fourth dimension, from above, was like learning new secrets about an old friend. *Everything is smaller from up here,* she wanted to tell Peter, but when she searched for him she didn't find him. She tried to look away but couldn't. Ahead, the forest took on shadows from a hollow break: the river. Her river. Agafia sat up. The pilot swung toward the water and positioned the helicopter over it, then followed it up toward camp, like a road. The river eased her into familiarity, a well-traveled approach to a well-loved home. When they landed, Agafia realized she'd been holding her breath, as if her exhales could blow everything away.

Galina greeted them at the camp and held Snow Crane and Agafia too long. She'd prepared lunch and ushered them to the table. Ivan rejoined the others, who absorbed him with their steady, familiar patter, barely allowing him to relate the trip's events. Galina, Snow Crane, and Agafia sat off to the side, picking at crumbs on their plates.

"Tell me everything," Galina said. The two of them stayed quiet. She placed a hand on Agafia's shoulder. She said, "It's okay," and "We can talk about it," and "How are you feeling?" and "It's not your fault."

Agafia walked the path home with the boxed kitten tied to her back, the goat pausing to graze. Peter returned, following a step behind. Hugo came to her; after just a couple of weeks' absence, he looked older, frailer, more diminished. The compound was clean, but Hugo said he hadn't been able to work in the garden. Agafia tied the goat to a stake by the front door, and brought the kitten in the house. All night he kept her up by climbing on the oven and pawing objects to the floor.

In the morning, early, she headed to the garden. Weeds pushed up between crop rows, reminding her of the crowds in the city. Fingers in the soil, knees sinking into the soft earth, she regained control of herself. Rootlets came easily out of the ground as she pulled, clearing space around the growing potato shoots and tall wheat. She relaxed into the soil, her muscles in control.

Agafia's world had been large and spacious, free of people. Her father had told the family their isolation shielded them, the steppe's vastness a protective cloak, flowing out like a generous train of fabric in all directions. Now that the cloth had shrunk around her like wool in a hot wash, the space echoed with vague threats, emptiness. Peter, her uninvited companion, always by her side, seemed like a cruel comfort in her new understanding of the world.

"You are worldly now," he told her. "A traveler, just like me."

She sucked air in through her teeth and glared at him without retort. Peter had spoken often about the world out there, his stories wild, the places he painted with his words illicit and mythical. They had tempted her. Agafia had allowed herself to listen, to imagine herself there, knowing she'd never visit the metropolises he described. But after her trip, the pull left her. She'd walked streets tangled like thread that led nowhere, unspooling into cement blocks that made it hard to breathe. The sky bore down like a lid rather than opening into heaven—it was hard to imagine traveling up to paradise from such constricted space. Maybe a city full of believers wouldn't be as bad, but Peter had done away with that. She sat back on her knees, then folded her body over them, stretching her arms forward.

Agafia worked all afternoon, grooming the garden until it looked as clean as the tended flower terraces in the city. To lessen the effect, she brought over dirt from her pile and threw it down. She tried to sing like the nuns had when they worked their land, but her voice rang thin and shy without anyone to join her. A rich soil smell rose from the ground in the warm heat of the day and she took off her scarf, letting her hair hang. Her hands slid toward her belly, seeking it under her dress, surprised at its smallness. It was hard to know what to ask for in prayer anymore: forgiveness for conceiving in such worldly sin, forgiveness for losing the thing that grew inside her, or something in between.

That night she dreamt of Dima, working like a metronome with his scythe, clearing a path to nowhere. He wore a loose white shirt that she'd embroidered for him with purple thread and he moved like a beautiful machine. In the dream he sang loud, even though he too was alone, and the song propelled him forward down the path that led to no known place.

■　■　■

Snow Crane and Galina, reunited, took walks. On a narrow trail out of camp they rounded the edge of a range and descended into a small cirque. He told her about the river, the nuns, Agafia's misfortune, how they ate pirozhki in the city. He told her everything in detail so Galina could be there with him, so that one day they could reminisce about the strange trip together. Galina listened, keeping her eyes on the horizon, distracted. The drill had been moved farther afield and she hoped Agafia wouldn't stumble upon it on a walk or hear it grinding into rock. The samples she'd reviewed looked promising. Black, iron-rich layers striped the cores from top to bottom.

Snow Crane found a mossy clearing in the sun and they

stretched out, their finger pads pressed together. Winter and summer in Siberia were two separate places, one flat with cold, one textured with the vigor of a short growing season. Galina wondered what it would be like to witness the transformation from one to the other. This field season was a short one and only a few weeks remained before they returned to the city. She'd miss this fragment of taiga, she knew. Her time there, and the place's very existence, were winding down, and she was already grieving them.

She'd been looking and looking, for some path away from dynamite and the taiga's gutting, but found neither answers nor reprieve in the landscape. It spread before her, indifferent, its usual resplendence on display. David's letter continued to haunt her. *What are we destroying in order to build? Look closely. You can do more. I can too.* She narrowed her eyes. The yellow-green of early summer had turned into a deep, shadowy jade, mature on the land. It was the green of the military helicopter, indestructible. Invulnerable emerald green. Soon winter would hide the ground cover, turn the landscape's palette to whites, to soberness.

"How beautiful it is here," she sighed. "Imagine if we could keep it this way."

Snow Crane had melted into the moss, sinking deep into the cool ground cover, eyes shut, forehead turned toward the sun.

"The Old Believers, they believe in keeping things the same," Snow Crane said. "That truth is preservation. Because what they know, God taught them."

"But we are not Old Believers, are we," Galina said.

She rolled back Snow Crane's shirt and laid her head on his stomach.

"Just leave it all to the Old Believers," he said, through his sleep.

"I'll just leave it to Agafia," she said, and curled into him.

■ ■ ■

Before they departed camp, Galina and Snow Crane pleaded with Agafia and Hugo to leave the homestead. They promised to settle them in a community not far from Moscow, but outside the overwhelming city. They promised to care for them and visit often and told them how much easier it would be if they were closer to them. Agafia and Hugo listened and nodded. Hugo cast his eyes in his daughter's direction, she now the one in charge of their destiny.

"It is worldly," she said.

She walked the geologists down the path toward their camp, and when they had left Hugo out of earshot, she told them, "Maybe if I hadn't lost the babe, I would have come."

That evening she prepared dinner and ate with Hugo in silence at the table. He was cold, and she helped lift him onto the stove and cover him with all of the blankets. At night she heard him wheezing, his soft snore pinched to a high note. When she rose in the morning she could still feel the warmth of his body on the quilts but his chest did not rise with breath. She rested her head on his hand and prayed for a long time. When she finished, Agafia prepared his tomb in the family cemetery. She worked the land, prying open the soil to make room, singing softly to herself. As if working a garden out of season, she mused as she crumbled chunks of soil in her hands. She carried Hugo's body, hollow as a bird's bone, to his resting place in her arms.

"I return you," she sighed as she laid him down.

When Hugo fled the village, he had brought his family. He'd never intended to face the Antichrist alone, nor to leave any of his children to the task unaided. He'd told Agafia, after Dima and Natalia died, "Go, find a village, make a home." Grief had drained him of his faith and his mass, it was the only explanation, Agafia thought. Perhaps her father had stopped believing in the glory that awaited him as a reward for his long fight. Or he'd been more human than she had realized.

When Agafia was young she'd pester her father by the evening fire, pulling his face toward hers by the beard until she could murmur in his ear. "Do you love us or God more?" she'd ask him, because he spoke frequently of his love for God and never uttered the word to the children, though Agafia could feel it on his skin and in his gaze. He'd stare into the fire and tears would glaze his eyes. He never did answer her, but she knew.

Maybe she'd leave one day, maybe she wouldn't. She'd have the whole winter to decide, to ponder quietly what it means to be alone in the world and whether worldliness could temper loneliness or if it would explode her, a quiet supernova, until she too emptied out.

CHAPTER 9
Глава 9

Moscow in fall, the dreary rains and pewter firmament. Galina and Snow Crane kept the windows covered with the blazing poppy curtains to block out the oppressive sky. When the still air grew too humid inside the apartment, she rolled thin cigarettes and leaned out an open window. The bright curtains reflected their cochineal hues into the wet street.

Each day the two went into the office to work, but progress was slow and uninspired. The cores, each a 300-meter extract of the underground, arrived in cylindrical rock sections laid out in wooden crates. How extraordinary to see a mountain packed into a box. Dust alighted from the packages when they unpacked the cores and laid them out on long tables in segments. Snow Crane's job was to log the cores in detail, inspecting them from top to bottom and noting fractures, each time the mineral or its hardness changed, or sediment size shifted in the rock. He ran a greasy red pencil down the core, marking the fluctuations with notches and scribbling his findings in a notebook. It felt almost sensuous to inspect the rock so intimately, but the repetitive nature of the task wearied him. The telltale stripes of the deposit appeared in each core, and he marked the mineral-bearing fragments with bold lines.

Meanwhile, Galina split the cores down the middle, ran metallurgical tests. She'd take pieces of the rock, grind it, and dry it, then peer at the powder through a microscope and run it through her machines. She measured the purity of the iron, its density in the matrix of the rock. Can we free the iron from the other minerals and make it ours? That was the question.

For inspiration, Galina and Snow Crane meandered along empty, rainy boulevards eating ice cream. The street vendors had long ago packed away their machines, but Galina splurged at the apparatchiks' grocery, where pistachio ice cream chilled year-round in humming refrigerators. She couldn't imagine a greater luxury than ice cream in the winter in a flavor other than the rich white plombir. On an unseasonably warm October evening, they walked arm in arm, silent, licking at their cones. Streaks of blue-purple the color of a heron's wings blazed across the sky. A boy in tall socks stuck his tongue out at them as he passed, as if calling out Galina's small bourgeois pleasure, and she stuck hers out back at him.

"There's a Café today," Snow Crane said. "Should we check it out?"

The Café was a doll-sized apartment whose occupant, a woman with shiny black hair, held a monthly literary salon. Galina didn't know how Snow Crane had learned of it, but they'd made a habit of attending in the past year. He seemed to feel at home in forbidden spaces, while she sat straight-backed in the din of this small bohemia, pleased and a little afraid to have found her way there despite everything.

They meandered to the apartment along pedestrian streets, the *click-clack* of trams crisp as alarm clocks somewhere out of sight, then ducked into a dark entryway and felt their way up the smooth steps. Nothing had changed at the Café since they'd last visited, before the summer field season. The same smudged wallpaper framed the room, the same Parisian posters hung askew. A few new faces accompanied the regulars who came there to lean into each other and talk. The host, an elegant woman with a deep, steady voice, kissed Snow Crane on the cheek to welcome him.

"Where have you been?" she asked.

"Who's on?" Snow Crane said.

"A poet. Someone from out of town. A looker." She winked.

Galina spotted an acquaintance sitting in the breakfast nook and joined him as Snow Crane greeted friends. The acquaintance, a man named Andrei who worked for the ministry of propaganda by day, passed Galina a cut crystal shot glass full of clear alcohol, and they toasted. A spread of salted cucumber spears and pickled watermelon lay before her, but the spirits were so clean she didn't touch the snacks.

Galina liked it best when poets read at the Café. They channeled old rabbis in their incantations, sing-chanting their verses as if they were Torah passages. That evening's poet would be reading from a new manuscript. He was in town from some far-flung northern village shopping the book to the Moscow publishing houses. Tucked back in the corner, she watched the man make rounds in the kitchen and living room, leaning over to introduce himself, doing little to conceal his nervous energy. He had a lupine quality, slinky. A pleasant buzz crept in as she swallowed.

Andrei refilled their glasses, the smell of fresh-cut grass and shaving foam rising from the new pour.

The poet approached and jutted his chin toward the jar.

"Got any to share with a poor poet?" he asked.

Andrei grabbed another tumbler to fill. The three of them clinked glasses.

"What do you do?" the poet asked.

"I work for the ministry of propaganda." Andrei grinned. "Means I'm a poet, like you."

"I was admiring your work today on the streets," the poet said. "Better advice than my mama ever gave me."

"The mamas are busy working, so we do our best to help them out," Andrei told him.

"Sometimes the mamas are just too drunk," the poet said.

"Lucky mamas." Andrei reached for the jar.

"And what about you?" the poet addressed Galina.

"I'm a geologist," she told him.

"Ah." The poet closed his eyes. "A mystic."

The host flicked the lights off and on and tapped a butter knife on a glass.

"Let's get started," she said.

When the conversations around her quieted, she directed the gathered people's attention to the poet. He dug a faded blue folder out of a leather bag, brought together several pages, and climbed onto a chair.

"My name is Marat," he said. "It's nice to be back in my dear, sad Moscow. You see, I've been working on one of the dams up north."

"A people's poet!" someone shouted.

Galina searched for Snow Crane across the room. He was deep in conversation, leaning in toward another man she didn't recognize, not paying attention. She motioned for Andrei to let her out of the booth, but he put a finger up to his lips in mock seriousness and settled his elbows on the table, blocking her.

Marat cleared his throat. He read to a rapt room for ten minutes. He read love poems—to places, women, work. The poems worshiped those entities all on the same plane, a love spread generously and evenly, like cream on a cake. His words spliced joy and misery. Galina could see the boy Snow Crane had described in the man before her. The flutter of his lids and the sway of his body. He was an atmosphere. He still sprinkled geology terms into his verses. His eyes were shiny and mischievous.

When he finished, he was visibly depleted and the audience was exhilarated. A live net stretched across the room, crackling with electricity. Andrei slapped him on the back and poured him another drink. People tried to approach Marat, to praise him and talk, but he took refuge behind Galina, still sweating, smiling shyly. Snow Crane squeezed through the crowd. "Hey, poet," he said. "Do you have a place to sleep?"

■ ■ ■

It had taken Marat a month to arrive. He hitched rides on trucks to reach a railway station, where he used years of meager savings to buy a ticket west, to Moscow. He had no permit to come to the city and slipped an extra bill to the ticket seller behind the glass. An attendant, her body packed into an army-green pencil skirt and a shirt with pocket flaps over her commanding breasts, took his ticket and escorted him to a compartment. A family was already slicing bologna on the shared table between their bunks. The matriarch offered him tea out of a floral thermos, as if Marat were one of her own, and handed him a sandwich.

The wood-lined cubicle absorbed the afternoon's golden light. Marat made his bed on the top bunk, where he could look down on the family below and through the window unobstructed. For days, he gazed out the window and sipped his roommates' tea. Pink dawns and dusks flared to illuminate miles of white fields, snow-crusted trees, and puffing chimneys, as if the train cut across Aiva-zovsky's Romantic canvases. At stations, bundled women boarded the train with towel-wrapped tubs full of pale pirozhki with potato, onion, mushroom. He bought some at each stop, to share with the family in his compartment. He'd fall asleep to the train's *chug-chug*. He slept soundly until the first light hit the mirror on the wall and flooded the cabin with a new day. Mornings, he'd make his way to the bathroom, the ground streaking by below the metal toilet bowl, then back toward his cabin, the pretty curtains in the train car's hall swinging side to side. More tea. The children cackling over a game of cards. He could have stayed on the train forever.

The dam where he'd labored had been a forgotten project, ma-terializing in starts and stops, out of sight of the public for decades. Prisoners had worked and died on it. Then volunteers like him had cobbled together plinths and great walls to hold back water. The vast-ness of the structure tempered the illusion of progress, as if some great machine destroyed each inch of wall that rose, like Penelope weaving and unweaving Laertes's funeral shroud. Marat hadn't cared much about the actual project, but he liked the physical labor of the days, the repetitive nature of the work that let his mind wander. He'd met the girl with chalcedony eyes. She was an apparition in the wild and ultimately not built for it. She'd died of exhaustion or cold, and when he kissed her blue lips for the last time, Marat had resolved to leave. He signed up for other projects—a railway, a road, a bridge, a town. Each more improbable than the last. The bigness of the land called for big infrastructure, the foreman of each project said. Marat looked out upon the construction sites and watched his fellow volunteers crawl all around them like ants. His mind stopped wandering, bogged down by the massive piles of mud, rock, timber, and rebar, unable to see over them.

Marat asked for time off but was not granted it. He asked for permission to transfer back to Moscow but was denied it. He'd found a way to go anyway. He didn't know what he'd find there, what exactly he was looking for, except a place already built, something not wide open to the elements or the capriciousness of shifting plans. The civilization around him was being remolded, remade, and as a ward of the state, first as an orphan, then a worker, he served as receptor, as guinea pig. But he wanted something primal, some way of being that did not have to be taught, did not have to be constructed. As he sped across time zones, he decided he was looking for deeper time. As if in going back west he'd find longitudes delineating centuries, universes, alternative versions of himself. He would backtrack to a different him, perhaps when he was more optimistic. More youthful.

Instead, he arrived at the terminal tired, lost. He stopped by the orphanage, the last place he'd lived in Moscow, and found one of the old nannies there. He and Vera were both grown now, just a couple of years apart. She took him home, to her room in a long-forgotten communal apartment, and made love to him on her creaky daybed. A vine wound round the room in a great spiral, its tendrils encircling the bed along the wall and ceiling.

"I took it from the orphanage," she said.

Vera cut back his hair, smoothed his brows with her firm thumbs, patched his pants. In the splotchy mirror of the shared bathroom, he inspected his face. White lines dug into the tanned skin around his eyes. Gray framed his hairline. He resembled the worksites where'd he'd wasted all his youth: somehow dated and old before they were ever finished.

The nanny didn't mind having him around when she returned from long days at the orphanage.

"The kids are getting brattier," she told him.

"You're just getting tired, like the rest of us," he said, laughing.

He prepared simple meals in the communal kitchen and they ate together in the evenings.

He began to work on his poems, by candlelight, while she slept.

"Still writing?" she said, chuckling, when she found his papers one morning.

Marat thought about his old friend, about where he'd ended up, whether the letters Marat had written to him in the army ever reached him. He wanted to dedicate his book to him—there was no one else.

When Marat laid eyes on Snow Crane, he thought him a mirage conjured by his loneliness. How many times had he summoned in his mind the woman that he'd loved? But there he was, the strange smell he always carried, of freshly peeled carrots, the serious open gaze, his voice.

They walked home that night delirious with joy, holding on to one another. They touched each other constantly, each assuring himself of the other's realness—the firmness of the skin, the tangle of hair, each with his calloused hands. Galina exulted along with them, infected by their radiance. Over tea, until dawn, cheeks rubied with delight, they basked in the unexpected return of the other into their lives. By the next day, Marat brought his small bag from Vera's apartment to Galina's and Snow Crane's and settled on the couch. He and Snow Crane reunited still as children, the elapsed time erased by absence, and so resumed where they left off, a place of chance encounters, hope.

They talked again about books they loved, passing between them tattered copies procured by illicit means. Marat read Snow Crane and Galina poems after dinner and took to asking them about rocks, so that his verses acquired new terms, new metaphors. Galina brought home Georgian wine and the best ingredients she could procure with her government ID, and Marat cooked while the two of them worked. They returned to spreads of cutlets, pickled salads, potatoes done up a thousand ways, and ate together at the big table as if it were a party each day.

Sometimes they had real parties. Snow Crane invited Café regulars, Galina called girlfriends from school and university, and Marat brought Vera. Dozens of people piled into the small apartment and leaned into each other and laughed. They debated the latest animation trends, economic policies, and where in the Arctic ice one could find the deepest blues. Galina's girlfriends pulled her behind the curtains, as if they were doors, and asked her discreetly about the new man in their milieu.

"Oh, him?" she'd say, smiling at Marat across the room. "We found him at the Café."

One night Galina cooked plov and everyone ate too much, so that one by one they began to drop to the floor and arrange themselves in a tangle of bodies until the rug was covered with limbs splayed in this direction and that. Heads rested on bellies and arms intertwined legs and hair fell across necks. A sensual sleepiness descended on the gathering.

"What is this?" Galina said in pretend incredulousness.

She put on a Beatles record she'd bought counterfeit and tiptoed between the bodies until she found Marat, squeezed between Vera and the couch.

"Dance with me!" she said.

Marat hopped up and took her by the hand, and they both climbed up on the sofa. They jumped up and down, shaking their hips and heads, sweat blistering their hairlines, until the human rug below began to shift, to rise. They played the record a dozen times, flipping it over and over until the neighbor began to bang on the ceiling with a broom.

"To feeling human," Marat toasted during an intermission, "when we're all just animals!"

"Don't insult the animals," Snow Crane said, and they all clinked their glasses so the room rang out like the joyous *trezvon* bells of a country church.

This was an intermission. Marat didn't know what would happen next. He had no place to live, no permission to stay in the city, which meant he could not legally work. He was not a member of the writers' union, so his poems would never see the light of day. He levitated in the in-between space as if it was a bonus life granted him, uneager to rush beyond the confines of the apartment, his friends, the suspended weeks that ticked by on the calendar. He took to reading tea leaves to make sense of the moment, to uncover some idea of what a future might hold. He'd slurp the last of a cup of tea and flip it upside down on the saucer before assuming what Galina called his oracle voice.

"We have to wait for it to dry," he'd say.

Then he'd divine: glory for Galina; another love, perhaps some children for himself; a trip to a faraway place for Snow Crane. He saw the same things each time, as if by repetition he could make them true.

But Marat also allowed the unknowable to overwhelm him. It came in like a tide, regular, every other day or so, and covered him. On those days he'd flip over the cup, fold his arms as the leaves settled into place, then sigh before peering inside.

"Hm," he'd say.

"What?"

Marat would gaze blankly at the Rorschach smudge of leaves covering one side of the porcelain, curling into jagged waves along the rim.

"What do you think it means?" Snow Crane would prod, sensitive to his friend's moods.

"Maybe," Marat would mope, "it all means nothing."

■ ■ ■

Galina liked having Marat around. She liked the person she became with him, the self to which Snow Crane returned—purer versions of themselves, unencumbered by their years. She got to see Snow

Crane in the glow of an old cheerfulness. This was new to her, and beautiful. At first she would sit back and observe them, smoking cigarettes, content with the pleasure afforded her through osmosis. They would flop down on the floor, on their bellies, scheming and cackling. She'd bring them tea and sweets, motherlike in her admiration. They made efforts to involve her, but they spoke in a boyhood shorthand she could not access and she'd wave an arm at them, relieving them of the pressure to include her. Some nights Galina would call a girlfriend and spend an evening at her house, often in the din of children and husbands and mothers-in-law, but the busyness of other people's lives made her feel lonely. A not unpleasant solitude overtook her. She began to walk the streets, thinking that just maybe she'd run into her old friend too, and they all four could be an island of happiness. It was winter, cold, dark, and she strolled the streets alone, passing like a shadow under yellow streetlights. The wind stung her face and lungs but she returned home refreshed, as if from a run.

On nights she didn't want to go out she'd curl up in the other room, away from Snow Crane and Marat, with tea and a stack of photo books. She'd taken to buying them when she was learning to use her camera, mostly for work. They were hard to find but she'd amassed a small collection that she liked leafing through. Her prized possession was an album of French architectural photos, which impressed her both with its foreignness and the richness of its black ink, the sharpness of the lines between shadows. She also had a book of portraiture, one by a travel photographer featuring every closed-off place she wished to visit, a few by a Czech named Vilém Heckel, mostly of mountains, and an album called *The Music of the Russian Forest.* In addition, she had two instructional manuals; they were both called *Photohunting,* but one inexplicably featured a mouse climbing out of a camera on the cover while the other had an etched owl. The first *Photohunting* had *Trigger Pulled, Beauty Born* printed on the inner flap.

She flipped through the books absent-mindedly at first, lingering on a detail, an angle, falling into reverie on favorite full-bleed pages. It was a meditation and she rarely read the text, if there was any. When she did, it annoyed her. In *The Music of the Russian Forest,* in particular, the introduction was sopped with romanticism and the swoony captions failed to provide even the most basic information about the captured moment or place. In one picture of a beaver, it read, *Even the beaver has his secrets,* which made her turn the page so forcefully it ripped. But what she liked about the book was that it was arranged by season, the Russian forest in some unnamed stretch of taiga through spring, summer, fall, that Russian condition between late fall and full winter called *predzimie,* then winter, then again spring. She flipped back and forth through the winter, searching for signs of people, as if the photos were a looking glass that might allow her to peer in on Agafia and, seeing nothing more than the gray calm, assure her of her friend's safety. She felt closer to Agafia being able to imagine her in the depths of that season, on that landscape.

With time, she stopped opening the French book and the portraits, lingering instead on the manuals, the book on forests, the other on mountains. She had looked at the books a million times but only now noticed how they idolized the landscape. Page after glossy page of breathless scenery, the soft green tips of a pine's new growth glowing against dark wood, sunsets in every hue of purple and rose gold, Vilém Heckel's mountains particularly pretty in black and white. As if in nature there was not an ugly corner to out. There was one photo of deep tracks in mud, the closest any of the books got to something unidyllic, and even that had the promise of rebirth, spring melt readying the fields, a beauty in the making. Had she chosen these books deliberately, subconsciously, each an ode to the very untouched wildness her work compromised? That's what she started to wonder as she thumbed the pages.

Sometimes she'd lay out her own photos from the field on the floor next to the open books and admire them together. There was beauty where she trod too, the same soft light, same bend to the grass and trees under the weight of wind, same river slicing through silence and wood, same wildflower-speckled horizons. They were the same pictures she used at work to trace her surveying routes and to verify maps. All it took was a shift in perspective to see heaven rather than lode.

She'd wander into the living room, a print in hand or a book open to a fingerprinted page, and set it down in front of Snow Crane and Marat. "I can't stand the thought of losing this," she'd say. "Of Agafia losing this." Snow Crane would smile at her, take her hand, say, "The landscape changes, it moves even without you." Marat would acquiesce, sigh, pull the picture toward him. "Progress proceeds," he'd say.

Galina wanted someone to agree with her, to punish her, to tell her to stop extracting mineral. She wanted to be with others who were troubled by the opening of land to sky. People who could put words to the vague emotions she'd been feeling since she started this job, an unwillingness to engage with the project, a new way of seeing the rocks that made her reluctant to blast them. She longed to protect Agafia and her home; in so doing it felt like she could protect some grander thing, a pureness of place, a well of pleasure, an unmapped space with room to dream.

She began to prowl the halls around her lab during lunch breaks or after work, listing from room to room like a lost ship. Sometimes she'd walk over to her old university building, as if she might find something to continue her education, prolong her inquiry into the meaning of a mine. One evening she was walking down a hall when people started pouring out of a basement classroom. They were talking seriously and excitedly among themselves, clutching each other by the elbow.

"Excuse me," Galina called out to a woman walking alone, "what was this meeting?"

The woman eyed Galina for a moment before answering. "It's a conservation club, we meet every Wednesday at six," she said.

"A conservation club?" Galina asked. But another woman had called out to the first, who was rushing off to join her.

When Galina returned home she told Snow Crane and Marat about the scene, the youthfulness and exuberance of the crowd.

"How mysterious and banal!" Marat was delighted. "In the basement!"

"I think I'll go next week," she said.

"David called," Snow Crane told her. "The American. He's going to be in Moscow on Tuesday, I told him to come by."

David showed up on a rainy evening with a soggy box of chocolates and a jar of his own potato vodka.

"I can't wait to get home," he told them.

"Your work is done?" Galina asked.

"My work is useless," he said. "And my mother is sick."

Marat prepared tea spiked with vodka and they picked at the chocolate squares.

"I've been thinking about your letter," Galina said. "You want me to sabotage the mine."

"Eh," he said, "in America we call it a Hail Mary."

"Sounds religious."

"Worse," David said. "It's an American football metaphor."

"We don't play that here," Snow Crane said.

Galina sipped from a chipped cup. The warm vodka went down thick and pleasant.

"Here it's complicated," Galina said.

"It's complicated everywhere."

"What are you in town for anyway?" Snow Crane asked.

"My handlers, they want me to give a televised address about our countries' relations before I go. Something about birds. It didn't sound like I had a choice," David said. "I have a few days to kill."

The next day he joined Snow Crane and Galina at the office. They toured David around and showed him all their samples. Snow Crane gave him a polished cross-section disk from a core. David seemed melancholy, more subdued than the gregarious person Galina remembered. They ate an early dinner at a restaurant downtown.

"I'm going to a meeting tonight," she told him. "I don't really know what it's about, but could be interesting. Why don't you come along?"

They rode the tram together, its windows fogged with riders' breath. It rocked precariously on the rails, jostling the people against each other. She wondered if she hadn't imagined the previous week's encounter, but when they descended to the windowless hall that smelled of mold and body odor, they heard the thrum of voices from around the corner. Approaching, they saw people with lustrous hair and pants that hugged their thighs ambling in in twos and threes, smoking cigarettes. By the time the proceedings started, they'd puffed a cloud of smoke so dense that their bodies materialized in the haze as mere mirages. The group was mostly students from the sciences departments. Young, incubated in the warmth of the post-Stalin thaw, eager to talk in full-throated voices. Galina slunk down in her seat, the oldest, quietest person in the room. David took on the liveliness around him, upright beside her.

A man rose and parted the smoke as he moved from the back of the room to the front and sat casually on a desk. He wore a beard and what looked like a field uniform—cargo pants, faded button-down. "I see a lot of newcomers today," he said, and held each attendee with his gaze as he scanned the room.

"We are here to talk about how we can protect the land," he announced. "Protect it from what?"

It was a rhetorical question and he began to answer it. The students shook their heads as he named the dams being planned across the Soviet territory. The list was long, a meditation. He narrated the Carpathian logging operations that shaved mountains of their pines. He painted a picture of virgin lands besieged by an army of slow-moving tractors planting row after interminable row of corn and wheat.

"And the mines!" the man said. David elbowed Galina in the shoulder and smiled. The man told of how they stained rivers red and moved whole mountains with no regard for the life there. Galina slid down in her chair. The images he summoned were terrifying. Dangerous.

As a student, Galina had attended conventions organized by the All-Russian Society for the Protection of Nature. The society, which had formed shortly after the revolution, had initially embodied the idealism of the 1920s. A vision of nature as something to be preserved and improved for the value-added benefit of man had already taken hold, but a dream of true utopias still hung like a wisp of incense smoke in the air. Science had already been co-opted as a tool for production, but scientists still had a seat at the table.

By the time Galina went to the meetings in the 1960s, party apparatchiks had almost completely taken over. They met to venerate nature in the rhetoric of numbers: how fruitful the forests, how giving the ore, how dense the schools of fish in the nets. The discussions focused on how to preserve productivity. She'd been invited to those gatherings as a miner, the face of future producers everywhere, as if to signal that the society and she, they, were united.

This meeting was different. The man described a biological world autonomous and violated, plagued by the nation's hunger for minerals, soil, energy. What had been noble goals in the mouths of the state's leaders were rotten deeds in his, aimed at destroying the land, the air, the essence of the sprawling Russian empire.

"We've named our sons Tractor and our daughters Electrification!" he exclaimed. "Because we are a nation blinded by the promise of progress. But what is progress?"

"He's good!" David whispered in Galina's ear. "Like an American preacher!"

The man went on, conjuring vast destruction, expanses of pillaged forest, denuded mountains and seas. *Such doom*, Galina thought, listening. Wasn't this what she wanted, someone to talk straight? But she found the man unsympathetic. The iron she mined would build tractors, so her people wouldn't have to break their backs. That's why people named their sons Tractor. Something noble in that.

She wanted less talk, more doing. She'd recently read a report about a group of Canadians who tried to stop a Soviet whaling ship. The way the Canadians spoke about the animals sounded just like this man, as if the whalers were despoiling a pure and wrathful Eden, but they did more than speak. Two Canadians in an inflatable boat placed themselves between the Russian whaling ship and its prey, raising their arms to make themselves tall. They thought their bodies would deter the kill. The whalers fired the harpoon cannon anyway, the rope arcing gracefully over the Canadians, who ducked in disbelief. The photos had made them look ridiculous. They didn't accomplish much, but Galina thought their attempts worthwhile, rather brave. She could hear her father going on about the activists' histrionics in her head. That's what her father had named any calls for reform: *histrionics*. She didn't agree with her father, which made her suddenly smile.

The man was still talking. She'd grown used to Snow Crane's peaceful demeanor, the unobtrusive way he communicated, his sparseness of words. She missed him when he wasn't with her. As if his way of being made the world kinder overall. She refocused on the man.

"You may think it is patriotic to take our natural resources from the ground, the water, the very air. But a true patriot knows when to stop," he said. "Because she is wonder and beauty and chaos and order all at once. Because we are part of her and she is part of us, and it's just pure, simple self-preservation."

He'd rolled up his sleeves and his eyes darted all around, frenzied. His pitch was to reestablish old *zapovedniks*, as well as to create new ones. The preserves had first been decreed before the turn of the century; the soil scientist Vasily Dokuchaev had proposed parcels of land free from human use, to study the soils. After the revolution, dozens more *zapovedniks* made up a Noah's ark of ecologies, bite-size undeveloped acreage of each wild ecosystem within the Union's borders. Scientists could enter and study and sample, but everyone else was to stay out, to let nature alone. As if divorcing people from nature was possible.

Stalin closed many of the *zapovedniks*; the scientists hadn't proved their worth. No big discoveries came from the fallow land, no innovations emerged. Friends—fellow scientists—told Galina that people used the remaining *zapovedniks* to graze cows or as hunting grounds. She'd never visited one but had liked the idea of them: an antithesis to daily life, a counterweight to the constant drumbeat of yield numbers. Something untouchable. She wanted to make her mountain into one, Agafia its caretaker. Yes, she thought, that singular blip of land, she'd draw a rhombus around her camp, like a great fence, and save it from herself. It was a funny idea, like a child's notion, and Galina smiled to herself again.

"You, the students gathered here, have the power to fight for the taiga, the steppe, the forest," the man was saying. "To protect them and protect yourselves."

The young people stirred in their seats, lit new cigarettes, and began to talk all at once. It sounded to Galina like an appealing but abstract provocation. What exactly was she supposed to do to protect them all, to protect Agafia? David turned to her and leaned in.

"I should've been hanging out with this guy the whole time," he said.

David wanted to talk to the speaker, but the man was mobbed with students, so he and Galina left and walked to his hotel.

"That was exciting!" he told her.

"I found him harsh," Galina said. "Maybe I'm too much of a loner for group rage."

She was in a talking mood, and as they walked she told him about the Canadians and the whales, the photo books she'd been poring over, Agafia, her father, and her own winter malaise, that settling discomfort within her that what she did for work should not be done, not there, not that way, not now. She hadn't wanted to burden Snow Crane with everything since Marat arrived, but David was comfortable to talk with, the easy smile, a click in his throat acknowledging her, telling her to proceed. He told her about his own underground work in America, the lack of understanding that had brought him to Russia, his father's years in the mill and the roses dusted with soot.

"We're both a little confused, aren't we?" Galina said.

"Plus daddy issues." David winked.

They walked in silence awhile, under yellow-green streetlights and the buzz of night. What Galina wanted was for the mine to be an option, not a destiny. It didn't seem possible in her country, so full of small, uncontested destinies. Galina had fought her fated path—her father's path—but she hadn't known she could ask bigger questions.

"What if we could be like the Canadians," she said. "Hold up our hands against the mine."

"They'll singe your arm hairs with dynamite," David said.

They'd arrived at his hotel. A woman in uniform stood at the entryway checking documents, and he began to dig his passport out of his pocket.

"But we can try," David said.

Galina took off her glove and held out a pinky to David. He latched his own pinky to hers and squeezed.

"To trying," she said. He disappeared through the door.

■ ■ ■

Galina worked on the reports for her bosses. The ore is abundant, she wrote. Iron and manganese could supply the nation's needs for at least a decade. The ore would have to be mined in open pits, shaving off mountaintops and burrowing down in spirals until the workers opened kilometer-deep voids, emptying them of the minerals. No nearby coal meant added expenses for treating the ore. A railroad would have to be built, she wrote, to deliver the ore to faraway processing facilities. That would certainly drive up cost on a per ton basis. A homestead, housing one family, would have to be destroyed.

She sat by her office window, early evening. The traffic noise, the loud honking and perpetual clatter of cars zooming past, made thinking hard. The risks are abundant, she wrote. An analysis of the destruction the mine would bring to the surrounding environment is necessary, she wrote. The biome has barely been studied and the project could jeopardize the survival of an intact ecosystem, she wrote. The deposit is academically interesting and should be investigated further to understand its origins before extraction. The endeavor is probably not economical, she added hopefully.

In geology, there are questions, and the rocks, with time, give up answers. The answers are mutable; new rocks refine and add insights to stories and timelines. Little by little, history gains footing on scree and rock face. But to get there, one must start with questions, not answers. In her work it had always been the other way around. First the answer: progress, technology, development. Then there's no room for questions. The report deadline loomed, just a week away, but she took the pages she'd typed and put them in a drawer, under a polished rock paperweight.

At home Galina obsessed about Agafia. Winter in Siberia had long since come and there was no checking in on her, no way to send word or receive it from the sealed white chamber of her land. She worked herself up and Snow Crane talked her down, recalling tremulously their relatively recent appearance in Agafia's life and the years she'd spent surviving without them.

"The taiga will kill her," Galina would say.

"It hasn't killed her yet," Snow Crane would remind her.

"She sounds indestructible," Marat would joke. Uncomforted, Galina would imagine the snow bloodied after a wolf attack, the hut collapsed under the snow's weight, the light footsteps, perhaps, of another visitor.

Agafia the person and Agafia the apologue; the fleshly embodiment of Galina's own uncertainties haunted her shrinking daylight hours. Agafia's needs were both primal—food, clothing, love—and existential—protection from the Antichrist, safety from the mine and the modern world—so that it was easy to paint Galina's own doubts onto her. To let her be the vessel for her own baggage.

That millstone was the mine, the other thing she obsessed over at work and in the confines of their brightly wallpapered apartment. To stamp her approval on the project would be to betray the mountain, that strange setting of her romance with Snow Crane, their friend's refuge, and an autonomous living world. She invoked Agafia's wind-worn face like a hologram, to consult her in her mind.

"What do I do about this mine?" she asked the hologram.

But Agafia did not know about mines or iron yields and she flickered in and out of Galina's imagination without a word, a silent half-smile her only guidance.

■　■　■

A couple of nights after the conservation meeting, Galina and Snow Crane sat watching the evening news. The anchor interviewed a young man with a mustache about a supercomputer he was building. Children with bows lush as peonies atop their heads performed onstage. In the following segment, a well-fed, gentlemanly battalion of dignitaries in dark suits faced the camera in a long line. They thrust out their arms at each other to shake and slap square shoulders. An American flag and a Soviet one drooped in the background, and taxidermied birds on little stands stood lined up on a wide, polished table. One of the men came forward to the microphone and cleared his throat.

"We are coming to you live this evening because our countries have put aside great differences for a common good," the man said. "That common good is the protection of the wild migratory birds of our great lands. These birds, unaware of the borders that divide nations, share flyways that bring us together. Recognizing that, we must protect their breeding, wintering, feeding, and molting areas, so these amazing creatures can continue to soar in great numbers."

"What is this?" Galina asked. Snow Crane picked up a book, uninterested.

The man on TV swept his hand toward the stuffed birds on the table, and the camera zoomed in on the specimens, panning across them slowly. Another man stepped forward from the line.

"Our great nations are signing an agreement to protect these birds," the man said.

He shuffled through his sheaf of papers and also cleared his throat. He started to list the names of bird species that would be protected by the agreement's signing.

Yellow-billed Loon

Red-necked Grebe

Black-footed Albatross

Red-faced Cormorant

White-fronted Goose

Green-winged Teal

He read in a sad, even voice, as if eulogizing the birds rather than setting them up for success.

New Zealand Shearwater

Bonin Island Petrel

Chinese Least Bittern

Baikal Teal

European Wigeon

American Wigeon

The man took a sip of water and read on.

Black Brant

Garganey

Shoveler

Whooper Swan

Sooty Shearwater

Fulmar

Another man thanked the reader, who folded up his papers and retreated into the line. Yet another man stepped out of the line, up to the microphone.

"David," Galina muttered in recognition.

"He mentioned something about birds," Snow Crane said, looking up from his book.

"I didn't recognize him in the suit."

Galina turned up the volume. David tapped the microphone with three fingers. He folded the piece of paper he'd been holding in his hand and withdrew an envelope from inside his suit jacket. He introduced himself.

"I'm so glad to see this agreement come to fruition," David said in his accented Russian. "But treaties and agreements and plans are promises. At pivotal times like today, we also need action."

The men in the line behind him exchanged looks, and one of them stepped forward hesitantly. David smiled and waved him back to his place in the formation before facing the camera.

"My father was a great believer in industry."

He approached the camera and removed a photo from the envelope. He held it up to the camera, filling the frame with the image of his father grinning in a hard hat. Then he held up a photo of Pittsburgh's skyline retreating into heavy smog.

"My city has given up its rivers and air to industry. And our health has followed with it."

"What the hell is going on?" Snow Crane asked.

Snow Crane put down his book. He and Galina held hands, scooted up to the television, rapt. David was talking fast—about the mill, the air—and sweating. He held up another picture of his father, this time in a hospital bed, ensnared in tubes. He was saying the mill did this, was doing this now to other men. When he lowered the photo, several of the suits in line behind him stepped forward, grabbing the microphone. David looked directly into the camera.

"You can do more," he said.

The men detained him by both arms, their mouths moving in exaggerated shapes, though no sound came from the TV. The screen blinked off. When it reappeared, a newscaster was shuffling papers. He began to read, but the engineer must have forgotten to turn the sound back on, so he moved his mouth silently, like a fish.

CHAPTER 10
Глава 10

Weeks after David's strange appearance on the main news program, people still whispered about it. Walking arm in arm in the bitter cold, at stores buying groceries, in the halls of the university, Galina and Snow Crane caught snatches of conversation about the strange American and his strange message that reverberated at a low frequency through the populace. Someone had an uncle who lived near a new dam who told of barren waters, and someone had a cousin who'd seen Lake Baikal bloom green with algae, and someone walked on the shore of the shrinking Aral Sea, and someone had a sister who worked on a timber operation and sent letters about the fields of fallen trees, which reminded her of war grounds after battle. An impressionistic sense of dread seeped into the city. Passersby talked about the handsome American and his worn photos, unclear of the exact outlines of his message, though intuiting its substance. David the oracle, cut short, leaving the city's information-hungry public grasping.

Others filled in the blanks for him. The Union of Soviet Writers published a call to amend the constitution to make room for new laws on nature. They'd convinced a group of prominent biologists to pen an article calling for the formation of an organ

in the Union's vast bureaucracy to take up environmental matters. This department, they wrote, would oversee projects from
other departments and make final decisions about plans with the
potential to affect the living world. The proposal was based on
other countries' systems and as such was an almost guaranteed
nonstarter.

Students from the university staged a demonstration demanding new *zapovedniks*. Galina recognized some of them from the
meeting when she walked by. They held hand-drawn signs, mouths
open in a long scream. The man who'd led the meeting was nowhere to be seen. Galina looked for David in the small crowd, but
of course he was long gone, deported with great fanfare to his own
land. Some punishment, Galina thought.

Agronomists published a letter criticizing soil rotation policies,
explaining that current practices depleted soils' natural minerals.
Ecologists at the zoo scared children and their parents, holding up
photogenic animals and announcing dramatically their expected
extirpation in the wild. It was as if the city, in the dead of winter,
woke to the world's aliveness when David appeared on their television sets. People breathed the land's vulnerability, palpable in the
very air, and burst to talk about it, like witnesses at the scene of a
daytime crime.

Galina and Snow Crane didn't partake. Between themselves
they marveled at the citizens' awakening, how readily the populace
jumped to defend the living world, something that had always been
there. But Galina didn't go to any more meetings, and Snow Crane
engaged little with anything outside their home—Galina, Marat,
and their small group of friends his entire universe.

The report was already late. Galina kept telling her bosses she needed to double-check the data. On a day when the cold frosted her office windows and blocked out the weak sun, she took out the folder of papers from the drawer. She closed her office door and reread what she'd written. Even with her caveats and qualifications, the mine was an inevitability. An apparition of Agafia's pale face shimmered in the half-dark. Her toothy smile and guiltless laugh animated the phantom. Snow Crane knocked on the door to see if Galina was ready to go home, but she waved him on.

"I'll be home late tonight," she said, and kissed him on the forehead.

Galina had helped open several mines. She rarely visited the sites once the diggers transformed the land, but once she'd been sent to consult on an operation years after her initial work there. She remembered driving to the site: a mud maw stretched where a craggy outcrop once parted land from sky. Machines belched out an arrhythmic strain in a steady drizzle. The air hung about her like boiled wool, curtaining off the familiar trees and ridgelines in the distance, so only the raw, oxidizing earth filled her view. The hole ran so deep into the ground that when she stood on the edge and peeked in she envisioned magma seeping into the bottom, like water leaching into a pocket of dug sand at a water's edge. With each scoop of dirt the dragline lifted out, she'd watched for molten rock to bleed through the brown muck. She kept a rock from that mine on her desk and fingered it as she turned the report's pages. What had struck her then was the permanency of the change—not a tear in the landscape, but a takeover. The mine became the terrain, the land, the thing on offer rather than a part of it. It didn't share space; it swallowed space.

The new project was expected to be bigger than the one she recalled. It would devour Agafia, the hut, the river, using the great pines as toothpicks. She turned to the first page of the report. She wished to write about the mine before construction. An option, not an inevitability. To capture the liminal space between landscape and lode, when something hung in the balance. About the land before transformation and how the alpenglow flushed redder than a smelter. How the wolf songs would disappear under a drill's echo. How Agafia might not survive the heartbreak of such imposed worldliness. She could dare ask: What would an iron mine mean out there? *What are we destroying in order to build? Look closely.*

She loaded a fresh sheet of paper into the typewriter and sat, smoking. She thought of Agafia's trust in her God and in Galina, the two bodies she should've trusted least. Agafia hadn't examined her trust but allowed her human heart to guide her. Though small and insignificant, Agafia had said, she contained the land and heaven in her, her people's past and future, their life and death, and so she listened when her heart spoke. That's how she knew to stay in the taiga, and there was no reasoning with that.

When Galina finally started typing, something wholly unexpected appeared on the page. Iron deposits are sparse and inconsistent at the study site, she wrote. While she could not be sure without further sampling in the remote taiga, she thought the existing deposits had been washed in from mineral-rich areas nearby. She wrote that she'd spent two field seasons trying to chase down mineral layers, but they thinned out and disappeared into rocky dead ends. While early analysis confirmed the belief that vast deposits stretched across this part of the taiga, more detailed scrutiny flipped our understanding of the mine's promise, she went on. The project would not make a return on investment once realized. Nearby areas could very well yield abundant quarries as the neighboring mountain ranges had proven to be rich in mineral, but this particular rock fold held little of value for the Union, she concluded.

She lit another cigarette and flipped through the sheaf of papers. She tucked in Snow Crane's core logs and her own mineralization reports. Her boss wasn't a geologist and she doubted he'd catch the discrepancy between the data and her conclusions. Would her colleagues contradict her? she thought. When she tried to lift the cigarette to her mouth, she jabbed it into her cheek. Her entire body shook. What did her heart know? Her teeth chattered and the heels of her shoes drummed on the parquet. *How tricky science is here*, she thought. Before Galina left the office, she slipped the new report under her boss's door.

■ ■ ■

Galina didn't tell Snow Crane about the made-up report, but when he rolled over in the morning her tense body alarmed him and he sat up, looking at her for an explanation. The morning was crisp but Snow Crane's skin radiated intense heat, as if he could not properly contain his own thermal processes, just like the city of M. She tugged him back toward her, under the silken, heavy quilt, and knotted herself around him.

"Let's call in sick and only do things we want to do today," she murmured. "All day."

She heaved the covers over their heads. His mouth found her shoulder, her neck. Her scent and closeness liquefied him.

"What will we do?" he asked.

"Let's go to a museum. Then maybe even a restaurant."

Marat had gone to spend the day with Vera, so they ate breakfast naked, wrapped only in blankets. They dressed, took the train to the Tretyakovskaya Station, hands latched. The marble bore down on them when they exited the train and Galina ran up the steps to the surface, rising from the depth toward air. At the Tretyakov Gallery they meandered through the wash of kids' voices echoing in the long halls. The old building was poorly heated and people kept their heavy robe-like coats on, lending the noisy processions a religious air. Galina and Snow Crane wound between paintings in thick frames without pausing, happy to shuffle in the grooves and scuffs of past visitors, until they drifted into a dimly lit dead-end room occupied by a passel of head-covered grannies. They stood all facing one direction, eyeing a painting.

A small sign by the piece attributed it to the icon painter Andrei Rublev. Three gold-winged figures seated around a low table, each in a voluminous robe—the first in matte pink, patchy like a rhodonite; the second the color of cherry flesh and dusky grape hyacinths; the last in the greens and blues of springtime mountains. The angels' heads, each in a white glow, inclined toward each other like flower heads bending to the sun.

"Granny," Snow Crane said, tapping one of the women on the shoulder. "What are we looking at?"

The woman took him by the forearm and led him toward the front. The others parted obligingly.

"Abraham's hospitality." The woman patted Snow Crane's arm. "He welcomed and fed the three strangers who came to his tent, and those strangers were angels. Here they are at their meal."

She pointed at the golden chalice in the middle of the table.

"There's a lamb's head in there," she said, and cackled.

"Is that why Agafia welcomed us?" Galina asked Snow Crane. He put his arm around her.

"Maybe she was just lonely."

They walked to another hall hung with paintings from the past century. Mother-of-pearl blues streaked snowy backdrops, morning light reflected from serene domestic scenes, dark woods with bears and droopy pines glowed in mist and moonlight, and women were wrapped in diaphanous chiffon, wispy as spring ice. Romantic Russia, all landscape and gauzy light. When Galina used to go to the museum with her mother, she found this hall boring. It was not a Russia she'd known and not one that fit with the time's mores. It was frivolous. But now the images pleased her. A sense of calm and laziness flooded her, and she slipped a hand under Snow Crane's sweater to feel his skin.

Everything Galina saw reminded her of Agafia—the icons, the forested and rural settings. Agafia was everywhere, traces of her in the very foundation of the country's DNA, though she herself had been nowhere. Or maybe it was the trees that were the foundation of them all, of Agafia and Galina and Snow Crane in their own ways. The report she'd submitted crossed her mind, some formless, looming menace, threatening the feeling that she carried at that moment, of a peace. She gripped Snow Crane harder with her long fingers.

■ ■ ■

In the morning, the mutt was waiting for them as usual. The dog walked them to the metro, but didn't get on the train. Stillness blanketed the office. At lunchtime, the man who'd invited Galina to the party knocked on her office door. He handed her a letter.

"Another party?" she asked.

He gave a slight bow, retreated. Galina opened the envelope.

The note dismissed her from her position, citing unpatriotic activity and sabotage of the project as the reason. The letter was written in the same elegiac prose as that initial job offer, as if the poet bureaucrat who composed these things was assigned specifically to her case and would send her such carefully worded missives for all the occasions of her life. Like a guardian angel. She was to leave promptly without taking anything with her.

Galina didn't know what she'd expected; surely she hadn't imagined they'd suspend all work in the taiga without further investigation. She packed some rocks into a box, refusing to evacuate empty-handed. She didn't feel like a traitor to anything other than the trees. *I tried!* she wanted to tell Agafia. *There's no more I can do!* she wanted to tell David. The dismissal's swiftness shocked her, affirmation of the mind-made-upness of the thing. No one even questioned her intentions, which stung. No one asked her any questions at all, because questions are not answers.

Snow Crane had no desire to stay on the project without Galina and he assumed the boss didn't want him there either, as it was she who'd fought to hire him on. He looked around the office, running his fingers along the heavy wooden drawers that lined the room floor to ceiling. He pulled a few drawers open and took out small white boxes where rocks rested on white padding. He threw several rocks in Galina's box.

"Souvenirs."

He took Galina's purse from its hook on the wall and gently placed it on her shoulder.

"Let's go," he said. "I'll buy you an ice cream."

Snow Crane kissed Galina on a wet cheek. He'd fought to make a life he wanted, something predictable and kind, from the chaos thrust onto him. He'd wrested it back, as if from some malevolent overseer—and here was that force again, pushing Snow Crane toward bedlam, away from the refuge he'd carved. It would be so hard to lose it all again.

■ ■ ■

Nothing changed and everything changed. They hung around the apartment with Marat, reading and listening to records. On the television they watched news and talk shows. In the evenings they strolled along Arbat Street and sneaked into the underground clubs to hear bards sing. Not knowing what would happen next and wandering the streets with their favorite people by their side filled the days with pleasant, youthful lassitude. Galina kept waiting for more beautifully written missives from the bureaucrat to tell her what came next, but none arrived.

They applied for new jobs—as geologists, Snow Crane as pilot—but supervisors shook their heads at them and said, "I'm sorry."

"For what?" she asked.

Finally Galina took a job at the natural history museum as a security guard. She walked the halls filled with dusty dioramas. She refused to shush the children and spent hours marking endless circles in her favorite rooms, darkened and full of backlit polished minerals, shimmering. Snow Crane took a job as a mechanic and returned home each evening covered in grease and dirt. They'd shower together, holding the nozzle for each other, washing away foamy soap from their bodies so that it retreated down the drain, a fleeing tide.

Without residency papers in the city, Marat hadn't been able to find steady, government-approved work either. He'd contemplated leaving, but Snow Crane and Galina persuaded him to stay. He started moonlighting as a handyman, working for moneyed apparatchiks with extra cash, building saunas on their dachas, renovating lush apartments in the city, hanging wallpaper and fixing parquet. Their dinners became less extravagant, the evening conversation more morose.

Spring came.

Galina hadn't told her parents about the loss of her job, but two months after the fact her mother showed up at the apartment with bags of groceries and books.

"How'd you know?" Galina asked.

"You must be kidding," her mother said. "I think your father can get you a visa out of here."

"Where would I go?"

"Anywhere."

■ ■ ■

There were things Snow Crane hadn't told Galina. Like about the night in Siberia when a guard sent him out with a few men to down a tree and the four of them walked deeper and deeper into the forest. Once a month they did this, volunteering for the extra work in order to walk the timberland on their own, freely. The four men were all young and had been sent to the snowy terra incognita with long sentences. In the months since they'd started talking, they'd spent hours and hours discussing their cases, trying to chisel into shape the reasons for their presence in the camp. They rearranged the same words and theories in different ways, but arrived at the same place, in the dark wood.

The four had the boots that they'd worn on their feet when they'd arrived at the prison and their thick coats. A moon lit the trunks, and the snowy ground sparkled like a cracked geode. An orchestra of creaking trees, heavy with the weight of a fresh snowfall, played. The boys had talked about escaping and told each other to be prepared every time they went out on these expeditions. Each outing they voted on whether the night was right. To attempt a flight, they'd need full consensus. They took turns voting no, stalling.

On this night, one of them, freckled and jumpy with energy, called for the vote as they stood around in a circle, resting.

"Tonight," he said. "Yay, or nay?"

He put his hand into the circle. That meant yes. Cold slid into their nostrils and lungs, freezing them fragile. Breath from their mouths condensed into thick, weighty clouds. Snow Crane ran his hand through the hanging billows, clearing it as if he couldn't see the other boys' votes for all the fog. In the middle of the circle three hands hovered. None looked at him, giving him the space to decide on his own. Snow Crane cleared his throat and jutted his hand into the circle. Consensus.

They had a plan in place even though they didn't know when they might decide to use it. Now they dug deep, searching for the pieces to set it in motion. They'd been like heavy stones—sunk into the ground, immovable—but once they started running through the woods, kinetic chaos burst forth from their bodies. A trucking ice road wove somewhere through the tundra. They had come in on it before veering off into the unknown, all those months ago. They'd conspired about that road, remembering where it lay in relation to the camp. How to find it. Collaborating, they'd cobbled together a map and now traced its invisible lines in their minds, navigating through the woods. Snow hushed their footsteps and wind masked their heavy breath. The elements were on their side.

An eagle-owl with heavy brows swept down from above and lit out in front of them, leading the group, they joked, to freedom. Snow Crane looked for openings in the forest canopy to peek at the stars and reset his inner compass. The others stood around him as he turned his head upward, pivoting slowly, then adjusted his direction and took off running again; the army's training in the mountains a blessing.

They ran and ran and ran until their lungs turned friable with the cold and the ground slipped out from under them like an un-secured rug. Hours, they ran. The forest suddenly stopped, as if fenced in. Beyond lay open tundra, just like their camp. For a moment, Snow Crane worried he'd steered them in circles all night long only to bring them back to camp, and without wood. But the moon lit a silver gash in the distance, tucked like a hem into the fabric of the land. The four stopped to catch their breath.

"We need to look for trucks going south," Snow Crane said.

They huddled together under a massive tree and swallowed handfuls of snow.

"Do you think they're searching for us?" one of the boys asked.

Winter obscured the time. Darkness lingered long hours in both day and night at this latitude. But soon a line of orange appeared on the horizon, as if someone had underlined the sky with a colored pencil. Pink gauze stretched into the distance, letting the season's blues shine through under it. Snow Crane spotted a vehicle bouncing on the ice road.

"Which direction is he going?"

"South," Snow Crane said.

"Let's go."

They made for the road, calculating where to intersect the truck. When it approached, Snow Crane stepped into the cone of headlights and waved his hat at the driver. The man stopped and cranked down his window.

"Mind if we catch a ride with you to town?" Snow Crane asked.

"Where you going?" the driver asked.

"Whatever town you can get us to. We're just looking for some work."

"You'll have to ride in back."

Snow Crane waved over the boys, and they climbed into the

haul bed. Canvas covered them, but the cold easily penetrated it. The cargo was a load of *tushonka*, cases and cases of the canned meat, stacked. They inspected the cans.

"From America!"

One of the men still carried the axe they had taken to chop the firewood and used it to open a can. The meat in its gravy was frozen solid, but they poked at it with their fingers until a brown slush formed in the can and pieces of meat fell out of the ice, like scree tumbling out of a melting glacier. Snow Crane picked at the mess until the roughly opened can cut his finger and blood rushed out.

"Still alive," he said, grinning at the others. They slapped each other on their backs. "Still alive!" they repeated.

The driver let them out a bit before town, so he wouldn't get in trouble.

"Here," the man said, and slipped a piece of paper into Snow Crane's hand. "Go there, they'll get you squared away. I was once like you."

They located the building on the town's periphery. A man covered in prison tattoos opened the door. It was a new structure, but the apartment already reeked of cabbage and diaper cloth. Snow Crane talked privately with the man while his wife served the group tea. More than anything, Snow Crane remembered the wife's braid—rich auburn, thick as a mooring line, wrapped around her head into a Flemish coil. Russian children's books, the old ones, drew czarinas with such braids, and this gave Snow Crane hope, as if she'd know the patriotic thing to do.

The man took Snow Crane into another room, where a spread of inks, papers, and photos lay neatly arranged. Passport booklets.

"I expect payment within three months," the man said. "Or else I notify the authorities."

Snow Crane acquiesced wordlessly.

"Who's first?" the man said. Snow Crane raised his hand.

He made them shave and wash. Then he pointed a couple of lamps at a white wall and took their portraits. They drank more tea as he developed photos in the tiny bathroom. A punched hole gaped in the bathroom door but it was neatly covered up on the other side to keep out the light. As the photos dried he assembled their documents under a magnifying glass, giving them Moscow addresses and new names.

"My husband, he's the best forger out there," the woman said.

"Whose name is this?" Snow Crane asked the man.

"Yours," he replied.

"Just put 'geologist' under occupation," Snow Crane said.

Snow Crane sensed that document in his pocket even now as he lay with Galina in a nest of pillows on the floor. It had served him well, but he'd never tried to board a commercial flight with it. He didn't know if it would pass muster in a visa official's hands, in an airport, in a foreign country. In the dark, he lay on his back. Shadows swam across the wall and ceiling.

■ ■ ■

While they waited for Galina's dad to work his contacts, Galina packed. A short stack of books, sweaters, her fur hat. A notebook full of yellowing glued-in recipes her grandmother had clipped from newspapers over decades. A jeweler melted down her silver forks and made crude earrings out of them with Snow Crane's polished stones. Those went in the suitcase, mixed in with her underwear, so the security personnel might have some shame picking through her things. A metal cooking pot sat in the pile. How does one pack a suitcase with a balance of material goods that soothe existential nostalgia and the need to boil potatoes in a new land? She took out one pair of shoes and replaced them with three books. She wrapped a couple of plates in a towel and tucked them into the metal pot.

Galina's mother brought more sweets and very little news.

"He's trying," she said. "But it's hard to secure permissions when you're already on a shit list, even for him. And you're on several."

"Just make sure he gets Snow Crane paperwork too," Galina said, and returned to packing.

The migratory birds had their newly installed protections. She imagined flocks escorted in the air by Aeroflot planes, the pilots smiling and waving at their winged charges with genuine affection.

Snow Crane held her in his arms. When he couldn't sleep, he folded paper cranes out of sheets of newspaper and strung them on thread in front of bluing windows.

■ ■ ■

Marat made some semblance of a new life. He roomed with Snow Crane and Galina. He and Vera came together once a week, made love, brushed each other's hair. The work, though technically unlawful, piled up, so that he spent full days beautifying spaces for people he thought blind to beauty. He read more poems at the Café, each time the warmth of the reception prolonging a bit his will to wake. And there were his friends; when he draped his arms over Snow Crane's and Galina's shoulders or they hunkered together in the small room with the poppy curtains, a certainty overwhelmed him of how a man should feel and the chasm between that and his daily state. The moments of joy were rare stars in a dark galaxy. He reasoned that he expected too much, that this was how people survived, traveling from one star to the next, the trips long silent journeys through harsh empty space. And yet he could not explain away the persistent depression that gripped him. It hit him like a raptor striking its prey and he was slowly tiring, giving up the fight. He'd come to Moscow for a new start, but the city bore down on him with the weight of his failures and the nation's, the oppressive forces of each diminishing him.

"All my life I've been helping build utopia," he told Snow Crane. They were lying on the floor, a record playing quietly, dust drifting in the ray of light that broke through the window. "But I feel like I'm living in a dystopia."

Snow Crane leaned up on his side and looked at Marat. *The world isn't built for people like him*, Snow Crane thought. He reached out and ran his hand over his friend's head, flattening his hair.

"And now you two are going to leave me too," Marat said. He pouted playfully, but Snow Crane could see the hurt.

"Maybe not." He shrugged.

Marat rolled over, took a sheaf of wrinkled papers from a pocket, and scribbled something under a protective palm. Lately he'd been writing furiously, short poems and long poems, one-line observations, pieces of overheard dialogue, as if he wrote to hold on to reality. At night he'd stroll and throw the day's sheets into the river from a bridge. He let go of the pages one by one. They turned translucent as they landed on the water and floated on the surface, downriver. Galina and Snow Crane came upon this ritual by accident one night while on their own nightly walk. After that, they tried to rescue what sheets they could, sneaking them to safety when Marat left something lying around.

"Who does such a thing?" Galina fumed to Snow Crane.

But Snow Crane understood the way Marat chose to hold on and to let go, to stay in place because it was harder to surrender.

One evening a police officer picked him up for public intoxication and he spent the night in jail. Another day he was handcuffed for reciting verses on the metro. The officers thought he was drunk again, or inciting a riot, but none of the charges stuck. At the station, he talked circles around the captain's questions, as if he was attempting to self-destruct.

"I think they let me go because I was such a pain in the ass," he told Snow Crane and Galina.

"Not funny," Galina scolded.

Marat began running, first around the block, then the neighborhood, eventually tearing out farther, to the limits of the city, where cement gave way to swampy flat horizon. He worked his breath into exaggerated fervor, flooding his brain with oxygen until he reached a meditative state, pumping his legs absently. Often he ended up in unfamiliar parts of the city without recall of his path there. It had become his preferred state, lost, unmoored, physically spent, an ill-fitting shoe, nipples rubbed raw, his brain preoccupied with corporeal discomforts that left no space for other, unwelcome thoughts.

One day he ran into a neighborhood where the five-story Khrushchyovki were in particularly bad shape. Façades crumbled into treeless courtyards. The quarter was empty, but children's voices drifted from open windows. He slowed to a walk. He imagined that he came from such a place, that his mother, who he had decided had abandoned him, still lived in such a place, unregretful of the decision to give him up. Marat didn't think about his father, as if he were the product of immaculate conception, but obsessed about his mother, who was a pathetic drunk, a mean hag, a teen mom, a saint in his mind.

"Mama!" he called out. "Mama!"

His voice boomed on the unoccupied street.

"Mama!" someone cried out from a window. Another voice joined in, from a different building. Then more, as if it was a game the invisible children were joining, each shouting from his hiding place. For a moment dozens of cries for "Mama!" rang out; the children laughed, then quieted.

Marat turned down a different street with newer buildings, and walked peering into windows. He saw pots on stoves, curtains blowing open to reveal shelves of books, an unmade bed, a rug hung on a wall. The rooms held signs of life but he saw no people, as if they'd all evacuated just minutes before. He turned onto a block where the buildings were painted a pretty pale blue. A woman leaned out on her elbows from a first-floor window. Marat stopped in front of her and watched her smoke. The woman had hair the color of rust, a bright-pink manicure, blue eye shadow heavy on hooded lids.

"Come in, come in," she said.

She put out her cigarette and disappeared into the apartment. Marat stepped into the entryway and waited for the door to click open. She was very tall.

"Are you here for your reading?" she asked.

Marat examined the small room. Curtains draped windows, doors, and, it looked to him, even solid walls. A dog, gray-muzzled and sleepy, dozed on a bright-orange couch.

"Yes," he said.

"Well, what are you waiting for?"

She ushered him inside and directed him to sit next to the dog. It raised its head, sniffed, and returned to its position.

"That's Jesus Christ," she said. "But I call him Mike. Do you want palm or cards?"

"I don't know," Marat said.

She exhaled heavily and held out her hand.

"They never know," she said under her breath. "Give it to me." She motioned to his hand.

She grabbed his wrist and drew up his palm toward her eyes. She traced his hand's lines, naming them: the hashed lifeline, the deep head line which split in the middle like a tree branch. A pair of glasses with scratched lenses slid low on her nose. She peered again at the wrinkled hand, ran her palm over his calloused skin, almost lascivious.

"You're looking for a woman," she said. "Everyone who comes to me, they're either looking for a woman or themselves."

Marat felt bad for not bringing something more interesting to her practice. She seemed exasperated with her clients, as if they'd worn her down with their predictable problems. Jesus Christ the dog stood up and scooched closer to Marat, then rested his head on Marat's leg.

"I found him in the trash, when he was a puppy," the woman said.

She tugged harder on Marat's wrist and concentrated on the lines. "Your hands are so rough," she said. "So many calluses, scars. You've done a lot of physical labor. The markings hide your original lines, what could have been." Marat pulled on his hand, self-conscious, but she held on to it. "Don't take it personal. That's true for everybody, we all shed or obscure the lives we could have lived as we age."

She held up her own hand. A shiny patch of skin stretched taut along its edge. "A burn," she said. Its surface was smooth, unmarked by lines, as if the skin itself had been erased.

"Imagine."

"Your future, though. More interesting. I can't make any sense of it," she said. "Never happened to me before, I swear."

She sat back and looked out the window.

"Make something up," Marat said under his breath.

CHAPTER 11
Глава 11

Galina's dad procured a couple of visas out of the country. Scientist visas, for a conference, with instructions to stay on. Her mom delivered the handwritten credentials.

"He won't come," she said. "He hates how this all turned out."

To leave a place is to bury it. Street maps get covered in the slippery mold of forgetfulness, and familiarity slides: which intersection binds what streets, where the buses run, the particular accents of a place's residents, how the river smells from the bridges that stitch neighborhoods into a city. To secure things in their places, Galina took walks with her camera and snapped photos of street corners, ice cream stands, the city's statues holding down plazas and promenades. She photographed the children's department store's tall windows, the Taganka Theater's triple doors, balconies obscured by laundry, and the long corridors that led to her friends' apartments. She photographed entrances and exits, as if their capture could delay her own passage from here to whatever lay ahead.

Sometimes Marat accompanied her on these walks. He offered to photograph Galina in front of landmarks, so she could remember that she had been there, that she had belonged, but she demurred.

"I'm not a tourist," she told him. "I'm a ghost."

"Fine. Then take a picture of me," he instructed.

He stood straight, under a streetlamp, tears shiny on his cheeks. He lifted his chin and looked directly into the camera, letting his lip curl into a half-smile.

"Now you'll remember me," he said.

"How could I ever forget?"

Galina had married Marat in a sham ceremony so he could take possession of the apartment. He could live legally in Moscow now, he could exist on paper, stop hiding out and perhaps work, but it was small solace if Snow Crane and Galina left.

"King of a haunted castle!" Marat said when she presented him with the papers. For days before their scheduled departure, the three of them wept. To gain some freedom, to lose one's self, a gamble either way.

Marat could see now what lay ahead for him. He would live an ordinary life, of average precarity. The fortune-teller had nothing to say about his future because it would be unremarkable. He'd toil perfunctorily, he'd love a woman, perhaps more than one, he'd walk the streets and drink in the company of strangers and friends, and there'd be flashes of joy, like fireworks in an otherwise unlit night. He'd endure loneliness. Like his compatriots, he'd suffer from the vagaries of the state: the food lines, corruptions, the indignities of stolen freedoms, big and small. What was there to complain about? Millions of people managed with less. It was just that he was a poet. He'd allowed himself to imagine something divine. Perhaps he'd been an amateur. A better use of one's imagination would be to create the divine out of the mundane. On good days, he promised himself he'd try.

The night before Snow Crane and Galina left, Marat threw a

party at the apartment, a surprise Galina walked into after one of her strolls. Friends brought over a couple of gallons of hooch, a guitar, and an enormous square Napoleon cake.

"But where did you get all this condensed milk?" Galina mused.

Snow Crane took the camera from around her neck and stood on a chair aiming the lens down at the familiar, happy faces.

"Gala! Galochka!" he called to her. She gazed at him, holding flowers a friend had shoved into her arms, her own cheeks now streaked with tears. When he pressed down on the shutter release, Marat blew smoke between them, so she peered through a veil, a fog.

Snow Crane climbed on the table, straddling the cake with his socked feet.

"Who is this animal you've chosen to love?" Marat yelled playfully.

"Galochka!" Snow Crane stepped down the shutter speed and held her gaze. The others swam about her like a school of fish, but she stood still, alone in focus in his shot.

He came down and put his arm around her, inhaled of her. She smelled like rain-soaked cotton and crushed mountain sage.

"Are you all packed?" she whispered into his neck.

"Yes."

Snow Crane had considered telling her about the false passport, his worries it wouldn't pass muster leaving this country, entering the other. A few nights before he had explained it quietly to her in bed, though she was already asleep.

"I wish we could say good-bye to Agafia," she said. He pressed her, agreeing. "I've written her a letter," she continued. "Ivan promised to take it, when he goes back."

Galina sipped the grain alcohol out of cut crystal stemware as if it were fine champagne. A coworker strummed the guitar. Another sliced into the cake, squeezing rich custard out of the layers with the dull knife. Fingers swooped in to scoop the cream.

"They don't have cakes like this where you're going!" a voice exclaimed.

The poppy curtains were thrown open and the city, in yellow, sat suspended in the window frame.

Galina's mother sat at the table, visibly thinned and sad. Lida had wrapped a photo album in a set of new bedsheets and stuffed it into Galina's suitcase without her knowing.

"Will we ever see her again?" she asked whoever happened to sit down next to her. She laughed after she said it, as if it was a trick question.

Most of the people there didn't know what had happened, why Galina and Snow Crane had lost their jobs and were leaving for good. It didn't matter. They escorted them out to a new beginning.

The flight departed at dawn. At three in the morning they started loading their suitcases into Lida's car. Everybody was a little drunk; Moscow streaked past the window, landmarks obscured by overpasses and tears. Galina aimed the camera at her mother's set face. *Click.* She pointed the lens at the windshield, focusing on Arbat Street. *Click.* Her mother toured them through their personal Moscow. Red Square. *Click.* The university's geology department. *Click.* Galina's childhood home, where she saw the window in her father's office illuminated. *Click.*

Then Lida turned the car toward the airport.

Lida kissed Galina's eyelids when she said good-bye, their

hearts bumping up against each other when they hugged. She held Snow Crane too, delivering private instructions to take care of her daughter into his ear.

"I'll be here," she said. "Where else."

The Moscow airport resembled a cross between an informal settlement and a penal colony. Whole families camped in the unwashed halls in small fortresses built of rope-tied boxes and plaid suitcases. Airplanes arrived and departed on no known schedule, like birds pecking at the runways' asphalt, finding nothing, taking off for the hazy skies. The airport employees' job seemed to be to make those planes linger. Women with tight buns sifted through travelers' belongings as if looking for deals at a flea market, before letting them up the jetway. Once a plane took off, workers and prospective passengers alike lined up by the windows and craned their necks looking for the next vessel to descend. The bird watchers stood for hours, days.

The ticket hall filled with chaos. By the door an Uzbek family distributed jewelry to the women and girls, layering gold chains around their necks so the customs officials couldn't grab them out of their bags. A Ukrainian family sliced pale bologna onto black bread, settling in for breakfast. An old man dragged a huge red suitcase as he crossed the hall. The unzipped bag flew open, revealing an empty belly. The man walked on, in a rush.

Snow Crane wiped sweat from his neck. If he had hackles, he'd have raised them.

"Why don't you go check about the plane," he said to Galina. "I'll stay here with the bags."

She approached the ticket counter, squeezed into the scrum

of bodies, first her arm, then her head, a shoulder, her torso sliding between others' backs until her finger followed the rest of her in. Other bodies swallowed hers, like quicksand.

Snow Crane looked around for police, for the secret service, half expecting to see the boxy woman who'd taken him the morning after his mother disappeared. He took out his passport and flipped through the clean pages. His name—he didn't know if it was stolen, made up, somewhere in between—appeared handwritten in black ink. This stranger would either fly, or he wouldn't.

There was nothing else to do now.

Galina emerged back out of the scrum and strode toward him, noticeably more disheveled than when she'd left.

"The plane's delayed four hours," she said. Snow Crane patted the suitcase next to him. Four more guaranteed hours with her.

Four hours can be a lifetime or a small gift. If these were their last hours together, Snow Crane hoped he'd already said everything that mattered. He laid a hand on Galina's leg but didn't talk. She was lost in her own worries. Fifteen minutes passed. Thirty. An hour. Out of a bag, Galina took a piece of cake wrapped in paper and unfolded it on her lap. They lifted it to their mouths, cleaning the paper of custard. There wasn't much to say, just the silence of new beginnings and the deafness of the past.

On the loudspeaker a crackling voice announced their flight.

"Already? It hasn't been four hours."

They sat for another moment in silence, clasping hands.

"For the road," Snow Crane said.

Then they rose and started to gather their bags.

"Documents in hand," Galina said. She held a pink folder full of inked and stamped papers documenting her Soviet life. She wouldn't need them in the future, perhaps, but it'd be evidence that she'd lived it. Snow Crane took out his passport.

They walked toward the inspection point. Bodies squeezed in around them, sweating and yelling, lifting their documents above each other's heads, as if they were fragile. The clerks worked slowly, touching their fingers to a wet sponge before they flipped through each person's credentials, squinting at thumbnail photographs of unsmiling faces and reading through the leaning narrow script that populated each sheet of transparent paper. The clerk hassled a family in front of Galina and Snow Crane, with four young children.

"Where are their pictures?" the woman demanded, hitting the visas with the back of her hand. The matriarch pointed at each of the children's names, listed below her own and her husband's pictures.

"They told us we didn't need pictures," she said. "They're just babies."

The clerk huffed. She pointed at a sleeping bundle.

"What's its name?"

The child's father answered. One by one, the clerk pointed, comparing the names to the list in her hand, testing the parents. Then she finally brought down her stamp on the loose pages and waved them through.

Galina and Snow Crane approached.

"One at a time!" the clerk snapped.

Galina handed over her papers. The woman inspected them in silence, her labored breathing rustling the pages.

"You've packed a lot of things for a conference," the woman said, though they each had just one suitcase.

Galina's mother had told her not to say anything, so she kept her lips pursed. The inspector turned over the sheets of paper, as if looking for more text, explanations.

"You're a scientist?" the woman barked.

"A geologist," Galina said, barely audible, unable to help herself.

The woman stamped the sheets and waved Galina through. A man on the other side of the barrier ushered her on. Snow Crane could see the crowd of passengers closing around her as he stepped up to the table and handed his documents to the same woman. She flipped through them slowly, her movements catlike in their desire to upend something. She paused on a sheet and brought it to her face, scrunching it behind oversized glasses.

"You're a scientist too?" she asked. He nodded.

"Geologist?"

The woman's glasses had slid down her nose, and when she looked up at him he could see the fine red veins in her eyes branching like a dried river delta.

"I can't let you pass," the woman said.

"I'm sorry?"

Galina had emerged from the crowd and stood waiting as people jostled toward the jet bridge.

"Next!" the woman yelled. She tucked his documents into a drawer and waved him to the side.

"Ma'am," Snow Crane said, "please explain."

A guard detained Galina as she tried to walk back to Snow

Crane. The clerk was already wetting her finger on the pink sponge, already flipping through a new stack of papers.

"Snow Crane!" Galina shouted.

"Go!" he yelled back, smiling. "Everything is okay, I'll catch up!"

■ ■ ■

Snow Crane never made it to the plane. Several times Galina tried to get up from her seat to check on him, but the flight attendant refused her passage. She threatened to kick Galina off. Galina was still arguing with her when the vessel began to move.

Galina recalled her dad's unkindness when she first introduced him to Snow Crane, the inexplicable sneer at his handshake and the relentless questions. Snow Crane hadn't answered satisfactorily, and that only brought on more questions. Her father did not like Snow Crane, she knew. Perhaps he divined that Snow Crane hadn't been a Pioneer.

The plane rose into the air, shaking and sighing, a bullet piercing thick clouds. She placed her hand on the empty seat next to her, searching with her fingers for the body that belonged there. She was a dandelion puff in high wind, finally free, undone. A body soaring.

When she was a child her father had been vindictive; he'd held grudges against Lida and Galina, punished colleagues in small ways and big, asserting his power sometimes to do good, but often to do bad. He hadn't come to say good-bye to Galina. He saw her as a traitor. Still, blood was blood. But Snow Crane? The unthinkable crept into her thoughts: Would her father really sabotage her lover's passage? Or had something else entirely transpired?

The plane's recycled air uncoiled passengers' nerves. Ten hours they'd spend in a sealed capsule, a merciful break before the past and the future asserted themselves in new ways. Some people cried, their sobs muffled by the hum of conversations. Others rearranged themselves in the seats, trying to sleep. A flight attendant rang a delicate bell but did not announce what was to come.

CHAPTER 12
Глава 12

The winter had passed without much to comment on. Agafia hoarded her family's blankets and slept under a hump of noisome quilts, not wanting or needing to move from under their great weight. Animals stayed away and Pavel did not return and no big sky objects fell, so that the darkness dragged on long and unbroken. She nursed memories of the nuns, pondering what they were doing in this moment and whether they too thought about her.

The geologists' help had made life easier, and yet she felt older, stiffer. When winter retreated for her brief slumber under the verdant cloak of spring, then summer, the relief was as welcome as ever. What would this season bring? Each morning Agafia stood on the rise of ground that protruded beyond the meadow and looked out on the land, prophesying.

Life returned around her; the shaggy rug of grass grew increasingly tall and disheveled, the animals released a furor of melodies into the great unfading skies, and the river shed the viscosity of the cold to run fast and clear. The garden filled with eager stalks leaning in unison toward the sun in neat long rows Agafia dug alone. The homestead was the only corner of the taiga that stood gray and silent, except for the goat's tender bleating. Agafia bustled around the hut cleaning and beautifying, but it was the first time she'd welcomed the warm season, the spell of life, without any of her family. The kitten had grown and followed Agafia around as she collected wildflowers from the meadow and laid bouquets on their thawing tombstones. Several times she walked the path to the geologists' camp, but the flat outcrop stood empty. She retreated, confused, ears ringing with the atonal march of loneliness.

One afternoon Peter showed up at the hut and knocked. She opened the door to him and he beckoned her outside. The sun hung high and bright.

"Something is happening," he said.

She followed him through the valley, hurrying behind his long strides, tingling. He marched toward the bend in the river, toward the geologists' camp, whistling a tune that gathered in his mouth like a bloom.

"Are they back?" she shouted from behind him, legs scurrying like a caterpillar's.

"It's not them!"

They walked around the bend, the valley opening up fresh folds for their eyes, rearranging her skirts into new and marvelous configurations. A noise muffled by distance came at them in spurts. Agafia stopped to listen.

"What is that?" she asked, turning her ears toward the source.

"Come on," Peter said, moving along. "We're almost there."

They had veered off the path that ran to the geologists' camp and stepped deeper into the mountains. Rock walls rose around them, shimmering in the inebriating midday light. Everything breathed, wheezing and gasping, exhaling deeply and gracefully, panting with exhilaration, steadily sucking up the perfumed air. Agafia was sweating. The noise grew louder, its origin more clearly stemming from some corner just around yet another bend.

When Peter slowed, Agafia almost ran into him because she'd been trailing along at such a blind clip. She followed his gaze to a cluster of enormous machines painted the same reddish-gray hue as the mountain, as if to blend in. One of them soared into the air vertically, puncturing the low-hanging clouds. Inside the metal cage, a spiral piece turned, boring down. Another machine roared nearby. Men milled about, all of them dressed in navy suits.

"What are they doing?" she asked.

Peter squinted into the distance. "I think they're drilling," he said.

Galina had used that word, but Agafia hadn't understood its meaning, its consequence. She stood staring, that spiral heart of the machine spinning round and round like a tenacious mole, burrowing.

"I'd grown to like this little nook of the world," Peter said.

"What are they doing?" she asked again.

"They're building a mine. They're going to eat the rock."

The drill stopped, and men milled about it. She heard a shout, a countdown. Then a blast shook the deep earth. Behind the hillock where the drill stood, a fan of dust and rock rose into the air.

"Dynamite!" Peter exclaimed.

Agafia crossed herself, then dropped her arms. She hadn't expected to meet the end all alone, on such a beautiful spring day. She turned to Peter.

"Did you do this?" she asked.

He stood watching the dust from the explosion float down in a cloud. Silence hung in the air. *What a complicated question*, he thought. History unspooled between them, a long thread coiled tight with time. Before them, the drill started up with a growl. The birds took flight at the sound and fled. *Can the sun fall out of the sky?* she wondered. She pictured the molten sphere falling with a thud, rolling down the path, burning everything in its way. Agafia lifted up her skirts and clutched them in her hands. She started running, feet thundering on hard ground, a dynamite explosion with every step. The scarf on her head loosened and fell so that her hair trailed behind her like a meteorite tail. She pictured the animals falling in line behind her, wolves and flocks of nestless birds and rabbits, a great army gathering. When she looked back she was alone. She ran and ran, putting distance between herself and her own reckoning.

ACKNOWLEDGMENTS
БЛАГОДАРНОСТИ

As I write, Agafia Lykov, now nearing eighty years old, is still tending to her homestead in Western Siberia. When I first read about Agafia and her family, who by chance met a group of geologists after decades of self-isolation in the Soviet taiga, I was drawn to their story of steadfast resistance to a modern world. What drove their tenacious hold on their solitude? This book is an exploration of that question. Although my protagonist lives in similar circumstances, she and the other characters—as well as the events and plot of this book—are fictional.

Many books helped inform my novel, particularly *Lost in the Taiga* by Vasily Peskov; *Old Believers in a Changing World* by Robert O. Crummey; *The Icon and the Axe* by James H. Billington; *Peter the Great: His Life and World* by Robert K. Massie; *An Environmental History of Russia* by Paul Josephson et al.; *Turizm: The Russian and East European Tourist Under Capitalism and Socialism* by Anne E. Gorsuch and Diane P. Koenker; and *The Life Written by Himself* by Archpriest Avvakum. Thank you to Father Pimen Simon for allowing me to pull from the Old Orthodox Prayer Book which was beautifully translated by him and others and published by the Russian Orthodox Church of the Nativity of Christ. Thank you also to innumerable scholars; I've amassed a toppling pile of papers on everything from cultural studies of Soviet geologists and alpinists to Old Believer ethnographies on Belovod'e. The real world is infinitely more interesting than anything I could make up. I also had help from geologists, including Sarah Carmichael and John Callahan, and scholars like Jeffrey D. Holdeman. I spent hours looking at the photographs of Ekaterina Solovieva as I wrote.

Friends and colleagues have been cheerleading this book and my writing for years. Mark Powell and Kayla Rae Whitaker provided much-needed feedback at a pivotal time. The University of Wyoming MFA program was a refuge that in myriad ways changed my life. Beth Loffreda, Andy Fitch, Rattawut Lapcharoensap, Alyson Hagy, Brad Watson, and others took me seriously when I didn't. I'm still in awe of the amazing work that comes out of that tiny but mighty program and grateful for the brilliant friends I met there. Also, to friends and family who've never read a word I've written but have nonetheless been checking on my progress—thank you for your generous and unconditional support.

Anna Stein has made this book infinitely better with her no-nonsense edits—you were right, that character was really boring!—and found it an excellent home. Sally Howe and the Scribner team have refined it with kindness and great intelligence.

Debra, Ronnie, and Savannah have been unwavering in their

ACKNOWLEDGMENTS

encouragement and care. Some of the episodes in these pages are inspired by and drawn from my parents, Galina and Arkady. Thank you for telling the best stories, instilling a love of the mountains and of moving my legs, for teaching me to always be open to whatever and yet methodical, and for allowing me to finish this book with a newborn. My brother, Mark, who is pure of heart, has never been skeptical about any of my plans. I wish I'd been as kind to you.

I very literally would not have written this book without my partner, Caleb, who taught me how to show up every (early) morning and has been bringing me coffee in bed for longer than a decade. Your profound love has taught me new ways of being in the world. Recently, my son Felix has exploded that world and I'm still reassembling the pieces. The new one is a wonder to behold. I love walking through it with you two.

ABOUT THE AUTHOR
ОБ АВТОРЕ

IRINA ZHOROV was born in Uzbekistan, in the Soviet Union, and moved to Philadelphia on the eve of the USSR's dissolution. After failing to make use of a geology degree, she received an MFA from the University of Wyoming. She works as a journalist, reporting primarily on environmental issues.